THREATENED WATERS

Kevin Land Patrick
River Walk Publishers

RIVER WALK PUBLISHERS
THREATENED WATERS
Kevin Patrick

Cover design: Victoria Salma

Published in the United States by River Walk Publishers
Electronic Format ISBN 9780578153001
Paperback Format ISBN 9780578152998
ISBN-10 0578152991

Library of Congress Control Number: 2014920170
Kevin Patrick, Besalt CO

ABOUT THE AUTHOR

Kevin Patrick is the founder and president of WATERLAW-Patrick Miller Kropf Noto, a law firm that practices exclusively in the field of water law, water rights, and water planning (www.waterlaw.com). He is an accomplished water attorney who has represented many of nation's most prominent companies, people, and water providers. He has appeared in state and federal appellate courts, including the US Supreme Court, and has written and spoken on water and infrastructure issues throughout the United States, Europe, and South America. He is also a PADI divemaster and avid traveler.

Things are not always what they seem; the first appearance deceives many; the intelligence of a few perceives what has been carefully hidden.
Phaedrus, Plato

There is nothing more difficult to take in hand, more perilous to conduct or more uncertain in its success, than to take the lead in the introduction of a new order of things.
Niccolo Machiavelli

However beautiful the strategy, you should occasionally look at the results.
Winston Churchill

ACKNOWLEDGMENTS

A lot of people have helped me get to this point. I suspect my interest in espionage and thrillers was spurred by my father, who was in counter-intelligence when I was a kid growing up. Of course, my family was a typical post–World War II baby-boomer family that really didn't know exactly what Dad was doing, which made it all the more intriguing to me. My mom kept my sister and me on an even keel no matter what country or state we were living in. My dad passed away when I was in law school, but I still need to acknowledge his influence. I owe the most to my beautiful and great wife, Andrea; without her support and encouragement, I probably would not have followed through with my desire to write this book. And to my son, I thank you for helping select a great book cover.

I have enjoyed a great practice in the field of water law and owe a lot to my law partners. When you spend a third of your life with business partners and still enjoy their company, call them your close friends, and laugh every day with them, you picked the right partners. I'd also like to thank Brooke Peterson, a longtime friend and judge in Aspen, for referring David Olmstead to be a reader of one of the early drafts of the book. David was a police officer in Colorado for ten years, the last three of which were with the Organized Crime Task Force, and is now a high-profile private investigator in Aspen; his observations were very valuable. I also want to thank Ray Peritz, one of my best friends, for reading and commenting on an early draft. Ray is a veteran of Mountain Rescue Aspen and a Pitkin County sheriff; taking the time out of his busy schedule to read an untested novel is the height of friendship.

Lastly, I'll thank Guy Kawaski, the author of *APE*. Reading that book gave me great insight into writing and book development.

Kevin Land Patrick

PREFACE

Water has always been a part of my life, from being on swim teams growing up in Hawaii to sailing, owning a few boats, becoming a divemaster over twenty years ago, and practicing as a water attorney for over thirty-five years. It has always entertained and fascinated me.

When I was in law school performing research at the National Energy Law and Policy Institute, I could see the volatility of energy markets and saw the possibility of switching from one natural resource to another (natural gas to oil, to nuclear, to coal, to solar and other renewables). But what was constant was the requirement for water in all food production and energy generation (as a nation, we use roughly half of all water for electricity generation). There is no substitute. It is the ultimate renewable resource. All the water that was is all that there ever will be. We have the same amount of water on the planet as the dinosaurs had. What we do with it and how we value it reflects on us as a society.

Working in the water industry and dealing with water infrastructure on a day-to-day basis has made me somewhat knowledgeable of its durability, value, and vulnerability. I have taken steps to omit critical information and locations as well as add a bit of misinformation to ensure this book is never used as a template for mischief. I hope it entertains and gives you an understanding of the importance of this precious resource.

Kevin Land Patrick

CHAPTER 1

The cold was sickening, pressing in on him, hunching him over. He gripped his coat collar, keeping whatever warmth there was from escaping. The hours before dawn are the coldest in the frigid wasteland of the Anatolia Highlands of south-central Turkey. Here, the wind sweeps the semiarid high plateaus much like the American high deserts. With nothing to stop the wind, the cold pressed into Akmed's soul.

He had little to prepare him for the weather—a light oiled wool coat and thin gloves. He crouched down behind a boulder, trying to keep his face protected from the blustering wind, his knee aching from the cold ground it rested on. He wondered if he would just go to sleep in this cold place before the sun rose. He had hallucinated at one point, seeing his father, sister, and older brother together, waving for him to join them. And then he had snapped out of it, realizing it was a vision, each having died by Iranian rockets in that war. His groan against the wind was met harshly by Uday, who hissed for Alea and him to be quiet.

He was close to the dam and the massive gray concrete pipes that extended downhill. Uday called them penstocks, a strange word that was difficult for him to say. He could make out forms, guards, moving above, lit by the lights on the top of the dam. The moonless and cloudless night was bright with stars. Looking away from the lit dam, he could barely discern whether hills were trees, rocks were shadows, or bushes were guards. He prayed to Allah for strength and for the night to be over.

The three had spent the night stringing wires that would bring the water back home to Iraq. The Turks had stolen the precious water to create farms and light their country in the Western way. Tonight they would change that, and the West would be powerless to intervene. Saddam Hussein had shown he was able to play the West. Uday had shown them a torn newspaper earlier. It reported the US Army War College just two weeks before had proclaimed that Iraq had adopted a peaceful nonaggression policy that would last a decade. Uday had read the tattered paper:

> Baghdad should not be expected to deliberately provoke military confrontations with anyone. Its interests are best served now and in the immediate future by peace....Force is only likely if the Iraqis feel seriously threatened....It is our belief that Iraq is basically committed to a nonaggressive strategy and that it will, over the course of the next few years, considerably reduce the size of its military.

Akmed knew that Iraq would act in ways the West never could predict, and it would begin with him tonight.

He had spent hours in the cold at the concrete pipes that extended down the hill, connecting charges to the plastic explosives. Ali Hassan al-Majid, whom he had heard sometimes called Chemical Ali, had provided the explosive, boasting it was "the most powerful NATO has to offer." Soon the water would be turned into these concrete paths for the last time. Detonated, the charges would ensure the water never stopped flowing. The charges were designed to damage, not destroy, the dam. Destruction of the dam would be devastating to Iraq. Damaged, it would not be able to impound water and would be forced to bypass the river's flow. Turkey and the West would blame the Kurds, and the distraction would allow Iraq to secure Kuwait's riches and unify the northern Gulf under Iraqi control.

The Euphrates and its tributary, the Tigris, had provided the cradle of civilization with all that it required for millennia, only now to be shut off by the Turks. For the last month, the river had been dry, stagnant pools collecting waste and mosquitos so the Turks could fill their new reservoirs.

And now it was war, and if it had an incidental benefit of the Turks blaming and retaliating against the Kurds, that was the genius of Saddam.

Saddam had long tried to eradicate the Kurds—in this he could find common ground with the Turks.

Akmed knew he needed to stop such thoughts...he needed to focus. Removing his gloves, he cupped his hands over his ears and rubbed his eyes. He needed to wake, be alert. He had allowed his thoughts to take over and his senses to be dulled in the cold. Brought back to the present by the hiss of water filling the penstocks, he never heard the footsteps or the sound of the safety sliding off the rifle ten meters behind him.

For Akmed, the sight of Uday's head exploding into mist next to him was surreal; it had come a split second before the sound of the shot. Akmed lunged away just in time to avoid the round meant for him, rolled behind an escarpment, and began to run down the hillside. He lost his footing, sliding and rolling against the jagged rocks. The RPGs exploded behind him, then in front of him. And then there was a burst of light as the grenade blast impacted him. He felt searing heat, smelled the acid stench of cordite, and slipped into blackness.

CHAPTER 2

COZUMEL, MEXICO, APRIL 2001

Jim woke to the weight of Maria's arm across his chest. He was surprised, as he could have sworn he had gone to bed alone. *Gone to bed* might not be the right phrase; passed out was more accurate. After eight years in Mexico, the days and nights were pretty much the same. Be at the shop at 7:00 a.m., work till 4:00, start cocktails at 4:30, and pass out by 11:00—earlier, if he was lucky. It was easy to fall into a routine here in Mexico.

It had become a routine for Maria as much as him. She managed a jewelry store on the San Miguel Square, having moved to the island four years before from Playa Del Carmen, where she had grown up, privileged by local standards. Her father was an *abrogado*, a lawyer. She had received a year of bookkeeping school, which was far more than most. To live in a tourist resort with a good job was more than any of her friends had. But they had families and children—she had Jim, a craggy ex-patriot from Michigan who had left his wife and three children behind for Mexico, with no intentions of another family. He wasn't a catch, fifteen years older. She doubted there was a future, but he was respectful, predictable, and good to her. She would get off from work about the time Jim was winding down his day. They would usually have a drink, catch a bite, and go back to his place. He looked at her brown, toned form and thought for a moment, a brief moment, that he should encourage her to find someone who would give her the family she wanted. He then deftly slid away, dressed, left her a note that he would meet her at her shop at 6:00, and left.

Jim's ownership of Cozumel Scuba World made him an early riser. His workday started at 7:00, when he started the compressor and made sure the staff had decided to show up and called those who did not. The advent of cell phones was a blessing. No one was without one in Mexico. When he'd arrived ten years ago, few had cell phones, and even fewer had land-line phones. Finding people was a challenge even on an island.

Today was turning out to be a good day for April. He had a party of four booked, and there might be a few walk-ins as well. They might actually pay for the boat today, he thought. April was the tail end of the season. As the weather became hotter, tourists became fewer. The weather warmed back in the States, with beach vacations giving way to new lawns, baseball, and the summer.

It was no accident that Colorado had more divers per capita than any other state. Active people with long winters made for sport div-ers, he had heard. The reservation log said today's group was from Colorado—somewhere. It didn't much matter, but he made a mental note to find out, as tips were his lifeblood and engaging customers was how one got tips.

The sun was just beginning to strike the square as Jim made his normal stop for a Café Americano at the Square's espresso cart and then balanced his satchel briefcase and the coffee on the rusting moped. The moped fit him. It and he had plenty of rust and dings, coughing fumes and disturbing the serenity of dawn along the waterfront. As he neared the store, he was surprised to see people, presumably his dive booking, waiting for him. The instructions on the dive booking were clear. Boats left at 8:30 a.m., shop opened at 8:00, yet here were four eager divers at 7:00. He clenched his jaw and resolved to be friendly even before finishing his coffee. He didn't like his routine being interrupted.

They didn't look like a group from Colorado, which the reservations log said. They looked Latin, maybe even Mexican. One was badly scarred, perhaps in his late thirties. The other three were young, in their twenties, an attractive couple, and another man who could have been the woman's brother stood to the side.

"Hola. I'm Jim Drake, the owner."

The man with the scarred face responded, "Hello. I'm Hector Dominguez, and these are my two cousins, Paulo and Edward, and Paulo's wife, Emilia. They don't speak much English or Spanish; they are from Brazil."

"Pleasure to meet you all, but didn't you get the word? The shop doesn't open till eight o'clock," Jim said.

"I'm sorry; we thought you would be open. We decided to come early and see about getting equipment," Hector said.

Jim replied, "Well, the equipment rental manager will not be here until eight, and he can fit everyone with what they need then. There will be plenty of time before the boat leaves to get your equipment together."

Hector replied, with an inducing smile, "Oh no. We would prefer to *purchase* equipment and take it home, not use rental equipment."

This *was* a good day. Customers *never* bought equipment, they *always* rented. The inventory was there in case some piece of equipment broke or someone just decided to splurge and buy something new. Whole sets were never sold. The heavy dive equipment wasn't worth lugging back home. Online and local dive shops back in the States could always beat island prices.

Yet here, four complete sets of equipment, from dive computers to regulators, BCs to wetsuits, were all to be sold. "What type of fins and masks do you have? We are a dealer for Mares and Oceanic, but we likely can get Aqualung from one of the other shops on the island," Jim replied, his attention now piqued with the thought that this booking could make his entire off-season, which was fast approaching.

Paulo, tanned and athletic, replied in very broken English, "We have no masks or fins."

Hector shot Paulo a glare. Jim saw it and made a mental note of the dynamic. He guessed that Hector had the money, ran the show, and didn't like the others speaking. Whatever, Jim thought. In nearly a decade, he had never seen or heard of a customer showing up to go diving with not even so much as masks, fins, and snorkel, buying all new equipment—and now, here were four at once.

It was nearly 8:30 when everyone was outfitted and the bill was being prepared when Jim asked, "Now, if I can just collect everyone's C-cards."

Hector pulled out his first, showing he was a PADI Basic Open Water Diver, certified almost ten years before. The other three dive certification cards were issued by SSI, not that common anymore. They all were dated the same day, just a month before. Odd, since one card was dated in San Paulo, Brazil, and the other two cards were issued in Los Angeles. The card issued in Brazil looked suspect, as it misspelled the word *International*, the *I* in SSI. But, Jim thought, a typo can be ignored when the bill is topping out at just under US$6,700, paid in cash.

At 8:45, with no walk-ins having come in, Jim decided to treat the group as a private and take them on some of his favorite dives. He told Heraldo, the divemaster, that he would go along as a second divemaster. Jim called Lisa to come and mind the store and have Ignacio power up the boat and load the guests.

When the boat reached the dive site, he stood on the stern, asked for everyone's attention, and explained, "The first dive is normally the deepest of a two-tank dive trip. Almost every diver coming to Cozumel asks to be taken to Palancar, but I will let you in on a secret. Palancar is actually a reef system with many sites. Horseshoe is my favorite Palancar site, which is below us. It is a beautiful site, at about eighty to one hundred feet in depth, calling for about a twenty-minute dive profile. For those of you who haven't been here before, Cozumel is pretty special—it's drift diving. When the boat drops you off, the dive party descends, drifting through schools of grunts, tangs, snapper, and grouper. Keep your eyes out for turtles and reef sharks. We almost always see both here. The boat will drift with the surfacing bubbles. The boat will be above you at the end of the dive. No one surfaces alone; pair up with a buddy, and I'll take you down. If anyone needs more time to descend, problems equalizing, no one goes ahead...we all descend together. Likewise, if anyone needs to surface, we all surface unless one of the divemasters instructs you otherwise. Understood?"

Everyone nodded, somewhat interesting since they supposedly only understood Portuguese, Jim thought. He asked Hector to translate whatever was said. Hector whispered to the other three, and they all laughed. Weird, Jim thought, but the funny thing about money is that weirdness accompanied by money just becomes eccentric.

Suiting up took longer than expected. They were inexperienced, and equipment checks showed rookie mistakes. Weight belts with way too much weight. Two put on their BCs, vests that can accept and release air to adjust buoyancy underwater, with no weight belts at all.

Jim announced, "Everyone, you should only use between twelve and fourteen pounds of weight. I only use eight to ten. If you load too much weight, you'll sink like a stone, fight to gain neutral buoyancy, and, if the weight belt comes off, you will launch like a Polaris missile. Better to take less. I'll have a few pounds with me in case you need it."

After he saw that everyone was ready, he announced, "Everyone line up on the platform, but don't get in. This is a drift dive, so we all need to get in pretty much at the same time to stay together. Remember, stay with your buddy. And remember, the first thirty-two feet is a full atmosphere. Take your time; you need to equalize. The technique is to yawn or gently add air to the nasal capacity, holding the nose—much like popping your ears when descending in a plane."

Drake tapped Hector on the shoulder, and he walked off the boat's platform in a giant stride, surfacing immediately and floating away as he gave the OK sign. Jim then went in, and the others came off the boat together.

Once in the water, the feeling of being swept away by the strong current was replaced by calm, a sensation of no movement. Everything moving at the same rate; the only sense of movement came from watching the corals sweep by deep beneath them. With nearly a hundred feet of visibility, the coral formations on the bottom were clearly visible below in the turquoise water. With the signal from Jim, they started letting air out of their BCs and descended, the turbulence and sounds disappearing in the calm just beneath the surface.

Hector began to struggle, holding his ear. Jim swam to him and raised him a few feet, allowing the pressure and pain to subside. The others descended a few feet with Heraldo. After a few minutes, it was clear that Hector was having difficulty equalizing. Jim signaled to Heraldo that he would take Hector back and Heraldo would proceed with the other three.

Jim signaled to Hector they were going back up the fifteen or so feet to the surface. Hector shook his head no. Jim held his BC and wrote on a small whiteboard, "Avoid ear damage, surface w/me."

At the surface, Hector inflated his BC fully and floated, exclaiming, "Why did we surface! My ears would have been fine."

Jim could see a tiny rivulet of blood in the man's scarred ear and replied, "It's better to be safe than lose an eardrum. We can try again, perhaps tomorrow or the next day. Let's get on the boat. I want to look at that ear." Jim knew Hector wouldn't be diving anymore this trip.

Back onboard the boat, Hector was agitated. Jim explained, "If you force it, your eardrum will just swell, making equalization impossible...and it can lead to more serious damage."

Hector finally calmed, staring over the edge of the boat at the bubbles making their lazy way up to the surface from the divers below.

After a few minutes of gazing down at the divers, Hector said, "Paulo and Emilia wish to learn night diving and buoyancy control. Can we rent your boat, and you do that over the next five days?"

Jim's reply was immediate. "Absolutely. I can take them to the cruise ship pier, which is a beautiful and very safe night dive; we can practice their buoyancy skills there and at a sunken plane not far away from the pier. Night dives are usually everyone's favorite, once they get over the initial fear."

"And one more request. Can you recommend transportation to get to Merida after our stay here on the island is over on Friday? We are meeting friends there at their home," Hector asked.

"Absolutely. I have a friend in Playa del Carmen who runs a tourist bus company. He has some smaller vans, and I am sure he would appreciate the business. I can take you to the ferry, and he will meet you in Playa del Carmen," Jim said with a smile. This *was* a good day. He was going to make money all week on this group and a get cut of their transportation on the mainland, he thought.

CHAPTER 3

ALONG A TRIBUTARY OF THE BLUE NILE, ETHIOPIA 2008

Ethiopia had been warned that its Chemoga Yeda Dam complex and proposed Grand Ethiopian Renaissance Dam would not be tolerated. Ethiopia's self-proclaimed title as the powerhouse of Africa attracted over five billion euros in investment in hydroelectric infrastructure, primarily from the Chinese consortium of Sinohydru and the Industrial and Commercial Bank of China, while Sudan and Egypt seethed. Egypt had publicly warned Ethiopia for over a year that hostilities were not off the table to bring the dams down. Egypt had warned that it "will not give up a single drop of water from the Nile" and in the same breath talked openly of advancements in technology that would allow retarded and delayed-action bombs to be deployed from low altitude to destroy the dams. A commission had even publicly been charged with enhancing "the concussive effect and pressure wave amplification" of munitions for dam elimination.

But Ethiopia and China proceeded, and that was why Akmed had received a quiet and lucrative nod to independently eliminate two of the recently completed dams. Paulo, Emilia, and he had trained for this sort of task for three years, first in Cozumel, Mexico, and then Hurgada, Egypt. Three years of buoyancy control, underwater navigation, night-diving exercises, and underwater demolition training. It had been Akmed's idea to develop a team for the eradication of dams in Turkey. But now, with Iraq was all but gone as a nation, he turned his trade to the highest bidder, and today, that was Egypt. His warnings that a direct military attack against Ethiopia would be not only constitute a traceable act of war but would result in devastating floods along the Nile inside Egypt had prevailed. He had assured them that in his way, the reservoirs would never fill or would be delayed for years, with no Egyptian fingerprint.

And so Akmed sat on the bank watching his team sink quietly underwater from shore, headed upstream toward the dam. His ear would not permit him to be anything but an observer in this final phase. He listened and watched the water surface and the bank for any sign of troops or the more dangerous Nile crocodile. The sounds of the river and surrounding marsh were alive with birds, monkeys, waterbucks, and the occasional hyena with its shrill call. He kept the silenced VSK 0.338 large-bore rifle ready. He had bought the weapon, specially built for the Russian FSB, on the black market just for this purpose. While the readily available, silenced Israeli Ruger would bring a man down with its .22 long-rifle shell, he needed something far larger to stop a croc. The underwater team carried shotgun sticks but was at little risk when underwater. Having been hunted to near extinction at various periods, crocs were stealthy hunters that attacked only what they were sure would not attack them.

The tall grasses moved to his left, not ten meters off. Taking his focused, red-lensed light, he scanned the surface of the ground and was rewarded with two sets of unblinking, glowing eyes. Then one pair disappeared. It would be slowly coming for him while the other moved closer one lumbering foot at a time.

Akmed stepped back from the water's edge three or four meters, outside the croc's lunging range, and slowly scanned in a circle. There. In the water not five feet from where he had been were two eyes and nostrils visible in the still water. Aiming the rifle, he fired for the eyes. The animal splashed violently several times, rolling, and submerged. He couldn't tell whether it was mortally wounded, dead, or fleeing. Then the other, not ten meters away, on land, its massive armored body slowly approaching. He walked toward it and fired twice. The animal fell still. Akmed's heart raced. Where there were two, there would be more.

He tried to adjust his eyes and ears again for any sound out of place, to focus. Just then, off in the distance, the staccato sound of automatic weapons, explosions. Not the sound of the explosives they had planned, but smaller—likely grenades or mortars. The sky in the distance was glowing with searchlights, explosions, tracer rounds. He waited.

A few minutes later an explosion, this time larger but muffled. He wondered, had it been theirs? Then the water in front of him, where he had submerged the red flashing locator beacon, erupted. He swung his weapon around at what he knew would be a lunging croc and saw Emilia thrashing to get out of the water. He ran to her and pulled her onshore and safety away from the black water.

"What is it? What happened? Where are the others? Where are Paulo and Abdul?" he asked.

Emilia threw the heavy tank and BC off, ripping at the light wet suit, shedding it as a second skin, all the while shaking her head side to side. "They are gone. They were waiting for us. They must have had sensors or night vision. There were many guards. The guards were Chinese; we could hear them," she said. "The charges detonated too far from the structure. We failed. I failed."

Helping her out of the wetsuit, Akmed said, "Quickly, get into these clothes. We have to get back to the vehicle. Leave everything here. Dry your hair, quickly, in case we are stopped."

They rushed down the path, Akmed keeping a careful eye out with his night-vision goggles for signs of crocs. It was their custom to wait along game paths sometimes far from the water's edge.

Getting to the Range Rover, they jumped in, started the engine, and drove down the narrow bush road, lights off. Akmed knew he would not collect the balance of funds, but they had learned from tonight. It was operational training. He would not make the same mistakes in planning again.

He could see Emilia was mad at herself. "Do not worry. You have done well; it was my fault. I should have had better intelligence, known their capabilities better. This was training for your real objective. When we get back to Hurgada, you will be briefed. You are leaving for America within days," Akmed said with a piercing look.

Emilia stared at him and replied, "God willing. I will not fail you again."

CHAPTER 4

TWO WEEKS AGO, LOS ANGELES, CA

Zach was one of two agents still on the floor, but even by his standards, it was late. He usually left between seven and eight to avoid the traffic on Wilshire and grabbed a bite on the way back to Santa Monica. When people commented about an FBI agent having an apartment in Santa Monica, he joked that his building had a partial ocean view, if you went up on the rooftop with a pair of strong binoculars.

"Take it easy, Greer. Don't spend the night here," one of the rookie agents remarked as she walked by his desk. Now he was the only one left, glancing around and seeing the rows of empty, darkened, tan government cubicles that stretched off into the distance before him. There wasn't much to rush home to, not even a cat. He'd immersed himself in the work, in part to forget the divorce. But there was something in these files that held his attention tonight. He couldn't see it yet, but it was there.

He flipped through the intercepts from NSA with phrases repeated from three different locations. What was unusual was that one intercept was in Arabic and the other two in Spanish, and each mentioned the word "canyon." And another referenced the word "waters." Besides the intercepts was a report from a month ago of two Canadian crew members of a Monrovian-registered freighter describing several fellow crew members who abandoned the freighter just off the coast of Veracruz, Mexico, in a lifeboat. One of the crew members described them as imposters, didn't know anything about crewing, and he swore he had overheard them speaking Arabic. Then there was the interagency threat memorandum issued describing the potential for an attack on infrastructure in either Europe or North America. He inhaled deeply and let out a sigh...it could all just be random coincidence. His eyes were blurry. Enough for tonight, he thought.

Zach walked out of the federal building toward one of the few cars left in the lot. The yellow security lights cast a dim glow across the parking lot. Suddenly a man's yell came from his left. "What the fuck? You bitch!"

He ran toward the voice. There, two young white women were struggling with a black man in his twenties. Zach pulled his nine-millimeter from his waist holster and yelled, "Freeze! Federal agent!" Instinctively, he charged in, grabbed the man by one arm, and kicked his legs out from under him, forcing his body to slam face down on the pavement.

The man let out a pained grunt, offering no resistance but murmuring, "Stop! Stop!"

Greer slipped orange plasticuffs on the man, reciting, "You're under arrest. You have the right to remain silent. Anything you say or do can be used against you in a court of law. You have the right to counsel. If you cannot afford an attorney, one will be appointed to represent you. Do you understand these warnings?"

All the while, Zach was searching him but found no weapon. Taking his wallet, he found his driver's license...and government-issued identification card. Greer stood up over him and looked around. The women, who had jumped away as Greer came at the man, were already three rows over in a car. Tires screamed as they barreled out of the lot.

Zach stared back at the man, who was obviously in pain. He bent down. "What's your name?" Zach asked.

"Thomas Eller. I, uh, work at Internal Revenue. They were trying to rob me, take my keys," the man managed to get out.

"The women? They were assaulting you?" Greer asked, reaching for his cutter to remove the man's cuffs.

"I, ah, I'm sorry...I thought," Greer tried to get out.

"Why? Because I'm black and they were white?" the man angrily asked.

"No. I heard you—a man's voice—yell, 'bitch.' It sounded aggressive," Greer responded. It was partially the case, but he knew the man was also right. "Listen, I'm sorry. Are you all right? I made a mistake. I hate to say it, but I guess I did make an assumption....I was wrong to do it," Zach admitted.

The man looked at Greer, his expression softening. He stood, brushing dirt off his clothes, and said, "It's OK. If you hadn't come along, they would have rolled me, robbed me, taken my car, maybe worse."

Greer extended his hand, saying, "Thanks for being understanding. I need to call it in to the LAPD. I got a make and model on their car, but I'm afraid no plates. Would you recognize them if you saw them again?"

The man nodded positively. Greer walked a few feet away and dialed the police while he castigated himself for drawing conclusions based on appearances. It was sloppy and led to costly mistakes, he told himself.

CHAPTER 5

PRESENT DAY, PAGE, AZ

Sandy gazed at one of the sights that drew her to her profession: yellow sunlight striking the muted sandstone meeting blue water in the American desert. The subtle sound of the wakeless ebbing of Lake Powell along the sandstone was meditative. Later, it would be unbearably hot unless you were one of the lucky tourists who were on the lake.

At over a half mile above sea level, the sun's intensity was startling. So was Sandy. At twenty-seven, tanned, with short blond hair, green eyes, and a head-turning figure, she was an anomaly here. She had an outdoor freshness about her but could pass as a model without makeup. Not many beautiful women chose living on the edge of America's largest Indian nation, five hours from the nearest sizeable city. Her Facebook posts were in sharp contrast to those of her college friends now living in California, New York, and Miami. The club scene didn't offer her the rewards that she could see from her light-green government pickup. Not a day went by she didn't stop, look, and appreciate nature before her.

"Wahweap NPS to Sandy. Over," her radio blared.

"Sandy here, Wahweap. Is that you, Mike? You sound a bit excited. Over."

"Aw, honey, I'm always that way with you. Over."

Sandy rolled her eyes. Mike was nearing retirement and at age sixty-five was a great-grandfather of two. They married young here.

"Sandy, go on over to the Wahweap Marina Hotel. There is a suit there that wants to talk with you by the name of Greer—Zach, I think he said. He will meet you at eight thirty at the restaurant. Over."

Sandy hesitated and then replied, "Mike, do you know what this is about?"

Mike's voice softened. "No, hon, but he didn't ask for you by name. Only wanted our best ranger."

She exhaled with a small smile and replied, "Thanks, Mike. Sandy out." After three years, she felt she had finally broken into the boys' club, recognized for what she was, not how she appeared.

Sandy walked into the restaurant, with its floor-to-ceiling tinted windows overlooking the lake. Looking around the tables of tourists, she saw a handsome, fit man in a suit. Midthirties, six feet with a muscled frame, he looked the part of an FBI agent with his short-cropped hair. "You must be Agent Greer," Sandy said, extending a handshake.

"Call me Zach, please." He hadn't expected her youth. He had requested the best park ranger in the district, which usually meant a soon-to-be-retiring man. Ranger Heller, standing in front of him, was young and striking, even in the less-than-flattering uniform of a US Park Service ranger.

"What can I help you with, Agent Greer?" Sandy sat down across from his at a table next to the window overlooking Castle Rock, a majestic butte that rose from the glassy surface of Wahweap Bay.

"I can't get over the view here. How big is this lake, anyway?" Zach responded.

OK, Sandy thought. It was either small talk, or he was like most people whose first impressions of seeing a vast blue lake in the middle of a Georgia O'Keefe colored desert landscape was simply to gape.

"It's over a hundred miles long but has more miles of shoreline than all of the states along the US's Pacific coast." Sandy knew the facts by heart. "Twenty-seven million acre-feet of water, two thousand miles of shoreline, it took seventeen years to fill. We manage one point two million acres here. But you didn't come in that coat and tie as a tourist. How can I help you?"

Zach smiled warmly. He knew he was meeting with a very quick-witted ranger. She was direct. He took a sip of coffee and said in a low voice, "I need to meet with the head of security for the National Park Service and Glen Canyon Dam and get a better understanding of what measures are in place to protect against a potential terrorist threat. And I need to understand the lay of the land—who is who in the NPS here."

Sandy thought about the reply before responding. "Well, the first part of that response is intriguing, as a normal review would not be undertaken by the FBI. The second part is a bit more concerning, as it implies that people within the NPS could be under investigation."

Again being direct, Sandy looked straight into Zach's eyes and continued. "Those are two distinct tasks and concerns. You want to tell me more? If I am going to help you avoid a specific threat, I need to be in the loop with enough information to do some good."

She was bright and right. Sandy had always been blunt. Raised by her aunt and uncle in Wyoming from the age of eight after her parents were killed in an accident. Graduated with honors from Colorado State University in forestry and land management. Loved horses, fishing, and all things outdoors. Above all, though, her quickness to dissect his conversation was both impressive and a little unnerving.

"I can only tell you what I know and then what I can," Zach said. "We have information that leads us to believe that there is a risk to the electric grid at several locations in the country, one of which may be here, at Hoover, or Grand Coulee." He went on. "NSA has picked up communication traffic similar to a level experienced before nine eleven, with specific mention of America's electric, and maybe hydroelectric, infrastructure. We have no specific intel on where, when, how, or by whom. The FBI is rechecking security at installations around the country."

Sandy replied, "Well, after nine eleven, the dam went through a number of security assessments. DHS has been here half a dozen times just in the last few years I've been here."

Greer responded, "Yes, I have seen their reports. But when Uncle Sam throws a mere billion at security for the nation's more than seventy-seven thousand reservoirs, hundreds of thousands of miles of pipelines, and nearly a quarter million water-treatment facilities, I'm not lulled into a sense of security."

Sandy understood, nodding, and asked, "So what do you need from me?"

"To start with, I need to talk with whoever runs security. Then I need to see the dam, all points of entry to the dam, and the electrical switch-yard," Greer responded.

"I'm curious why you didn't talk to the security folks first," Sandy said.

Greer smiled and said, "Well, I am not sure from the file that you actually have security. Looks like a couple of security guards, periodic drive-bys of NPS rangers, and security cameras manned by Bureau of Reclamation guys. I was counting on you introducing me to ones that you feel have the best insight into site security now that you know the threat."

Sandy had never thought about it in those terms. When recapped that way, there really wasn't that much security. "OK, let's start with Rich Stanway at the dam's visitor center."

CHAPTER 6

MARSEILLE, FRANCE THREE MONTHS BEFORE

The café was dingy, dark. Wooden slats across the windows filtered the sunlight while the dark wood of the furniture seemed to absorb whatever light made it in. The floor was a dust brown overlaid by dozens of worn Persian rugs. The smell of decades of Turkish tobacco permeated the café even though smoking had been outlawed for the last five years. There were a dozen tables, two occupied besides the one he sat at. Josh discretely glanced at two men who were occupying one of the tables and drinking tea, talking in hushed whispers. Josh's senses had been correct. He had seen his picture before, staring at it now in the file on his tablet. Not knowing the connection wasn't good. He read the text beneath the picture: "You now have two assignments, at least for a few days. By now, you have the file. We are sending Anna—she will be there in 48 hours. You can't keep an eye on both Ivan and him alone. Be careful."

Josh appreciated his handler's concern. He was on his second café in Marseille's 3rd Arrondissement, which was now overwhelmingly Muslim. The French government had even begun referring to this neighborhood and others as "no-go" or "sensitive" urban zones, dangerous for non-Muslims. Josh's appearance, that of Mediterranean descent and dress, didn't reveal his Israeli ethnicity. He loved France; his only complaint was the beloved croissant was being replaced by pita bread. Wrong, very wrong, he thought.

His tablet revealed a dossier on Akmed Halabi, a.k.a. Akmed Mahbeer Waddid. A picture showed him in a hospital bed, his head swathed in bandages; the caption read: "ANKARA MEVKI ASKER HASTANI (21/01/1990)." That was Turkey's third-largest military hospital. The dossier indicated he had been severely injured and captured in an attempt to sabotage Turkey's Ataturk Dam. The attempt had failed. All other members of his team were killed. A memo authored from the CIA noted that the explosives were military grade, traceable to Iraq's Republican Guard.

As he scrolled through the file, only one other picture existed. This picture was grainy, but a scarred and disfigured-faced man was visible standing among a handful of other men. The caption read "05/02/1996-Unidentified S1, Akmed Halabi, Unidentified S2, Imad Mughnijah, L to R." Anyone standing that close to Imad Mughnijah was a threat and enemy. The fact that the dossier revealed that no further observations and no links to his identity or whereabouts after that date was a cause for concern.

Mughnijah had been a senior member and the military commander of Hezbollah in Lebanon. Until his assassination in Damascus in 2008, he had been targeted by the United States and Israel, although each denied involvement in the more than six attempts to kill or capture him. Each sought him for good reason. He had been linked to the 1983 Beirut Bombing that killed 241 US soldiers, sailors, and marines; the Khobar Towers bombing in Saudi Arabia that killed nearly 500, including 19 US servicemen; the hijacking of TWA flight 847; the 1983 US Beirut embassy bombing; multiple kidnappings; and even the 1992 bombing of the Israeli embassy in Buenos Aires, Argentina. The Argentinian bombing showed just how bold Iran and its proxy, Hezbollah, had become.

The file didn't say whether he was in Marseille. And what connection he might have to Josh's current surveillance target, a former Spetznas operative turned ex-FSB operative sitting before him in this foul café. Once a member of Russia's Federal Security Service of the Russian Federation (FSB), successor to the KGB, the Russian appeared to be working on his own with elements of the Hezbollah forces now fighting in Syria. Josh assumed Russia had sanctioned his business or at least turned a blind eye in support of Assad. Josh winced at the implications...he had full days ahead.

"Le café est excellent," Josh said as he left money on the table to leave. The waitress, in full niqab, peered nervously at him. French was not spoken much, and even less common would a man speak to or thank a woman waitress. Josh made a mental note to not do so again. As he swung the door to the café open, the glass shattered. Instinct told him gunfire. Josh dove sideways behind trash cans on the curb. He could tell rounds were coming from two points several meters apart and above...directly across the narrow street. The fire wasn't accurate. At this distance, he should have been hit. He wanted whoever was firing alive.

A bus was approaching, which he could use as cover to escape his weak position. He leaped up from behind the trash cans as the bus went by, took several steps to get behind the bus, and dashed across the street. He would be exposed for one, maybe two seconds. His advantage was that those firing weren't professionals, nor did they know when or exactly where he would appear.

Gunfire rang out again. From below, against the building, he could look up. Two barrels—one floor above, two windows apart. He burst into the smoke shop as Arabic screams rang out, through the store to the back exit, and out to the alley. They would exit to here. He saw the first one, small, a teen, with white running shoes. A second, larger, slower one; he would be the muscle. He went for muscle, the smaller and smarter one deserting his lumbering partner. Josh put one silenced round through his thigh as muscle swung his AK47 up. The jolt of pain and surprise caused him to scream, drop his weapon, and slide face down in the alley.

Josh kicked the weapon away, keeping an eye out for the partner he knew would not return. Holding the Ruger Mark II LR, an internal silencing weapon of choice, against the base of the man's skull, he whispered in Arabic, "Who do you work for? Hezbollah? Hamas? Quds?"

In pain, the man managed a grin through bloody, clenched teeth. Josh pushed his thumb into the man's thigh—in the wound—and the man went white with pain. He asked again, "Who do you work for?"

The answer was puzzling. "The Twelfth Gulf Service, praise Allah."

Josh pressed, "What is that? Who is the Twelfth Gulf?"

The man laughed and reached for the gun while pressing against the barrel with his head. He wanted death, and despite Josh's efforts, in an instant he met it.

CHAPTER 7

PRESENT DAY, LONDON

Elle's trim six-foot frame strode into his office without knocking on the open door. "Our friends have been a little more talkative lately."

Franklin looked up at Elle, who was dressed in a form-fitting navy pin-stripe pantsuit. He guessed Armani. Elle was a knockout, even at 9:00 a.m. With black hair swept back, high cheekbones, and piercing blue eyes, she possessed a walk that accentuated her long legs, as if daring others not to notice. "Which friends are we talking about?" he replied.

"Our friends in Tel Aviv. I just spoke with Evan. Seems one of his people located Ivan Romescki...in France. Ivan has been on both the Mossad's and the Agency's radar for some time now. We believe he has developed a new trade selling services to anti-Assad rebels—that is, until ISIS eliminated most of his customers," Elle explained.

"Interesting that Evan would reopen channels. They must need us pretty bad," Franklin said, knowing that Israel had voiced its displeasure with the current US administration by shutting off all but essential intelligence sharing. He couldn't blame Tel Aviv. He had a hard enough time trying to understand the recent US policy of abdication that had plagued US Middle East policy of late. As a carrier intelligence officer for over twenty-five years, he had built confidences and relationships, which were difficult to maintain when policies were fluid.

"What do they need from us?" Franklin asked.

"They need us to run intel on an Iraqi who was arrested by and escaped from the Turks in '92. We interrogated him for the Turks," Elle replied.

Franklin pushed back from his desk. "What is his name?"

"Akmed Halabi," Elle responded.

"Not ringing a bell, but it's something, or Evan wouldn't have asked. You oversee it, and let's keep it between us for now," Franklin directed.

"Already on it," Elle quipped on her way out his door.

The file before Elle showed interrogation reports from two sessions in January and one in February 1990 with Akmed Halabi:

Age 18, severe burns to left shoulder, neck, and left face. Loss of hearing—left ear. Minimal interrogation, supervised by Agent J. Wilcox, Ankara Station. Exec. Summary: Suspect claims he was recruited by the deceased team leader only two weeks before and told they were to probe the dam's security. Claims he knew nothing about explosives. Explosives confirmed to be Iraqi origin military grade. Detonators of Russian manufacture. Companions deceased by gunfire, Turkish forces. Munitions not exploded but found at inlets of four penstocks. Threat Impact: Had attack been successful, damage would have been severe, loss of operational pool of dam. DNA and fingerprints on deceased no matches.

Not much to go on, Elle thought. She clicked on the reference folder that accompanied the briefing paper and saw that the dam Akmed Halabi had attempted to bring down was one of the last major dams in Turkey, immediately above the Mosul Dam that had been the subject of fierce battles with ISIS just a few months ago. This piqued an interest. It showed that a simmering dispute had flowed from a half-century-old colonial agreement to allocate the waters of the Tigris and Euphrates, which had been the subject of sabotage and armed conflict for decades. The paper detailed that with 90 percent of the Euphrates's flow originating in Turkey and the rest flowing from Syria, those countries felt little obligation to deliver water to Iraq.

The reference folder continued: Akmed Halabi had been caught trying to blow up Ataturk Dam, one of twenty-two dams in modern Turkey's Guney Dogu Anadola Progesi, or GAP. Turkey had shut off the entire flow of the Euphrates for over a month to fill the reservoirs. The slogan for GAP had been "Turkish Water for Turkey." Similar slogans were always used to describe water battles. Since Turkey was a NATO member, the West cast a blind eye to what otherwise would be labeled an act of war.

The briefing paper ended by describing similar conflicts: Forty years before, Syria had attacked Israel's moves to construct a canal to harness the Jordan River. And a dozen years after that, Israel shelled and bombed earthmoving equipment staged to divert water away from the Jordan River, depriving it of the flow of the Hasbani and Banias tributaries. Indeed, one of the major contributors of the June 1967 Six-Day War was access to the waters of the Golan Heights. Iraq was only repeating history.

While historically interesting, Elle didn't see the connection the Israelis were concerned over. She dialed Franklin and relayed her observations, adding, "I'm meeting Mossad's man here in DC, Evan, in an hour. I told him I owed him a dinner the next time he was in town. I suggested he make reservations at the Grill at the Dorchester. I'll see what I can get on what connections the Institute sees with him in person." Elle always referred to Mossad by its literal translation, the Institute, and had no doubt that cocktails and perhaps dinner would reveal more than a phone call.

Franklin responded, "All for God and country." Oh to be twenty years younger, Franklin thought.

Elle walked into the Dorchester, her heels clicking on the hardwood floor. All eyes turned to observe her frame in the dimly lit room. Looking around she saw Evan sitting alone at the long rich wooden bar. He didn't look the part of a spy or Elle's date. Fifty, bald, a few pounds overweight for his five-foot-seven-inch frame draped in a gray Brooks Brothers suit. He stood up as he saw Elle approach, his height coming only eye level with her breasts. "Elle, you look stunning, as always. More so at this level. People will think I must have money."

Elle smiled sitting down next to him. "Evan, you always are so gracious. What are you having?"

"A twelve-year-old Macallan. May I order you one?" he replied.

Elle nodded yes to the bartender, who was looking in awe at the oddly matched couple.

When the bartender placed Elle's scotch on the fabric cocktail napkin and walked away, Evan started to speak, leaning a few inches closer to

Elle. "We've uncovered some disturbing information. Has your agency ever encountered a group that calls itself the Twelfth Gulf Service?"

Elle put her drink down and replied, "Not that I am aware of. I will check, but who, or what, is this group? Who are they aligned with?"

Evan proceeded. "That is what is disturbing. We've never heard of this group before. We know nothing about them except they tried unsuccessfully to take out one of our agents in France when he was tailing an arms dealer, Ivan Romescki. You may recall he was former FSB, who, we believe, has been selling arms to the rebels in Syria fighting Assad. The Russians have been looking for him, but we located him in Marseille. This group attacked our agent when he was watching Romescki. But it doesn't stop there. Our agent wasn't tailing Romescki. He was tailing members of an Islamic cell who we didn't know would be meeting with Romescki. Everyone in the cells disappeared the next day. The cells' members were engineering students."

Elle asked, "Engineering students? What is the connection with Ivan Romescki?"

Evan sipped his scotch and slowly replied, "We don't know. The apartment the cell was based in was wiped clean. We located a bag of shredded hard drives and papers located in a dumpster. We were able to reconstruct a few words, phrases: 'Mount Sannine,' 'Sinaloa,' and 'special packages.' I don't have to tell you that Sinaloa points to the Mexico-US border."

This time it was Elle who drank. "Thank you, Evan. I need to get back. Is there anything else you can give us?"

"I'll have a file sent to Franklin. And I would like to have the agent who was attacked follow his leads in the US. Franklin knows him—Joshua Marcus," Evan replied, standing up and throwing sterling pounds down on the bar. Elle nodded, patted Evan on the cheek, and walked briskly out.

CHAPTER 8

TWO MONTHS BEFORE, VERACRUZ, MEXICO

The lights of Veracruz flickered on the horizon. With no moon, blackness surrounded the freighter as it droned toward the coast, gently rising and falling on the swells. They had departed three weeks ago from Marseille and were sick most of the first half of the trip. Their references and claims as deckhands were discounted soon after they sailed. It had cost them €15,000 to keep the captain and first officer quiet.

The vessel had slowed as it began its approach to the outer channel marker. It would be met by the Port Pilot boat at 07:00, thirty minutes after sunrise. After three weeks at sea, the vessel approached its destination within a few hours of its scheduled docking time.

Hector looked at his watch, which read 3:00 a.m., and decided the time was right to wake the others. He walked from the aft crane, where he had been assigned to lubricate the gearbox before docking later in the day, to the crew aft quarters. The walk was dark, smelling of diesel fumes and degreasers. The fumes from the degreasers were particularly vile. A brew of bilge-cleaning agents, tank degreasers, and descalants was ever present below deck. Most crew members never gave the fumes a second thought, but Hector thought he was more likely to die from the fumes than the packages they had brought with them.

"Leva'ntate, es hora!" Hector proclaimed.

Amante woke and threw his legs over the berth. Victor looked confused, clearly not understanding.

"Get up; it's time," Hector repeated in English, continuing, "You must speak Spanish from this point on."

Amante was the smaller of the two, in his late twenties, thin, perhaps five feet eight. Victor was the muscle, a weight lifter. He was stocky and wore several scars on his face and hands that revealed the type of person he was and the life he lived.

"Be quiet and move to the aft port-side lifeboat. I readied it for us," Hector whispered in English, making sure both Amante and Victor understood. "Take my duffel, and I will take the packages," Hector said to Victor.

Amante grabbed his duffel while Victor threw the other two duffels over his right shoulder. Hector unscrewed the ceiling panel and removed the two gray dry boxes. Although the same size, the size of a small suitcase, one was much heavier. Although it had wheels, they couldn't afford the noise of rolling it. Hector strained and began to sweat profusely in the warm Caribbean air. Seeing Hector's discomfort, Victor exchanged the duffels for the dry boxes with Hector.

They walked up the steps to the lifeboat entry platform. The vessel carried two free-fall motorized lifeboats on the aft and a number of raft pods positioned along each side the vessel. The two aft free-fall lifeboats were positioned to launch behind the boat and normally would carry up to eighteen crewmen.

They approached the orange free-fall lifeboat from its aft entry point and opened the rear hatch. The hatch was about two feet wide and four feet tall. Amante carefully crawled in, a difficult task when the boat was at a seventy-five-degree down-angle, nose first. Amante motioned to Victor for him to pass through the three duffels and next the two dry boxes. Amante strapped each down inside with seat belts and strapping cords. Hector had volunteered to maintain the two free-fall lifeboats, a dangerous job aboard. More than one crewman had lost fingers or a hand near the winches and slide while maintaining and lubricating the mechanisms. But it had given him more than the cursory lifeboat drill understanding of the launching of the boats.

After sealing the aft hatch, Victor made his way between the two rows of seats to the captain's chair. Amante had taken a seat midway in the vessel, as instructed, with Hector near the rear. Each fastened his seat belt and shoulder harness. Hector peered out from the open hatch for any sign that their exit and loading had been discovered by the crew. When he was certain no one had seen them enter the lifeboat, he eased the hatch shut and latched the watertight bushings.

"Ready? We launch now. Brace, brace, brace," Victor said loudly after receiving a nod from Hector.

Victor began to pump the hydraulic lever near the captain's seat up and down, increasing the hydraulic pressure needed to raise the plunger, which would release the boat. The release pressed them against the back of their seats as the boat slid off the davit and fell fifty feet to the black water below. The boat hit the water, its bow dipping below the surface and quickly surfacing away from the moving ship. As the boat came to stop in the wake of the receding vessel, Victor started the engine and set a course for shore.

Veracruz is not an easy port to approach in a large vessel. A string of small islands, shoals, and wrecks presents a maze that cautions toward a daylight approach from the north around the small islands of Cancuncito and Isla Sacrificios. It was when the freighter was slowing to wait for daylight that they had planned to disappear from the boat. Using an aft launch ensured not only the sound of their escape would be behind the freighter but behind the ship's radar coverage.

With the handheld Garmin GPS chart plotter-compass, he knew both his relative position and the heading needed to scuttle the boat before sunrise near the deserted stretch of beach just north of the channel into the Port of Veracruz, where the freighter was set to dock in less than four hours. The missing lifeboat would be noticed within two hours when the shift changed at

05:00. They needed to disembark and sink the lifeboat before sunrise, which gave them less than two hours.

The lifeboat's top speed was only a few knots. It wasn't built for speed, but the currents were helping, and Victor guessed they would just make their appointed landing time.

As the boat neared Playa Norte, it banged hard against something. Amante, who had released his shoulder harness, flew forward, smashing his face against the metal seat in front. "Aiiieee! Kahlet!" Amante yelled out. Blood poured from an obvious broken nose.

Victor reversed the prop and eased the boat back. Water began flooding in from the floor panel and a gaping hole in the starboard side below the water line. Hector popped the top hatch and stared out into the still dark. He thought he could see shore and waves crashing. "Where are we? What did we hit?" Hector asked Victor.

Victor popped his head out of the top hatch and raised the GPS unit. One, two, three satellites locked; that was enough. He read the coordinates and then the coordinates of the radio tower appearing off in the distance to the southwest. Seeing the location plotted on the screen's map of the coast, Victor pointed, saying, "Those lights are just beyond Lergo de Tejada, our destination. We must have hit a reef. We are close to land, but we need to find a path through the reef before we take on too much water. We can't swim through the reef without knowing where it is." Victor's years in Hurgada, Egypt, had taught him respect for the ocean, reefs, and currents. Knowing the direction of land was no assurance that one could swim to shore—no matter how close it might seem.

"Give me the phone," Victor barked to Hector.

Hector wasn't used to being talked to this way by a subordinate but handed him the smartphone, knowing this was Victor's realm, not his. Victor powered the smart phone up and got a signal. They had been given the phone with instructions that it would be compatible with most carriers in Mexico. He Googled "coastal charts Puerto Veracruz." As a website came up, he saw a string of small islands and shallows, not a reef system and not a barrier to their approach. That was good.

Nautical twilight allows the human eye to begin to make out shapes and the horizon. When the sun rose another six to ten degrees, civil twilight would be upon them, and they would become visible. Hector could now see the shore was close. He could make out what appeared to be a jetty to the south and a beach with few lights dead west. They were close. He would scuttle the lifeboat here and swim if it were not for Amante's injury. Veracruz is an area where two of the most polluted rivers in Mexico discharge to the ocean, the Rio Blanco and the Rio Jamapa. The pollution brings sharks. While most sharks are harmless and afraid of humans, bull sharks are ever present in the waters and not the least bit afraid of man. From what he had read, learned earlier in Mexico, and saw off the coast of Sudan, they feed at dawn and dusk. Hector did not want to swim several hundred yards in these waters at dawn with Amante's bloodied face and clothes. They would get closer. He resolved that Amante would take care of scuttling the lifeboat after Victor and he were ashore.

The shore was no more than two hundred feet off the bow, and the depth was shallow, very shallow. They would do it here. Hector leaned down into the hatch and instructed Victor, "All stop."

Victor cut the engine and turned the wheel to starboard to slow the craft's approach.

"Victor, pass up the bags and the boxes," Hector said. Victor untied the cargo and handed the duffels and dry boxes up to the waiting Amante and Hector. "There are two survival suits in the aft stow. Get them. We will fill them with the duffels, seal them, and try to keep the duffels dry and buoyant. Bring all the life preservers also," Hector instructed.

Hector tied the duffels inside the dry suits and then sealed the legs, arms, and necks of the suits in knots, tying a life preserver to each. They then each put on a life preserver and tied the remaining life preservers to the two dry boxes. "Amante, you pass them down to Victor and me in the water, and when we are halfway to shore, scuttle the boat the way Victor explained," Hector instructed.

"Si," Amante acknowledged, wincing in pain.

Hector and Victor slid into the black water. It was colder than expected, and the pants Hector had on filled with water, weighing him down. He was glad he had the life preserver. He swam, pulling the two dry suits and their cargo, while Victor dragged the two dry boxes toward shore. Pulling themselves through the water in life preservers with dry boxes trailing behind was exhausting.

Finally, Hector's feet touched bottom, and he struggled through the surf to shore. Twice he swallowed a mouthful of saltwater, lashed by waves, his eyes stinging. At last he made it. He fell on his knees in the sand and looked back. Amante was standing on the lifeboat as it appeared to be easing below the surface, filling with water. As the water level neared the top hatch, Amante jumped in. The sound of a boat filling with water and splashing are sounds of distress. And sounds of distress attract sharks.

Amante struggled under the weight of his bloody shirt. His breathing was labored as the swelling prevented him from breathing through his nose. He spit blood. He unbuckled his life preserver and thrashed to get out of his shirt. After what seemed like minutes and several mouthfuls of seawater, he had the shirt off and his life vest back on and began swimming toward shore.

There was a noise behind Amante. A ripple. As if a slight current had broken the water's surface. He kept swimming, only this time being careful not to splash. He had learned to breast stroke when he was a child in Aqaba. He swept his arms forward and cupped his hands, dragging himself through the water. He tried to not ripple the surface. Suddenly, the water erupted behind him where he had discarded his bloody shirt near the lifeboat. He was only halfway to shore. Panic enveloped him. He prayed silently. Knowing, feeling, the mouth that would be opening behind him to take his legs. In the twilight, the water all around him was black, concealing the predators that he knew would take him. Pull him apart with double rows of teeth as sharp as needles. Every stroke seemed to make noise. And then there was the sound...surf. As Hector and Victor charged into the surf to retrieve him, they saw a dark shadow two meters behind Amante turn and disappear.

Exhausted—there was no time to rest—they split the weight between Victor and Hector and ran from the beach, with Amante gasping through near-closed eyes. The swelling cut off his breathing and made his eyes water, which already stung from the saltwater. He struggled to keep up. The instructions had said that there was one highway near the beach, Poza Rica Veracruz 180. There, buses ran to and from the center of Veracruz every twenty minutes. The could see headlights crossing from left to right and headed to a point in between to reach the highway. Praise to Allah, a bus, the very first vehicle to come, approached. Hector waved, and the bus stopped.

"Donde? Esta' a 30 pesos cado uno con el centro de la ciudad," the bus driver said with a quizzical look, observing the men's wet clothes and cargo and Amante's swollen and bruised face. Hector had studied Spanish for two years, but they spoke it so fast here. Understanding "30 pesos," he handed the driver 100 pesos and accepted the change.

The bus was nearly empty, a few passengers obviously on their way to work. They went to the back of the bus and fell into the seats, exhausted.

A few minutes later, they approached the outskirts of Veracruz. They stared out at an industrial city. Warehouses, truck yards, equipment yards. The highway names changed with every bend in the road; Poza Rica Veracruz turned into Boulevard Fidel Vela'zquez. Fear erupted in Hector as he looked out the left side of the bus. The bus was approaching the port, and he could see their freighter being piloted into its berth. The bus had to keep going; it must not stop here. Then the bus took a hard right turn onto Ignacio Zargosa, and he powered up the smart phone once again. He touched the square on the screen marked Maps, and a blue dot appeared just as he had been told it would. He looked as the dot moved south toward their destination. The bus driver looked in his mirror and yelled back, "Su tarifa so'lo te lleva la estacio'n de tren."

Hector waved and pointed to his ear, the universal sign he hadn't heard, to have the driver repeat what he'd said. The bus driver repeated, slower this time. He understood. They had paid only as far as the train station. That was perfect. Their destination was only a few blocks from the station, and he could see that on the map on the phone. "Si, gracias," he yelled from the back of the bus.

The bus approached an overpass, taking them over train tracks leading to a large train station. Once on the other side, they would get off. Hector stood, motioning the others to get off. They had been instructed to speak only when required, as dialect was everything in smaller towns and cities. "Aqui' es Bueno," Hector said as he walked up to the front. The bus came to a slow stop in front of a Holiday Inn, the driver assuming this was their destination. They were a sight as they got off, their damp clothes impacted with sand. Victor carried a duffel over his shoulder and the lighter of the two dry boxes. Hector rolled the heavy dry box with his duffel on top. Amante walked a step or two behind, wincing, rubbing his eyes, his nose turning blue and bruised.

He looked at the smart phone and hit the Recall Locations button. An address appeared, and he clicked on that address. The map flashed, and the phone spoke: "Proceed to the highlighted route; make a right turn in forty meters onto Calle Benito Jua'rez." He marveled in the irony that the West's technology would aid its enemy. They walked past street vendors and people walking to work, each staring at the three of them in their wet and sandy clothes. Victor tried to shake and sweep the sand from his shirt and pants as he walked. Walking past a glass storefront, Amante caught his reflection long enough to gasp at his appearance. All he could do was straighten his hair. That caused Victor to laugh, for which he received a shove from Amante. "After thirty meters, proceed two blocks to Avenue Cinco de Mayo. Your destination is on the right," the phone spoke again. As they approached, Hector could see the sign: Hotel de Centro Veracruz. "Wait outside with everything," he said to Victor.

Hector walked through the open doorway into a foyer with green-and-brown floor tile, a wooden crucifix on the wall, and a single desk with a bell. He tapped on the bell, and a small, elderly woman appeared, saying, "Necesita una habitacio'n?"

"Si, una habitacio'n para tres," Hector replied.

"Sera' 25 dolares," the woman replied. She assumed by his accent he was an American.

He reached into his money pocket he carried around his neck, handed her the money in American denominations, and replied, "Gracias," taking the key with the number 25 on it. He walked out to the curb and motioned Victor and Amante to follow.

The hotel was small, maybe a dozen rooms, with dark hall walls painted deep blue many times over in a thick, glossy enamel that covered the plaster's imperfections and scars and time's gashes. The floors upstairs were alabaster gray. Hector was struck by Mexico's vibrant colors and hard surfaces, so opposite his world's muted tan and brown colors with rugs covering every floor surface.

The room was large, perhaps eight meters long, with three small beds. Two floor-to-ceiling French doors opened out onto a courtyard below. If the room had been in a tourist town, it would have fetched ten times the rate. They each fell upon a bed, exhausted. Amante closed the thick, heavy drapes, blocking light from the French doors. He hoped they could sleep; there would be nothing they would have to do for the day.

A sound woke Hector. Someone was in the hall opening their door. He looked at the sleeping Victor and Amante, and there was another movement of the door, almost imperceptibly opening. He threw his pillow on Victor to wake him. Victor groaned, and the door burst open. Four shapes in the dark rushed in.

Victor turned his body sideways and down, using the charging shape as its own weapon. The shape stumbled at the declining target and was slammed to the floor. Victor took the man's life with one blow to his neck. Hector ran toward the approaching shapes, his knife cutting into the first man's carotid artery, then to the following shape, plunging the knife under the xyphoid, where the bottom of the rib cage joins. He twisted up and to his right, where the heart should be. A rush of air into the man's lungs was

followed by a bubbling sound as the man collapsed. Amante awoke in con-
fusion, his nose and eyes swollen. He wrapped both arms around one of the
shapes, wrestling the man to the ground. In seconds, it was over. Hector
flipped the light switch to see a scene of horror. The room was flooded red
with three corpses.

"Is anyone hurt?" Hector asked.

Victor was covered in blood but didn't think it belonged to him. He
replied, "No."

Amante called for help with the wrestling man, and two sets of arms
held the man down.

"Who are you?" Victor demanded in English.

The man's eyes widened. He hadn't expected English.

"In Espanol," Hector said to Victor.

Victor asked again, "Quie'n es usted...para que' esta's aqui," he said,
asking what the man was here for.

The man, really just a boy of sixteen or seventeen, replied, "Pensaron
que había dinero porque de nuestra cara maletines."

Amante squinted toward Hector. Hector translated. "He says they
thought we had money because of our expensive bags." It was obvious the
dry boxes looked out of place.

"Kill him. Let's go; we need to be in Merida before the maid gets to this
room," Hector said.

Victor did as he was told. They washed their stained hands and
changed clothes, leaving the blood-soaked clothing behind. It was three
in the afternoon, and they needed a car. They walked back to Via Ignacio
Zargosa. Amante lay in the street with Hector standing over him as a car

approached. Hector waved his arms in distress, and the car slowed enough for Victor to rush for the driver's door and yank it open.

They had a car. Merida was only a few hours away. Hector wondered if it would look the same after all the years.

CHAPTER 9

SOUTH BEACH, FL

Gustavo sat in his limo staring at the South Beach scene. It was nearly three in the morning, and the streets were jammed. He had been working since six the previous evening. He had picked the couple up at the airport and taken then to the Mandarin on Brickell. Waited for them there until nine and taken them to dinner at Casa Tua. They had been in the club since midnight, and he was tired. It was good money, though. He had three limos working tonight, and business was hot. The recession was a distant memory. The street outside Rewind, or whatever this club was called, was strewn with limos, Bentleys, and Maseratis. The Floridians were all about their cars, he mused.

His cell rang. Finally, he thought, they're ready to go. He answered.

"Gustavo Torres," a woman's voice spoke.

"Yes, this is Gustavo Torres. Can I help you?" he asked.
"Stand by for a ship-to-shore call, please," the woman said.

The line clicked several times, and a man's voice came on the line. "Gustavo, this is Paco. *The times are upon us at Mount Sannine.* Please change your schedule and meet us on Wednesday in Fort Lauderdale. I will send you a reservation confirmation through your company's website with the details of our arrival." The call disconnected.

Gustavo sat, his heart racing, fatigue replaced by adrenaline. It had been so long, he hadn't thought he would ever hear those words. After two years in Rio and six years in Miami, a series of green cards and finally citizenship, it felt like a lifetime.

He was ready. He had developed the plans and studiously attended all the public hearings for each and every plant upgrade and expansion. He was ready.

CHAPTER 10

LANGLEY, VA

Shaw arrived at his normal time: 07:00, noon in London, midafternoon in the Middle East. He stepped into the marble foyer of the Central Intelligence Agency and presented his identification. The guards, of course, knew him but asked that he lean into the scan so his retina could be paired with his ID. Harris, the senior security guard, smiled, saying, "Skins sucked last night. I'm going back to being a Raiders fan."

"Skins need a QB...and a coach...and maybe a front line," Shaw replied. "My Broncos did pretty well, though," he gloated.

"Yes, sir. They look like they could take the AFC again this year," Harris said, handing Shaw's coat and briefcase back.

Shaw always marveled in the power of football in communication. When he was dating his former wife in Austin years ago, he had to study up on college football whenever he flew to Austin just to communicate with anyone. In Idaho, football was not a defining theme. He had been the outdoor type, quiet, graduating with a dual degree of English and political science, which hadn't brought many job opportunities to his door. When one day he was approached to join the Agency, he jumped and had never regretted the decision after nearly twenty years. The Agency had paid for a master's degree and more than his share of world travel.

"Good morning," Alice said as he passed into his office. Alice had been his assistant for several years now, and he was convinced she lived behind her desk. No matter what hour of the day or night he came to the office, she was there. They needed to pay her more.

"Morning, Alice. Anything happening?" Shaw responded.

"There is a dossier from London SC on your desk. Arrived about an hour ago...arrived by diplomatic pouch, not transmission," Alice said.

"Ahh, the old-fashioned way. Guess we have Snowden to thank for people not storing and transmitting sensitives. Did you look at it?" Shaw replied, knowing she had.

"Yes. It's bad if true, but there are a lot of links that don't yet have a lot of support. It's more a hypothesis. It was sent from Franklin and Elle."

Shaw looked at the file, slowly turning to its four-page summary and then skimming the support folder and pictures. What he saw was troubling. The Israelis had linked the sole survivor of a botched sabotage of a Turkish dam in the nineties to a cell of terrorists in France and another cell in Italy. The cells had been tight and appeared to be well trained, with several members attending vocational and college classes in electrical engineering, mechanical engineering, and fluid dynamics. As scary as that sounded, it wasn't the real problem. The problem was that not one member of either cell could be located. One day the Israelis were watching them, and the next, all were gone from both cells on the same night. And one member of the cell may have been in contact with a former member of the Spetsnaz and KGB who was now in the arms business on his own. The bells were going off.

He picked up the phone, dialed the London station, asked for Franklin, who was in a meeting, and then asked for Elle. "Elle, I received the file. I've had everyone here drop everything, reassign everything. We need to be on this full time," Shaw said.

"I agree. Franklin has me on this 24-7. He noticed the EAC. He wants to meet with them on what we have in the next twenty-four hours,"

Shaw was surprised by how Franklin and he thought alike. The Emergency Action Commission was seldom called on such short notice, but Shaw had a very bad feeling on this, as Franklin and the Israelis must have had or they wouldn't have acted so quickly on it.

Elle had already gathered the best analyst in the London station and called in Langley's best, Sarah Tashkent. Sarah was always in high demand, and people would not be happy having someone usurp all of her time. "Sarah, Elle Hardwicke here. I know you are likely slammed, but I need to pull you off everything for the time being. Shaw Ellis has already been briefed, and you need to report to both Shaw and me on this immediately."

Sarah knew her workload had just doubled, but she knew from Elle's tone that something big was going down. She called her sister and asked her to pick up her daughter from school and spend the night with her. She had a feeling she would not make it home tonight.

CHAPTER 11

PAGE, AZ

Dylan was sitting out on the porch under the shade drinking a beer when Sandy drove up to his house. "You look relaxed. I thought your shift ended at eight," Sandy said, smiling as she stepped from her National Park Service truck.

"Supposed to, but Billy offered to let me off a couple of hours early in case I wanted a Friday-night date...and I was able to get a sitter," Dylan said in a drawl that he knew she liked.

"Well, I just learned I have to work early tomorrow, so it will need to be an early one, but sounds good. I could use a drink." Sandy continued, "Give me a half hour. I need a shower and might even girlie up for you."

Dylan smiled. How he had ended up in Page with a catch like Sandy amazed him. He had moved here three years ago from Grand Junction, Colorado, or more to get *away* from Grand Junction, where his ex-wife continued her less-than-discreet life. One weekend, she announced that she neither wanted the kids nor him. He didn't want Ally and Samantha to grow up where they could see that self-destruction. As an experienced police offer in a city of sixty thousand, he had no problem getting a job on the Page police force, which oversaw a tenth of the Grand Junction population. It didn't hurt that his parents lived in Flagstaff a few hours away; the kids needed family, grandparents.

After sitting and looking at the lake off in the distance, he went inside to change his shirt and push a comb through his hair. He was met at the door with a transformed Sandy. "Wow, what nightclub are you dressed for?" he chuckled.

"Well, let's see. We have a choice of Pizza at Strombolli's, the bar crowd at the Dam Bar, or the Blue Buddha, all of which close by ten, so we'll have to hit the clubs another time," Sandy said.

"Well, I guess it's bait time then, sushi," Dylan laughed. He knew that was always her choice. The Buddha was really *it* in town. It was one part sushi restaurant and one part lounge/nightclub, having lights and even go-go dancers and music on some weekends. Page didn't offer much in the way of a date spot, but this was close. On a Friday night in May, it would be quiet, with just the locals. The tourists really didn't start coming until next month, and that was fine with Dylan. He loved Page this time of the year. The weather was good, and the beauty of the surroundings was there just for the locals.

They drove Dylan's Ford F150 the six blocks to the restaurant and walked in. "Hey, Sandy, Dylan, you guys look all dressy. Is it an occasion?" asked Briana, the bartender.

"Friday night in Page," Sandy quipped back, which brought a chorus of laughter. The place was actually pretty busy. The sushi bar was nearly full, and about half the tables were taken. The place catered to mostly tourists, as sushi, even at Page prices, was still pretty pricey for a town that bordered the largest Indian reservation in America. Covering over twenty-seven thousand square miles in three states, the combination of the reservation's low wages and 40 percent unemployment meant it wasn't the driving economic engine. The tourists, hospitality, and service industry that catered to the Lake brought the customers.

Dylan shook hands with Ed and his wife, Cathy, who were at the sushi bar next to an obvious tourist dressed in slacks and a three-button Tommy Bahama shirt. People didn't wear slacks in Page unless they were selling something or paying last respects. Jeans and shorts were business attire.

"Zach?" Sandy said.

The tourist turned and stared at Sandy for a second before recognition cut in. "Ranger Heller, I, ah, almost didn't recognize you without your uniform," Zach said with a smile and wide eyes.

"Zach, let me introduce you to my boyfriend, Dylan Owens. Dylan, this is Agent Zach Greer," Sandy said.

"Please, just Zach," Greer said.

"Agent? Is that CIA, FBI, or Allstate?" Dylan good-naturedly said, extending a hand.

"FBI," Zach replied.

"Dylan is an officer on the Page police force," Sandy chimed in.

"Well, nothing like three law-enforcement types to kill a party," Zach added.

"So what brings you to Page?" Dylan asked, his curiosity piqued.

"Just some infrastructure inspections and interviews. Sandy was good enough to give me a briefing this morning on the dam and hydro operations the Park Service administers with Bureau of Reclamation," Zach said.

"Hey, Sandy, you want a table?" Briana asked.

"Come join us," Dylan said to Zach.
"No, looks like you two are out on a date. I know free Friday nights are rare in our line of work, so I wouldn't feel comfortable. Besides, I'm almost done," Zach said.

"Well, join us for a drink when you are done, at least," Sandy said.

"Thanks. I might do that," Zach replied.

Sandy left for the table, tapping Mannie Calamos on the back. "Hey, Mannie, good to see you out," Sandy said. It had been almost three months since his wife suddenly disappeared, to be found a week later in the lake. The coroner had determined she drowned after a blunt-force trauma attributed to falling as she took her favorite hike along the shore cliffs. It had affected him greatly. Once a pretty likeable and talkative person, he was a shell of himself after she died. This was the first time she had seen him outside of his work at the dam's visitor center.

Mannie looked up and replied, "Hi Sandy...Dylan. Haven't been out much. But thanks, I'm better." He averted his eyes from Agent Greer, perhaps embarrassed, Sandy surmised.

CHAPTER 12

DENVER, CO

Joshua Marcus sat at the bar, feeling a bit old. How had this happened? he thought. At forty-six, he used to feel at ease in a hip bar. Now he felt invisible. At forty, he had still been able to mingle with the bar set in most places. Women would look at him from across the bar. He always could develop a reason to fit in at a bar for several hours if he needed to. Somehow, now, he had gotten a few years older and less visible to the bar crowd. He was perceived as an older guy sitting alone. He didn't care as much about the awkwardness of sitting alone as he did his inability to casually fit in and be there to observe. "Guess I'll have to develop a new image of being a sad old guy drinking alone," he thought. It didn't thrill him.

Josh had been at the LoDo Sports Bar for nearly an hour following these two. Mossad had tracked them from France to Houston, and he had followed them from Houston to Dallas. He'd lost them outside Amarillo but reacquired them this morning in Denver. He had the consent of Franklin Harbour to operate in the United States on the condition he check in and brief him if anything happened. So far, he was operating on a hunch and a partial face-recognition tape that had been shared when one of the two entered Texas City at the Container Customs Office.

The two were in a sports bar with dozens of TVs. They sat in front of the only TV with soccer playing. Pretty unusual when a repeat of the AFC Wildcard Game Denver won last season was playing on all other sets—particularly in Denver, where Bronco fever is a religion. Josh didn't understand American football but appreciated its complexity. These two couldn't be bothered by it. They were focused on a game between Iran and Brazil, playing *real* football.

Josh was sipping on a cold Stella when all hell broke loose. The two suspects dropped to the floor as if they had both slipped on ice a split second before the sound of gunfire. The backbar mirror and half a dozen bottles shattered. Josh dove off the barstool before the shattered glass hit the floor. Years of training and experience had saved him from the fate of others at the bar, all dead or dying next to him.

A flash grenade went off, and more gunfire. Despite being temporarily blinded and stunned, Josh leaped over the bar. He could see the two he was tailing run for the door; they obviously were a part of the attack. He ran after them as they jumped into a panel truck. People screamed, running from the bar. He looked around, feeling responsible. They knew he was following them. It was he they had been after. He had seen the panel truck outside but assumed it was a delivery truck. They had lured him into the exposed bar. He had been a target...for the second time.

He wasn't going to stick around for the police. By the time the police were done, this group would be in another state. He walked briskly toward the Rockies' stadium, hit the speed dial on his phone, and spoke quickly and clearly. "Task my location five minutes ago. Blake Street and Eighteenth Street, Denver, Colorado. Dark-gray panel van. Late model. Last three license plate 459, Colorado. Advise present location."

The computerized voice replied, "Confirmed data input, checking... checking...." Three long minutes passed, and then the computer spoke again: "Target vehicle southbound on Interstate 25 approaching Speer Boulevard Exit."

Josh placed the call on hold, not wanting to lose the connection. He selected another line and dialed Franklin's contact at Langley. "Institute One, authority Harbour, I have an event in Denver involving my suspects. Multiple civilian casualties, have tracking on suspects and am in pursuit. Need backup assets; advise."

The computerized voice was unnervingly calm, replying, "Wait one... yes, assets notified...ETA two hours thirty minutes."

"Negative. Need Franklin Harbour on voice now," Josh barked at the computer.

Twenty seconds passed, seemingly an eternity, until Franklin's voice came on the line. "Franklin here. Josh, what's going on?"

"I am in Denver trailing our two tangoes. A third or more shot up a bar I was in—in broad daylight. They were after me and hit civilians. Your people have the vehicle real-time. Need help, transit, and backup. Franklin, they've tried to hit me twice. It has to have something to do with my identification of Romescki or who he was meeting with in Marseille," rattled off Josh.

"We don't have on-ground assets there. FBI has a field office. We have your location; walk to a safe point. As I recall, the train station is a few blocks from your location. Get there and wait for my call," Franklin said and then disconnected.

"Elle, get me Zach Greer in LA, at FBI. An event has just occurred in Denver. And come up to my office," Franklin said into the phone.

Elle called back two minutes later. "Greer is in Arizona. His office is trying to reach him, but his phone goes to voicemail. His last cell-phone track was four minutes ago. FBI believes he might be inside a dam with no coverage. FBI is tracking down a hardline for him," Elle relayed.
"Inside a dam? That's a new one. What dam?" Franklin asked.

"Glen Canyon. It is at Lake Powell, a large Bureau of Reclamation lake that straddles Arizona and Utah," Elle continued.

"What's a senior field agent doing that for?" Franklin said incredulously, then continued. "Get the Denver FBI field office to tail the van and any bolters, but advise them NOT to arrest or be seen. Tell them it is a national security matter. Find out who is in charge there and have him, or her, call me...and get Shaw Ellis on the line."

After a few minutes, a familiar voice came on the line. "Shaw here."

"Shaw, this is Franklin in London. Where are you?"

Shaw put the coffee cup down as he reached for the wheel. He knew his long weekend was over before it had started. "I flew out this morning for a weekend with my son in San Diego...motoring out past the jetty as we speak," Shaw said. He loved being on the water. He didn't get much time anymore with his son after his son went off to college, and the offer of a friend's boat for the weekend, just his son and him, had been on his mind for weeks.

"We have a situation, and I need you to back at Langley in the morning. We think it has to do with the file we sent last week. I'll send the updated file and our notes. I'll send a plane so you can have the day. The plane will be at Coronado at 04:00. I'll meet you at the EAC in Langley at 11:00 local time. Sorry to do this to your weekend." Franklin hung up.

Shaw looked at Sam and thought of all the times he had disappointed him. The missed practices, the canceled trips. It wasn't fair to Sam or him. In his freshman year at the University of California San Diego, Sam was studying environmental systems. Sam wanted to be as far away from his dad's line of work as he could be. He was a bright son who had been raised as much by Shaw's sister as him. Shaw had him when he was only eighteen. His mother was also eighteen but not cut out for being a mother. She left one day when Sam was two. Shaw raised him, worked two jobs, and put himself through college in two years, getting a master's in international affairs. The master's was courtesy of the Agency and was more the development of a cover than an education. All that took time, something he never had for Sam.

"It's OK, Dad. What's up? Do we have the day?" Sam asked.

"Yes. I leave early in the morning. But at least we can get out and run up to Oceanside and get some time on the water. We have the boat for the weekend, so we can come back to the slip tonight. I'm sorry," Shaw said, his voice falling off.

"Dad, it's OK, really. I should study tomorrow anyway," Sam said.

Shaw looked over to his right, at the Point Loma sub pens, seeing the string of floating barriers installed after the attack on the USS *Cole*. Terrorists had not caused much damage across the world, but they had caused a way of life and a sense of security to be lost.

As he cleared the jetty, he set the trim and brought the boat up on plane. The Formula 37 was a nice boat. The twin duo-prop Volvo Penta diesels quickly brought it "out of the hole." With its deep V-hull, it sliced rather than bounced through the waves, even at only thirty-seven feet in length. Shaw flipped the captain's seat up into a bolster and arched the boat over to starboard, mindful of the kelp fields outside the harbor.

Sam stood next to him, looking at the chart plotter. "Dad, don't forget the submarine surfacing zone...like last time," Sam said with a wry grin.

"Yeah, yeah," Shaw remarked, laughing. The last time they had been boating here together, the water seemed to bulge, and a voice had bellowed from the wave: "Attention, small craft, you are in a restricted naval zone. Turn hard port and exit immediately." That announcement had been joined by a submarine surfacing at what must have been twenty knots not a hundred yards away. Scared the crap out of both of them. Shaw imagined the twenty-year-olds driving the sub loved "buzzing" unsuspecting small craft.

The feel of the salt-laced wind and sun was soothing, interrupted only by the nagging thoughts of what might be transpiring for Franklin to have called. He kept himself from making calls to his office; they would already be on it, he said to himself. He didn't want to lose the moments with Sam; they came so sparingly. He asked, "So, Sam, what are you studying in that major of yours?"

"Geology, hydrology, biology—pretty much all of the 'ologies' one can," Sam replied.

"But what is the job or profession you are looking for when you get out?" Shaw asked.

"Environmental science is broad. You can do lab work, be a consultant, get a master's in engineering or hydrology, or teach," Sam said.

"I was with you until the 'teach,'" his dad said. "You know I believe teaching is an admirable profession—perhaps the most, when it comes to grade and high school. But college? Seems they are students who can't leave." Shaw felt himself lecturing.

"I don't agree, Dad, but it's OK. I have no plans to teach. I think sixteen years, eighteen if I go for a master's, is enough," Sam said.

They sat in silence. The drone of the engine, calm shore to starboard, as the throaty hum of the Formula gently cut through the small swells.

CHAPTER 13

CHULA VISTA, CA

Pedro had dreaded this day. He knew it would come. With the passage of years, his zeal was gone. He had become content with, even appreciative of, his new life. He turned the alarm off before it went off and slid out from under the covers. Mary turned but didn't wake. He knew she would be up in another few minutes to get Anna to day care and Claire to school before going to work.

In the garage, he pulled the spare tires away from the wall and worked the paneling free to retrieve the King James Bible he had kept all these years. It was not a book for prayer. He took the order he had received by e-mail for a new sprinkler system and traced each of the part numbers. Part 4P200L50W2 was the first part. Striking the zeroes, he turned the Bible to the fourth page, paragraph two, line five, and looked at the second word. After he was through with the part list, he stared...comes—two—days—from Sunday—Noah-the—prophet—Sunset—Holy Trinity—Church.

It was a perfect code. No two versions of the King James Bible had the same page numbers corresponding to Psalms or verse. Each Bible version, due to size and font, had a different page, paragraph, and line. And the e-mail invoice, sent years after the Bible was printed, looked innocuous. He asked himself, what time is sunset on Tuesday? He checked the Weather Channel app on his phone: 6:52 p.m.

He walked back into the house to make coffee and checked the phone book for any Catholic churches named Holy Trinity...yes, there it was, in El Cajon, less than an hour's drive. He dreaded this. He had a family now. He had been in America for nearly a decade, since he was eighteen. The country had brought opportunity. He had created a successful business installing and maintaining lawn sprinklers and had just purchased their first home. Jihad wasn't what he was anymore...and perhaps never was.

But he knew what they would do to his family if he did not comply.

CHAPTER 14

FORT LAUDERDALE, FL PASSENGER TERMINAL

Gustavo sat outside the gate of the Royal Atlantic Lines Terminal in his limo as a steady stream of pedestrians walked out to cabs, limos, and buses. He held a sign reading Mr. & Mrs. Blanco.

A man and woman in their late twenties approached. The man was tall, thin, of Mediterranean appearance. The woman was tanned, tall with chiseled Persian features. The couple pulled four hard-sided metal suitcases behind them, as if they would be on an extended holiday. "Hello. I am Alex Blanco, and this is my wife, Lateef. You are Gustavo?" the man asked.

"Yes, I am Gustavo, your driver. Please let me take those bags."

The man opened the door, and the woman got into the limo with its heavily tinted windows. The man walked around to the other side and got in, waiting for Gustavo to load the bags. Gustavo sat down in the driver's seat and turned to look through the partition window. "First things are first—Mount Sannine," Gustavo said.

The woman responded with a smile, "33.80. It is good to be here."

Gustavo smiled and asked, "How was the voyage? Any problems?"

Alex responded, "No, none at all. We were delayed a day on the trip from La Spezia to South Hampton. But they shortened the layover in England from three days to two so our arrival here wouldn't be off. Customs didn't even check our luggage. They only X-rayed it."

"Excellent. I booked you a room at the Marriott in South Beach. It is convenient and a place where tourists stay. But first, would you like to see the objective?" Gustavo asked.

"Only if it is on the way and you are sure we aren't followed," Lateef said.

"It's in Hialeah, a little bit out of the way but near Miami International Airport, so a limo is a common sight in that neighborhood," Gustavo responded. Gustavo drove in silence to a nearby Wyndham Hotel with a parking structure. He drove into the parking structure, paused, and then exited. It would look to anyone following that he had let his passengers off. He then accelerated onto I-95. "We are fine; no one is following. I checked; we were the only ones to get on the interstate, and in this traffic, it's impossible to follow us," Gustavo assured them.

After driving for about a half hour, he exited off at the NW Seventy-Ninth Street Westbound exit. "This is a common route to the airport when traffic is high on 836," Gustavo said. They drove west a few miles and then went south. The traffic was congested, and they stopped for many lights. "There, up on the right. That is the Hialeah Preston Water Treatment Plant, which supplies Miami and Dade County with all of its water. I have done much research on this. All of the water comes here from wells and is treated. There are two pipelines in and two pipelines out. In the past couple of years, they advertised for bids to replace these pipelines on the Internet. I have detailed maps of where these pipelines are," Gustavo proudly reported.

"We have studied the plans and specifications of the plant and the locations of the chlorine tanks," Lateef said. "That was the original plan, yes, but after 9/11, they strengthened security around the plant, particularly the chemicals, and it is well guarded. The pipelines, though, are not, and with the shallow groundwater here, they are very close to the surface. One of my drivers works for Comcast and moonlights driving for me. He has a company truck. Comcast has underground lines, so any work we might do near the pipelines wouldn't draw attention," Gustavo said.

Alex smiled, replying, "Gustavo, you have done well, very well. You have thought of everything. We are in deep gratitude. Praise be upon you."

They drove through the outer lots of Miami Airport and onto the highway to South Beach. They needed to get to their hotel room and assemble the weapons.

CHAPTER 15

NOGALES, MX

Interstate 19 was over the rise. They had walked for nearly six hours and were exhausted. Amante was the weakest. His nose was just beginning to look normal, but he was dehydrated from a week of dysentery or Montezuma's revenge. It was likely just that his gut was not used to the food. They had made the trip from Veracruz to Merida three weeks ago, meeting up with cartel smugglers who had taken them over the border just west of the Nogales checkpoint. They were in America. The smugglers left the group of eight just over the border. Hector pulled Victor and Amante aside and let the other five walk ahead. Four men, ages twenty to thirty, and one young boy, not more than ten. They wore sandals and had one bottle of water between them. Nothing but the clothes they wore and small daypacks filled with their limited possessions. Hector could not understand what would cause men to endure such hardship to be a part of Satan's America. The desire for freedom and betterment was a false goal, a goal not expressed by Allah, he thought.

The going rate for the smugglers was $3,000 a head. A sum that took years to amass for most. They had paid triple, with another $10,000 to be wired on the condition that no questions would be asked and no attempts would be made to relieve them of their belongings. All of them had heavily laden backpacks—old Kelty frame backpacks that had been left for them years ago in Merida. Victor carried the heaviest, at about 120 pounds. Hector's was also heavy since he had to take much of the weight for Amante.

It was May, and the snakes were coming out. They walked carefully, making sure to make noise. He was glad they were not here in warmer months, as it was already sweltering. Hector said, "We are here. The highway is there.

Go to the southbound lanes. We will rest next to the backpacks while I get us a ride." Hector stuck a thumb out as Amante and Vincent sat against their packs on the shoulder. If they were seen hitchhiking north, they would be assumed to be illegals, and the United States Border Patrol would arrest them.

Vincent asked, "Why are we hitchhiking south to Mexico?"

Hector smiled, replying, "Our location here isn't visible from the northbound lanes. See that small hill? We are hidden."

A pickup truck slowed, and the driver yelled out in Spanish, "Going to Nogales? Jump in the back."

Hector and Amante loaded the packs into the back while Victor reached in and pulled the man from his seat. With a twist of his neck, he was dead. Victor carried the body behind a mesquite tree and removed the man's driver's license. They piled into the truck, cut across the wide median, and made a U-turn to the north.

Hector began to relax; they were only couple of hours from their destination. "We can buy a prepaid phone easily in Tucson. The city has a large illegal immigrant population that use the phones out of necessity."

As soon as they reached Interstate 10, Hector saw a sign to a store with a funny name: Walgreens. The sign read, "Prescriptions to Hardware, We Have All Your Needs."

At the designated exit, they pulled the pickup off the highway into the Walgreens parking lot. Vincent got out of the truck and returned with medication for Amante, two bags of pita chips, bottles of water, and two prepaid cell phones.

"Ibrahim, this is Hector, your uncle's nephew from Mexico," Hector said into the phone.

"Yes, I remember my uncle speaking about you. How are you?"

"Good. I am in town and would like to see the you," Hector repeated by memory.

"That is good. I can meet you in one hour at the Starbucks coffee shop on the corner of Fifth Street and Mill Street, in Tempe. If you put that address in your phone, you won't get lost," Ibrahim said.

"It will take us two hours. We will meet you at Starboards at Fifth Street and Mill Street," Hector said, typing the address into the phone as he was talking.

"Starbucks, not Starboard," Ibrahim said and hung up.

Hector thought how vulnerable the Americans were to invite students from any country to study at universities and how easy it had been for them to send these "students" years ago.

CHAPTER 16

BLACKSBURG, VA

The walk from Torgerson Hall to the War Memorial Gym across the drill field had changed overnight. The drab, overcast drudge of a late spring had been replaced by warm spring sunshine. Something happens in the spring, but more to those lucky enough to be twenty and in college. Vibrancy, love, and the feeling of possibility burst on a day like this. Javier looked at the chosen ones. The ones who had won the lottery. To be born in the United States, that was the lottery. To be born with intelligence and wealth in the United States...well, that was the Powerball. He loved his research work but hated the idyllic and privileged life of campus. His path here had been far different. Born in Spain to a Syrian mother and Spanish father, he had never belonged. It drove him to achieve, but it distanced him from everything and everyone. This country had given him a visa and a tuition-free degree from Cal Tech, then MIT, leading to his professorship at Virginia Tech. He owed much but resented more.

"Good morning, Professor Estaban," a passing student said.

"Good morning, Ms. Helton," Javier acknowledged. He avoided the dogs, students, and Frisbees that surrounded him and passed the residence halls to the Duck Pond and Golf Course. It was a trek, nearly a mile. He needed to find Eduardo, Ed, and be back for class in less than thirty minutes.

"Professor Estaban, can I help you find someone?" a student said.

It never ceased to amaze him that college credit was given for taking golf. "Yes, I'm looking for Ed. He...ah...was to help me move some materials around later today, and I need to tell him what time to come," Javier said.

"I saw him a few minutes ago, out back working on one of the carts. You might try there," the student said.

"Thank you," Javier said, walking out the door.

"Eduardo, there you are. We need to talk. *The times have come.* Be at Jimmy's Grille at six o'clock tonight."

Eduardo nodded. Javier looked around and, seeing no one, started the journey back to his office.

Javier never came to him or left the central campus. Something must have shaken him. He called Ellise from the clubhouse phone. "It's me. I will be to the house later tonight. I'm meeting Javier after work. *The times have come,*" he said.

"I understand. I'm ready," Ellise replied.

Ellise had never liked her new name or this country. She hated the people in southern Virginia. She saw them as redneck and uneducated, always looking down on her for her darker skin. They were too dumb to know the difference between Hispanics and Syrians, she thought.

CHAPTER 17

SOUTH BEACH, FL

"I have been thinking. If the pipelines are damaged, it will take them only a week, maybe two, to repair them. The same goes for the wells. If the wells are also destroyed, they can redrill them in a few days. We need to make it harder for them to merely repair the damage," Lateef said.

She was right; they had studied enough in their engineering classes to know pipelines were easily repaired and replaced. "What about poisoning the water supply itself?" Alex asked.

"The wells withdraw water from the Biscayne Aquifer; I have read that," Gustavo replied.

"No, that is impossible. Water sources can't be poisoned. The poison would be diluted too much. Don't you remember what Professor Marshan used to say? 'Dilution is the solution to pollution.'"

Lateef continued. "No, we need a reason why they would *hesitate* to do the repairs, a reason they would be *fearful* of doing repairs."

"A dirty bomb," Alex said.

"Yes, but where can we obtain radioactive materials?" asked Lateef.

"Hospitals. Miami has many hospitals. I have a friend whose wife is a nuclear medicine technician. I can tell her I have a nephew who is thinking about getting an education in nuclear medicine. Ask her what hospitals have the largest nuclear medicine use," Gustavo said.

"This is a good idea, but be very careful. Do not ask too many questions that would attract attention. We don't need much material; we can spread misinformation on the amounts to the media at the appropriate time. Tell them that the concentrations are far higher than they are. We just need enough to result in the detection of nuclear material. That will cause them to delay and study what must be done. That will be all the time we need," Lateef replied.

"I suppose we will have to assault the hospital to get the materials. This will be dangerous; it will take planning, time...and time is what we do not have. We have three days until the *times*. Gustavo, get us weapons. We will set the bombs in advance with timers. In the event we are caught in the assault, the bombs will still go off as planned," Alex said.

"Getting weapons in this country is not difficult. I will do this today," Gustavo replied.

CHAPTER 18

PAGE, AZ

Zach exited the elevator that had lifted him from the powerhouse inside the dam. The sound of several pings from his handheld meant he had been out of touch and people were looking for him. Squinting, he walked out into the sun, grabbed his laptop from the car, and tried to focus. Five secure e-mails, three from DC and two from the LA office. All within the last fifteen minutes.

He had just opened the one from the DNI entitled "Threat Matrix US Grid Elevated" and begun to read when his cell rang. "Greer here."

The voice on the line sounded mechanical. "Hold one for the Deputy Director of National Intelligence."

A few seconds later, a voice came on. "Agent Greer, this is Deputy Director Maxwell Howard. I understand you are in Arizona."

Greer responded, "Yes sir. Page, Arizona."

"I understand you are investigating security at Glen Canyon, Hoover, and Davis Dams. What led you to the need to do this?" Howard asked.

"Sir, about one month ago, the FBI field office in Phoenix received a call from a woman stating she was a neighbor of an electrical engineering student from Pakistan. She said she had overheard the neighbor and three men who arrived in the middle of the night to their apartment asking questions about the generating capacity of Colorado River dams and whether a disruption in generating capacity could be replaced by other generating facilities in the West," Greer said.

"Go on," Howard said.

"Ordinarily, that would be investigated but would not be cause for alarm, but a few days later, just two days ago, the woman was found dead in Tempe's Town Lake. Her head was severed violently, and the neighbor had moved from the apartment and left grad school, where he was a teaching assistant. Interviews with his coworkers raised flags, as he was a loner and had voiced his displeasure with America's involvement in the Middle East," Greer paused.

"Not much to go on," Howard responded.

Greer interrupted. "Sir, there's more. The grad student took Spanish classes, something you don't often see—Muslims taking Spanish."
"Agent, I don't believe there is anything suspicious with an Arab taking Spanish in a border state," Howard said.

"Sir, he's Pakistani, not an Arab. Most Pakistani are Muslim but were originally Hindus who converted. This person was a practicing Sunni who reportedly looked down on Hispanics. And there's more." Howard was silent, letting Greer continue. "On the day the three men visited his apartment, a pickup truck was carjacked near Nogales on the US side, its driver killed. That pickup showed up abandoned in a university parking lot near the Tempe Town Lake two days ago, with traces of blood, which the lab confirmed matched *both* the neighbor and the Nogales pickup truck owner."

The phone was silent. Then the deputy director spoke. "Agent, NSA reports that its Blarney and Stormbrew programs have shown an increase in traffic interest on electrical infrastructure. At the same time, the Israelis have been tracking electrical engineering students in Europe who have disappeared off the radar. We had two partial facial recognitions. One on one of those students in Times Square and the other at the Port of Houston. Your report of last week made it to the action committee, and the commonality is of concern."

"Sir, what can I do?" Greer asked.

"Continue your good work, but from his point on, send daily reports to my office as well as the FBI chain. My office will e-mail you contact information as well as a list of substations, transformer yards, and balancing authority sites. I've spoken with FBI Director Tankerfell, and he is bringing an additional twenty-four agents into the region and placing them under the LA office's supervision. Protect us. We can't afford to visit the dark ages even for an hour," said Howard, and the line went dead.

Greer put the phone down. His mind swimming, he took a deep breath. He saw the icon for a voice mail and missed call—it was unfamiliar—and listened to Franklin Harbour. He hadn't spoken to Franklin in years. There was a time when agents and spooks didn't interface, but Franklin had been a mentor back when he was in the service, and after 9/11, agencies learned to communicate. What he heard next sent chills down his back despite the oppressive heat. He hit the callback button and was connected.

"Franklin, this is Greer. I just spoke with my office, and the events you describe were never mentioned. Sir, what is going on?"

Franklin responded, "Zach, all I can tell you is that an Israeli agent, with my blessing, has been tracking two from France through Texas. They and their cohorts just tried to take him out. Multiple civilian casualties in Denver. We don't have a presence in Denver. Who do you know there who can help and keep this between us, not the FBI command?"

Greer thought for a moment before responding. "Sir, keeping this from command would be a career killer. I know someone, but she might need a job when this is over."

"She'll have one, and you will too, of course," Franklin said.

"Her name is Carol Manning, former California state trooper. She's tough and smart. Can you send me details, or should I have her call you?" Greer said.

"I need both of you in on this and on the line. I'll hold," Franklin said.

Carol had just returned from the gym and was drying off from a shower when her cell rang. She recognized the number. "Hey, Zach, why the call? Does it have anything to do with the drive-by here?"

Greer replied, "It wasn't a drive-by. I have a friend, the London station chief of the Central Intelligence Agency, on with me. Are you somewhere that you can speak privately?"

Seconds passed while Carol sought to make sense of what Zach had said. Not a drive-by, CIA—what?

"Yes, I'm home. It's my day off, but it sounds like that's changing. You have my attention," Carol said, grabbing a pad and pen.

"Ms. Manning, my name is Franklin Harbour. I'm with the Agency, and I have asked Agent Greer for someone who can help the Agency on a matter of national emergency there in Colorado. Ordinarily the CIA does not operate domestically and certainly not without the Bureau, but this is an exceptional matter. We need to act first and bring the Bureau up to speed later. We are working with a Mossad agent under our supervision there in Colorado. He was the target of the incident in Denver. He wasn't hit, but civilians were, as you know. We need to make sure this stays perceived as a local incident, and we have reason to believe that someone in law enforcement, perhaps the Bureau, was involved."

Carol swallowed and replied, "Sir, what makes you believe someone in law enforcement is involved? Can you tell me anything more?"

"Not now, Ms. Manning," came Franklin's reply.

"Sir, you are asking me to keep my superiors in the dark, to break every protocol, and risk my career. I think I deserve—no, *require*—more," Carol said, trembling at her bold reply.

"Bob said you were tough and smart. Yes, you probably deserve more, but first I have to know you will not reveal what I am going to tell you to anyone, even under direct orders from your superiors. I know that this may result in your career being terminated with the Bureau, but I can assure you that my agency will have your back and a future for you," Franklin said.

"OK. I wasn't going on the fast track here in Denver anyway. What can I do?" Carol said after a moment of thought.

She towel dried her hair listening to the details of this morning's assault, the role of Josh, and chatter that had been picked up. The intercepts NSA had picked up between a cell phone in the LoDo bar and a phone outside an Au Bon Pain breakfast place on Tenth Street, across the street from the FBI's J. Edgar Hoover Building, jarred her. That intercept could have come from anyone, as the cell phone was of the prepaid variety, but the intercept revealed a detailed description of a Mossad agent matching Josh. The coincidence was too much to ignore. Both Greer and Manning were silent after Franklin finished the briefing. The Bureau was compromised.

The briefing described the location of the panel truck and Josh. Carol was already dressing, holstering her nine millimeter, and was out the door in ten minutes. She stopped in the apartment hall to wait at the elevator. "I'm on the way. Text me the Mossad agent's contact number and let him know I'll be there in ten to fifteen minutes."

"Be careful, Carol, and remember, we can't let these people know they are being watched," Zach said.

"Thank you, and report in to Elle Hardwicke here at the Agency or me if anything develops," Franklin added, hanging up.

It took Carol ten minutes to get to the Asian diner Josh was waiting in a half block from the old Gates Rubber plant.

Josh looked up at and saw what could only be described as an FBI agent. Navy pantsuit, dark-brown hair swept back. She was mildly attractive, midthirties, broad shoulders. Josh could not understand how all FBI agents looked alike and in so doing always stood out. In his profession, the object was *not* to stand out. He smiled and rose to meet her. "Agent Manning? I'm Joshua Marcus. Please call me Josh. Franklin said to expect a smart and tough agent, but not someone this beautiful."

"Does that work in Israel? Call me Carol, but let's leave the compliments out." Carol smiled and sat.

Josh was in the same jeans, blue T-shirt, and black leather jacket he had been in at the bar, only now the jeans had food stains on them from diving over the bar. He looked the part of an informer meeting with a cop.

"I followed the people who shot up the bar in LoDo to an abandoned warehouse up the street. I observed cameras on two corners of the rear of the plant near the loading docks. The cameras are new. It looks like someone is intent on not being surprised. The two I was following are engineers, or at least were engineering students in Europe. They were part of two Islamic cells we were monitoring in France and Italy," Josh said.

"The plant is being demolished, but it's still big for two people to recon. We need more assets," Carol said.

"I know, but given what has occurred, I'd rather not risk it," Josh responded.

"Well, let's assume that the cameras record their entrance *and exit* and watch that. It fronts on Mississippi Avenue, and there is a new five- or six-story apartment building there. Maybe we can convince someone to give us keys to one of the apartments," Carol said.

"My thoughts exactly. I went in the lobby, and there are two mailboxes that are full of mail. One apartment has two UPS notices on the door," Josh said.

"Sounds like our place," Carol said, standing up. She asked herself if there were Fourth Amendment search-and-seizure implications when a federal agent wasn't actually searching and seizing but commandeering an apartment without a warrant. She decided no, it was simple breaking and entering.

The van pulled behind the abandoned factory. It had been the number-one employer half a century before. Now, the old Gates Tire Factory sat vacant. It was a deteriorating shell in the process of being demolished. Its industrial history precluded restoration; demolition was its fate. For Estaval and Savano, it was perfect. Its rear access was all but invisible, and Estaval's uniform as a rental cop made access explainable. Several weeks before, Estaval had entered the factory and installed the rear security cameras, which he slaved to his IPad.

Estaval drove the van while Savano closed the gate. Rose simmered in the back of the van, studying Estaval, wondering if he could be trusted. Estaval marveled at the fact that they were in downtown Denver and yet hidden and safe. He had come to Denver from Pakistan twelve years before with a student visa, receiving bachelor's and master's degrees from the Colorado School of Mines. After 9/11, he changed his name from Abdul Hisbani to Estaval Hisbano. He told friends he had done so because his Middle Eastern name held his career back. He had shaved his beard and slowly adopted the appearance of a Latino American. He was invisible, just another commuter no one looked at. America's class system had served their cause. He kept to himself and had few friends outside of work at LCM, a regional civil engineering firm. He had fit in and had begun to almost enjoy some of what the country offered: women, television, freedom of movement, a centuries-old disdain for required credentials.

Savano, on the other hand, didn't look at all Hispanic. With light-brown hair and light skin, his Avarian roots dated many centuries back in the Caucuses. Rose too looked European. They appeared an exceptionally good-looking couple, which had allowed them to gain employment with Qatar Airlines for the past year while attending occasional classes in Milan and having access to international travel.

"Savano, this is too exposed. We would fit in better in plain sight, not hiding like bums in an abandoned building," Rose said.

Estaval was deflated. He had spent months creating a hidden spot, and they didn't appreciate it. "This is a perfect place. It is central and deserted, and my uniform as a security cop makes it a controlled environment. I am supposed to be here to make sure no one else can disturb us." Estaval continued, "Besides, we will be gone in three or four days' time."

"He's right. This is secure and will do for our short time here. We will be gone *tonight*. We need a secure site to assemble the materials," Savano said.

"American cities have radiological detection," Rose fired back.

"Yes, but that's why I chose Colorado and this site. The natural background radiation will mask the small amounts that might be emitted," Estaval replied.

Rose wasn't convinced, but she said no more.

Estaval's mind raced. *Tonight.*

CHAPTER 19

HIALEAH, FL

Lateef sat behind the wheel of the Comcast van using Gustavo's pocket-knife to clean the dried blood from beneath her coral-painted finger-nails. She had felt nothing when she killed Joseph, Gustavo's employee of three years. It had to be done. They needed his Comcast van, uniforms, and ID. Gustavo had not wanted to do it. She understood. It was nothing to her.

Alex and Gustavo were behind the van, digging in the soft sand on the edge of the highway. They had called a locate service to come and mark the utilities in the area. They knew the two pipelines closely paralleled each other on the map. The service painted the pipelines' alignments in blue spray paint on the highway and curb. One was two feet away, and the other four feet from the hole they were digging on the side of the highway. They would place the bomb in a plastic box that had been spray-painted with the Comcast logo. They just needed another foot of depth. Three feet was plenty.

A Miami-Dade Water & Sewer Department pickup truck slowed, and a man rolled down his window, letting the hot, humid South Florida air in. "Hey, what are you doing? That's pretty close to our lines here."

Gustavo looked up and stepped up out of the shallow hole. He wiped his forehead with a bandana and replied to the man, "We know where your lines are. Ours run perpendicular above them. Don't worry. There's four feet of vertical separation, but that's why we are out here hand digging. They won't let us use equipment because of your lines."

The man appeared to think a moment before replying, "It's probably OK, but I'm going to need to call it in. We are supposed to get notice of any digs in our right-of-ways. We need an inspector onsite at all times for any activities in our right-of-ways."

"That's fine, but first come over and look at our survey. I'm not so sure your right-of-way is located *actually* here," Gustavo replied.

The man parked his truck in front of the Comcast van and walked back to the yellow-tented structure behind and attached to the van. Gustavo pulled the flap aside to let the man in. The man commented, "Well, I know where the lines are. I helped install upgrades not two years—" His sentence was cut off by the five-inch blade piercing his carotid artery.

Alex laid his shovel down and stepped up out of the hole and pulled aside the tent flap. "Help me throw him in the back of the van. I'll get rid of his truck," Gustavo said.

Alex covered the body with a white tarp while Gustavo drove the man's pickup two blocks away to a coffee shop's parking lot. He wiped the truck of prints and walked back to the site.

By the time he arrived, Alex was done with the dig. "Help me with the box. Keep it level. The charge is directional," Alex said.

They placed the box into the hole and began to backfill the sandy material over the box. "Nine kilos of HMX will do it. It will leave a massive crater. Leave a shallow hole for the second box at street level. If we get the nuclear material, we will place it in the box at the surface to be dispersed when the bomb goes off. We have one more pipeline to take care of, the one from the well field," Alex said.

CHAPTER 20

PAGE, AZ

After hanging up, Greer thought he should be anywhere but Page. Things were occurring in Denver and Phoenix, not here. He had seen the dam and electrical switchyard. It was reasonably secure, as much as any electrical yard could be. The dam was secure, requiring a key and employee security card. Each of the employees had been issued a card, but only five had elevator keys. Those five had each been with Reclamation for over a decade. There were only eleven employees, and they knew one another other well. The public tours were limited to sixteen at a time due to the elevator size and were well chaperoned, yet there was light security and no metal detectors in place. He would suggest an end to public tours for the duration, under the cover of budget cutbacks.

He phoned Sandy to tell her his recommendations and let her know he would be leaving in the morning. Her phone went to voicemail. He left a message to call. As he entered his motel room, the AC was a welcome reprieve from the heat. It was only two o'clock and already in the midnineties. He resolved to get on his laptop and do some hunting. He needed a shower but was suddenly overwhelmingly tired. Perhaps just a quick catnap, he thought.

He awoke to bright lights, white surroundings, and a pounding in his head. He tried to focus. Where was he? What had happened? He tried to sit up.

"Whoa, wait a minute. You are all hooked up," the voice said.

He struggled to focus and saw Dylan. "What's going on? What happened?" Greer asked.

"Carbon monoxide poisoning. If Sandy hadn't come over to your room when she did, you probably wouldn't have made it. The doctors said it was close," Dylan said.

"You're alive," Sandy said, walking in the room with two cups of coffee, adding, "You've been out for over twelve hours."

"Twelve hours? How? How CO2?" Greer stuttered.

"Well, that's why Dylan's here. The owner of the hotel's brother was the plumber, and he was pretty distressed that something like this had happened in his place. His brother immediately drove over from Tuba City. He said the hot water heater vent had *intentionally* been disconnected and ducted into the room. He swears it had to be intentional," Sandy said as she stroked his hair out of his eyes. He was conscious enough to see Dylan fidget, not liking that contact.

"When can I get out of here?" Greer said through the oxygen mask.

"Good morning, Agent Greer. I'm Dr. Nez. I'm glad to see you awake. You've been on oxygen therapy since you were brought in. There is a danger of stroke in the first twelve to twenty-four hours, and you need one hundred percent oxygen until your blood results are better. I will need to keep you here today. You can likely be released in the morning. Is there anyone I can call for you?"

"If you would please call Agent Davies at the FBI in Los Angeles and let them know of my accident and that I have been out of communication," Greer said.

Dr. Nez, a tall, good-looking Navajo, nodded and walked out.

"Sandy, are my laptop and phone secure?"

Dylan responded, "Yes, I have them with your weapon."

He needed to get a message to Shaw and Franklin. First the attempt on Josh, and now him. Someone was serious, *if* they were linked, and *if* the plumber was correct. Only the FBI and CIA knew he was in Page.

"You get better. I have to go on duty; Page just got a little more interesting," Dylan said, walking out.

Sandy walked out and in a low voice said, "Let me know if you want to grab a late bite. You're off at nine, right?"

"That's the plan. I'll text you later," Dylan said.

Sandy went back in the room. "I instructed the nursing station that no visitors are allowed and to call Dylan or me if anyone asks about you."

Greer interrupted. "Sandy, I need your help. First, I need my gun, and I also need to confide in you a bit more about what I am working on."

Sandy nodded, saying, "Your gun is in my truck. It's outside. That's not a problem, but why me? Why not call your office? I'm sure you folks have reinforcements."

Telling a white lie is almost like not lying, he told himself. "It's complicated. I am tasked to another agency, as my office may have been compromised. I can't take a chance. I need someone outside the loop, someone who has no connection with the Bureau. Someone here."

Sandy looked at him. Was there a touch of fear, mortality, something sincere? She could see it. She was surprised by her reply. "Zach, I'm a park ranger. My experience is in botany, geology, and drunken boaters. Of course I'll help, but why not Dylan or—"

Greer interrupted. "Because I think I know you. Because you *aren't* a cop. If I talk to Dylan, he talks to his superiors, files a report, and in this town, everyone knows everything before I'm out of this room."

He was right on that; the town was small. For the past twelve hours, all everyone had been talking about was the federal agent who had almost died in Al and Ellen's motel. "All right, you have my attention. What can I do?" Sandy replied.

"Not here. I need to get out of here—now, not tomorrow. We can take oxygen, whatever I need, but I can't stay here. Things are moving too fast to be here another day. Do you know this doctor well enough to convince him?" Bob said.

"Maybe. Charles is a good guy. One of the few Navajo to leave and come back to help his people. I know his wife and him pretty well. She's in a yoga class I sometimes take. I'll talk to him. But what is moving too fast?" Sandy asked.

"I'm here because of actionable intelligence of a possible attack on the grid, the electrical infrastructure. We—or at least the good guys—have been investigating what may be a plan that would make 9/11 look insignificant. I think my 'accident' *may* be related to that plan. And I may not be the only good guy to have been targeted in the past twenty-four hours," Zach confided.

Sandy stared into his eyes. He was telling the truth. She could see it. It wasn't fear, it was more determination mixed with anxiety.

He reached for her hand. "I'm serious. I really need your help," Zach said.

Sandy felt a shiver, something. Was it fear or the excitement of his touch? He wore no ring. She told herself to snap out of *that*, surprised that even crossed her mind. But she didn't withdraw her hand. He wasn't trembling. His touch felt solid; perhaps he too had felt it.

"Well, you can't very well go back to your room, and Dylan will not take it well if we go to my place. Assuming I can get you out of here, we can go back to the park trailer. No one will be there till tomorrow's morning meeting. We can make a plan there. There's a sofa that you can sleep on till we get you a more secure place to stay," Sandy said. She looked at him intently and rose. "I'll go find the doctor."

Zach used the buttons to raise his bed to a full sitting position and looked around for his clothes, finding them in the side table next to his bed. He also found his phone. His phone had forty-seven e-mails, and his voicemail looked full, all but two from his office; the other two were international numbers, no doubt Franklin. His head pounded but was clearing. He needed some time before dealing with the office. He slid his pants on, but the shirt was out of the question with the oxygen monitor and mask. He didn't want nurses running in if the monitors showed he had removed them.

"I see you're tired of our hospitality, Agent Greer," Dr. Nez said, entering the room.

"Hospitality has been great. I appreciate everything, Doctor, but in my business, leads and information dry up quickly," Greer responded.

"Ranger Heller said as much. I don't like it, but I understand it. I'll release you on two conditions: First, you need to be on pure oxygen for another eight hours, no exceptions. I can lend you two of our four-hour tanks. And second, I want you back here in the morning at eight for blood work and an O2 monitor. If there is any residual CO_2 in your system, I am readmitting you. I want your promise," Dr. Nez said.

"I promise, and thank you, Doctor," Greer said as the doctor turned and left.

Almost immediately, a nurse came in with a scowl and removed the oxygen monitor, barking, "Keep the mask on until we get you a travel tank."

Sandy smiled from behind the large, overweight nurse, mouthing the words silently, "Nurse Ratched."

Zach tried to keep himself from smiling.

CHAPTER 21

BLACKSBURG, VA

Javier arrived at Eduardo's apartment building parking lot at 5:00 a.m. as planned. It was still dark and cold for Virginia in May. He threw his duffel bag in the backseat and got in with it. Eduardo nodded to Ellise. Javier handed him a thermos of coffee. Javier watched in the dim reflection of the rearview mirror as Eduardo glared at him. Javier knew his beliefs didn't permit coffee. They drove in silence, through the sleepy college town, out on Highway 460 to the interstate. It would be an eight-hour drive north. Eight hours and a dozen years of sacrifice for all of them.

CHAPTER 22

PORT ELIZABETH, NEWARK

Phillipe and Marza walked arm in arm from the freighter. Three expensive Rimowa rolling bags identified them as well-heeled adventurers. The captain watched them; he was dark, probably from Southern France, he thought. The woman, she was definitely Eastern European with her high cheekbones, full breasts, and stocky legs. "Eurotrash," the captain spoke to his first officer, watching them walk away toward the Customs Office. "Why anyone with money would think freighter travel is adventurous—two weeks on a cargo ship when you can fly in seven hours—is beyond me," the captain continued.

Phillipe and Marza showed their French passports to the two customs and immigration officers, who asked them how long they were staying in the country. "Three weeks, sir. We want to see Las Vegas and the Grand Canyon this time," Marza excitedly said.

The officer's stone expression belied his first impression, which was to roll his eyes at these two. "Are you carrying currency over $10,000, any fruits or vegetables?" he asked.

"No, sir. Just a bottle of French wine we brought for our hosts here," Phillipe said, showing the bottle to the officer.

"That's fine. You are allowed the bottle; have a nice vacation," the officer said, stamping their passports and waving his handheld scanner over the bar code on the passports.

They smiled and walked to a waiting cab. Amazing, Phillipe thought. No checking of bags, no search. They had expected, planned, for so much more. Marza grabbed his hand as they strolled away, completing the charade.

CHAPTER 23

OVER NEVADA

He was the only passenger on the C-20G from Coronado, the military-government version of a G-III. He loved "flying private" but hated being torn once again from his son. Shaw promised himself that when his twenty were up next May, he would retire and get a security or desk job, something nine to five, near his son. There was still time.

He stared at the electronic dossier on his laptop. Ballistics from Denver showed one shooter, an M-4 with armor-piercing .223 rounds. Why these were available on the market he couldn't understand. Their only use was killing two-legged game...as most shooting targets and big game leave their armor at home. As a hunter, marksman, and former army ranger, he couldn't justify these weapons, particularly these rounds, in the general public's hands. Ballistics showed these were not *sporting* rounds.

He scanned past the Denver synopsis and read the NSA intercepts. Could the Bureau have a mole? What were the odds of someone purposely making that call within the shadow of the FBI's building in DC?

The "eyes-only envelope" folder was opened with his employee code. In it was Franklin's report on Joshua Marcus, a Mossad agent allowed to operate under his direction in the United States. Then he scanned the materials provided by Israel on the cells they had been watching in Italy and France, thinking that had a familiar sound to it.

He went through the NSA and JTTF briefing folders, each about five pages in length, describing what communications had been intercepted by NSA and what the Joint Terrorism Task Force had assembled for their daily briefing paper. The *chatter* was at a higher-than-normal level and included noise within the hemisphere. No hits with customs and immigration that were out of the ordinary in the past twenty-one days. In general, nothing solid to go on other than the Denver attack. For a moment, Shaw wondered if the Agency hadn't overreacted. Maybe it had been a drive-by; street gangs were known to possess weapons corresponding to the ballistics. Could the Denver attack have been nothing more? No, Franklin vouched for the Mossad agent's abilities, and the NSA intercept from a location in DC to the Denver bar was too much of a coincidence. If Franklin was concerned, he needed to be.

CHAPTER 24

TEMPE, AZ

Ibrahim sat in the window of the Starbucks and watched as the pickup backed into the parking spot and tapped the white BMW 650i coupe, causing its alarm to go off. Then he saw the three occupants of the pickup, matching the descriptions he had been provided, get out of the truck. He looked in both directions as he walked out of the door toward them. A few people had stopped to look at the commotion. He overheard one girl tell another, "A couple of Mexicans banged into that beautiful Beamer. Wow, is that a bummer."

He motioned for the three to get back in the truck and follow him in his Honda Civic around the corner. He glanced around the corner to see if anyone was following. It would not be good to have his car seen. Not seeing anything, he quickly got in, turned the ignition, and pulled out.

After getting back to his apartment building's parking lot, he walked over to the pickup. "I hope you can do better than that entrance," he scowled at the three.

Vincent glared while Amante looked down. Hector was not used to being talked to in this way and was the first to speak. "Give me your code, or you will die here."

Ibrahim looked at the larger of the two in the far seat, who was leaning forward. "Mount Sannine," Ibrahim said.

"33.88," Hector responded with the reply code.

"Relax. You are safe. Once we take care of a task, we will go to a safe place. You've probably been traveling without food or sleep. A good meal is waiting for us," Ibrahim said; he knew he needed to be careful with these three.

They tied up a loose end and drove the pickup out to Tempe's Town Lake. After wiping the car of fingerprints, they all got in the Honda Civic. They drove north on North Scottsdale Road, past the Old Town with its not-so-authentic western facades. The two in the back stared out, wondering if Americans were really like those they had seen in westerns. Hector stared straight ahead, taking in the direction of travel and driving customs, trying to absorb as much as possible should he be required to take over.

They drove by saguaro cacti and finely manicured green lawns. The comfort, amenities, and wealth of these Americans were apparent at every glance. The car slowed to a stop at a red light. A police cruiser came up alongside, and the officer in the passenger seat looked into the car.

"Look relaxed. Don't look back," Ibrahim said under his breath.

The light changed, and Ibrahim deftly accelerated to 40 mph. The cruiser, accelerating slower, pulled behind them. Two, three agonizing blocks passed, and then the cruiser's lights came on, signaling for them to pull over.

"Do not speak unless they ask a question to you, and make no sudden moves. I will handle this," Ibrahim instructed. He leaned over and grabbed a folder out of the glove compartment in front of Hector.

The police stayed in their car. They would be running his plates. After what seemed like too long a time, the officers both got out, one walking to the driver's window and the other staying back of the car on the passenger side, his hand on his holstered gun.

"Good afternoon. License, registration, and insurance card, please," the young officer said as he scrutinized the three other occupants.

"Yes, sir. Was I going too fast?" Ibrahim asked, handing the paperwork to the officer.

"Remain in the car," the officer said, walking back to his partner.

"Two in the rear look real nervous, and they don't fit with the driver. They have worn, scuffed boots with plenty of dirt. Laborers, probably illegals. Front passenger looks calm. The plates match. Ibrahim Shastani, Middle Eastern graduate student at ASU. No outstandings," the officer said to his partner.

"We have nothing on them and no cause to detain or check the others. The way they were looking back at the light, I expected we'd have more. Give them a warning, and let's go," the older officer said.

The officer handed Ibrahim back the papers and license. "I'm going to give you a warning on crossing lanes without a signal. Be more careful in the future," the officer said and then turned and walked back to the cruiser.

As the officers watched Ibrahim pull away, the radio came alive. "All units, DHS reports an MRD radiological detection in Phoenix at 11:35; approximate location North Scottsdale and McDowell. The detection was broken and has not been reacquired. Any overweighted vans, light trucks, and similar vehicles should be reported for HAZ review."

The older officer whistled and said, "That was only thirty minutes ago. That close to Arizona State and St. Luke's, it could just be a medical shipment."

CHAPTER 25

WASHINGTON, DC

The DHS notification of the radiological detection came across his screen at the same time his phone rang. Franklin's voice on the line was firm. "Shaw, Franklin here. Have you seen the DHS notification from Phoenix?"

"Yes, just now. What do you know?" Shaw asked.

"It's the second detection in as many days. Yesterday, there was an unconfirmed detection near Newark's Liberty Airport," Franklin said.

"What do you mean 'unconfirmed'? How does one confirm a detection?" Shaw asked.

"I asked that myself. What I am told is that the detectors are actually composed of two detectors: a scintillation detector that measures radiation one way and a gas-filled detector that measures radiation in a completely different manner. Suffice to say it is a redundant detection device. If both means detect radiation, it is a confirmed detection. But if only one means detects and it's not above a certain level, it is assumed to be a false positive," Franklin recited.

"Given that we have two detections in two days, both in major metropolitan areas, and with the event in Denver, we are assuming the New Jersey alarm now might not have been a false positive and we are under a possible attack. Elle Hardwicke and I are about two hours from landing at Andrews." Franklin continued, "I'll meet you at Langley at 16:30."

Shaw pushed back from his desk, taking it all in. He messaged Kathy Corre, Sarah Tashkent, and Brian Culbert: "Meet in my office in fifteen minutes. Drop everything else you're doing."

CHAPTER 26

"Greer, Davies here. I need you back in LA ASAP. Are you fit to travel? I heard you had an accident. Some kind of CO leak?"

Greer replied, "Wasn't an accident, according to the locals here. What's up?"

After a second of silence, Rob Davies spoke. "What do you mean it wasn't an accident? Are you telling me someone intentionally tried to do you in?"

Greer replied, "According to the local cops, yes. They said the venting was intentionally disconnected and vented into my room. I don't know if I totally believe it, but I'm not supposed to travel until tomorrow. Something about blood levels."

Davies tried to digest what was said and how that might fit with what he had called about. "Greer, we've had two radiological detections in less than two days. Newark and Phoenix. With what happened in Denver, the Bureau is going ape. I can't just dismiss the idea that someone intentionally tried to kill an agent. That would mean you might be close to something. What do you know?"

"That's the problem. Nothing. Security at the powerhouse and dam isn't bad, and we strengthened it with what resources they have. Not enough population to waste a dirty bomb on, and a terrorist wouldn't waste a nuke on a hydro plant. It's protected by over five million cubic yards of concrete. We can see to it that boats cannot get near the dam. That's all I can see that's missing," Greer said.

"OK. Make the recommendations law. I'll send a plane for you in the morning," Rob said.

Greer looked over to a wide-eyed Sandy. "You said dirty bomb and nuke. What the hell is going on?" she asked, almost in a whispered voice.

Zach replied, "You sure you want in on this? Still time to say no."

"Well, let me think. Stopping nuclear terrorism or going back to checking campsite littering and boat registrations. *Of course* I'm in," Sandy replied.

Zach smiled. He needed the levity, and he needed the help. He also found himself wanting to spend time with her.

"First, I'm not accepting that my little accident was anything more than that—an accident. But if it wasn't, who in Page has a beef with the FBI enough to kill? That's something Dylan and his office could assist with. Second, can we barricade boats from getting close to the dam? I'd like to restrict them from getting a thousand yards from the dam in both directions," Zach said.

"Yes. On the lake side, a buoy line stretches across the channel about a hundred feet from the dam, but it would be possible to anchor a buoy line and cable just below the mouth of Wahweap Bay where it feeds into the main channel. That's about a mile from the dam. It would piss a few boaters off who like to see and fish the dam. There's also road access to the channel just above the dam that would need to be restricted, but that's tribal land, so we'd have to involve the Navajo authorities. Below the dam, we can restrict that pretty easily.

"But the bigger problem is the bridge. The main highway in and out of Page goes right over the dam. Highway 89 is the major feeder from I-70 on the north and Flagstaff and Phoenix to the south," Sandy said.

Phoenix to the south, Greer thought. He needed to find out how heavy a nuclear device would be. The road had to be closed to all but small vehicles beneath that weight limit. They needed the Highway Department to close the bridge.

Without replying to Sandy, he dialed Davies back. "Rob, I can secure this installation, but only by closing a state highway. The major artery that goes in and out of Page traverses a bridge that is right next to the dam. Can someone find out how heavy a nuclear device is and get the Arizona Highway Department to close the bridge over the dam to vehicles large enough to carry one? I don't have much information on how large these weapons are. Does someone need a truck? Perhaps we can make up a story about bridge cracks and a bridge inspection."

Rob replied, "I'll see what I can do. I'll get back to you."

Sandy frowned, remarking, "I'm not sure the bridge idea is going to be convincing. Start thinking about another white lie. I'm going to need you to explain to the Park Service and Page PD why we need to close the channel to boaters and banks to fishermen *and* the bridge."

Greer let out a sigh. Sandy was right; he hadn't thought about that. One white lie would be believed. Two would not. They needed to come up with a single reason to close the channel and bridge without alarming the local population.

Sandy was the first to speak. "What about a spall? That might work!"

Zach stared back asking, "What's a spall?"
"The geology of this area is that it is all sandstone, middle to late Jurassic-era formations. The Entrada, Navajo, Kayenta, and Wingate formations are the rock formations you see here. Sandstone is soft and absorbs water, as it once was the bottom of an ancient sea that covered inland America. The pressure of the overlying ocean compressed the sand into sedimentary rock. When you put water and steep canyon walls together, you get sections of rock that slough off—sometimes they can be massive. They call them spalls. A few years back, the Park Service

banned low overflights by the military. The vibrations were resulting in dangerous spalls to boaters. We might be able to spin a story about a potential spall near the dam, which would necessitate closure of the channel to boats *and* the bridge to trucks to reduce vibrations," Sandy said.

"I'm not sure I followed all that completely, but it sounds convincing to me. We can round up some folks to act the part of experts. I'll make a call for that." Greer continued, "Not to change the subject completely, but I'm pretty famished. I haven't eaten since that lovely breakfast at the hospital. You don't suppose I can convince you to grab an early bite of dinner, can I?"

Sandy's response was almost too quick. "Sure, particularly if Uncle Sam is picking up the tab. But I need a few minutes to clean up. I want to get out of the uniform." She smiled. "I'll swing back here at six and pick you up," she continued.

Zach felt a pang of excitement, which surprised him. It had been a long time since he had felt this sort of feeling. He didn't think it qualified as a "date"...but she was going to change for dinner; that was a good sign. He hadn't seen anyone in almost eighteen months, since his wife had left him. She had said she "needed to grow." While he had thought she was fully grown when he met her, he knew the real reason. His job kept him occupied ten hours a day, often away. He had never been there for her. When he did get home, he was too exhausted to have a normal conversation. It wasn't to be.

He hadn't looked at a woman since then, confining—or maybe *distracting* was a better word—his attention to other thoughts. He really didn't expect to be thinking or feeling like this. He was approaching his relationship with Sandy as work, but there was something more that caused him to feel alive and a bit human around her. On the other hand, he thought, she had a boyfriend...a big one who carried a gun for a living. That was something to be mindful of.

Sandy manhandled the light-green pickup. The US government didn't pay for power steering. Talking on a cell and trying to turn the pickup was a challenge. She needed to call Dylan to let him know she was going out to get dinner. His shift ended at 9:00, and she remembered she had tentatively told him she might wait and have dinner with him. She dialed. "Dylan, I'm going to grab a quick bite early with Agent Greer. There have been some developments that he is going to want to involve the Park Service with. I didn't get a lunch and can't wait till later. Do you mind? I can meet you later, when you get off."

She could tell from Dylan's voice that he did mind but was trying to mask it with sarcasm. "Agent Greer? Hmmm, I'm not sure if I like that idea. I get off at nine. If you are still out, let me know where you are, and I'll join you—*if* that wouldn't be interrupting."

Sandy felt controlled and a bit upset by his tone but replied, "Sure. Text me when you are leaving." She knew that he was right to feel that way. It was she who was feeling as if his joining would be an intrusion. She had forty minutes to get home, take a shower, fix her hair, put some makeup on, and get back to the Park Service trailer by 6:00. It was a good thing she wasn't like a lot of women, or she'd be two hours late, she thought.

She pulled into the drive, unlocked the door, and started for the bathroom, dropping her light-green ranger uniform in pieces along the way. She pulled the shower curtain aside, stepped in, and felt the hot water through her hair. She lathered and rinsed and then slowly rubbed an oil over her taut and tanned skin, which seemed to absorb the oil with a soft sheen.

She got out of the shower, dried her hair briskly with the towel, and stared in the mirror, thinking not of Dylan but of Zach. She needed to shake that off. The dry desert air had dried her hair almost before she picked up the hair dryer. In ten minutes, she was out the door, a light-blue lace bra barely visible beneath her blouse, which was tucked into a tight pair of blue jeans.

CHAPTER 27

JERSEY CITY, NJ

They pulled off the Jersey Turnpike at the Lincoln Highway exit. After eight hours in the car, they were stiff and exhausted. Their senses now alive again, they pulled up to the tollbooth to pay the fee. Eduardo pulled out a twenty and handed it to Javier, who gave it to the attendant, who gave change without a word. They pulled through and took the first right onto Lincoln. They drove through warehouses and industrial yards, then crossed a bridge over the marshes famous for slowing the advance of the British several centuries before. They turned onto Stuyvesant and eased back, looking for the address. It was a poor neighborhood, where hardworking Americans came back to after their shifts were over.

Seeing the address, they went around the block and drove into the alley. Javier walked to the door and dialed a combination into the lockbox hanging from the door handle. The first breath inside was a mixture of mold, rotting wood, and years of dust. He stifled a gag and went to the front room, softly parted the sheer drapes, and raised the side window a few inches for air. No one was on the street; no one had observed the entry. They likely were still hard at work at this hour. The late-afternoon sun was dim through a gray sky that seemed to touch the low rooftops, adding to the oppressive staleness of the old house.

The residence was attached to an electrical supply warehouse. Eduardo peered into a bedroom that had a small bed, nightstand, and lamp, with nothing on any of the walls. It would do. He put Ellise's duffel on the bed and heard the knock. They froze. Then the knock again, and the song they had been told to listen for, "Fortunate Son," Credence's iconic antiwar song. Javier knocked back three times. They heard the sound of a latch being opened in the next room and rushed to it. A door swung open to Phillipe and Marza. They embraced without a word.

CHAPTER 28

LANGLEY, VA

Franklin walked into the glass room, its walls embedded with electrical fiber to contain any communications, a room safe from listening devices. He shut the glass door, and an electric current rendered the glass opaque, shielding their words from the outside. He shook hands with Shaw and Sarah and was introduced to Kathy Corre and Brian Culbert.

Franklin started the meeting. "Let's get to it. We have had two radiological detections in the last thirty hours, one in Phoenix and one in Newark. We have had a sanctioned Mossad guest almost taken out in Denver. The perpetrators are believed to be under surveillance now in Denver by that Mossad asset and a trusted agent on loan from the Bureau. There is anecdotal evidence that the Bureau has been compromised, in DC. NSA has picked up a high volume of chatter. The Israelis were tracking two cells believed to be extremists made up of Chechens and Syrians that suddenly disappeared four weeks ago from Italy and France. They both disappeared overnight—the same night. The Mossad agent believes at least two of the missing cell members made their way into this country. Lastly, about three weeks ago, we started hearing chatter about an attack on infrastructure, bridges, the grid, in the homeland. There also is a mention of a Mexican cartel. I don't have to tell you what all this points to."

Sara spoke first. "Why were the Israelis following the cells? What do they know? Do they know or have recognition on any of the members we can run through our databases?"

Franklin responded, "They decided to share all with us only a couple of hours ago, after their asset was targeted in Denver. Sarah, you'll take the lead on getting that information and analysis of that data."

Kathy spoke next. "What is the tac situation in Denver? You said they were under surveillance. Are we going in? We need to take them alive."

"Actually, the Israeli asset needs to take them alive. If the Bureau or this agency seizes them, they go to ground and call their lawyers before we get any answers. The foreign asset is, shall we say, less familiar with notions of constitutional rights. Mind you, we will not condone such activity on US soil. I am sure that at some time in the future, we will express a very strong condemnation of such conduct to the Israelis," Franklin said.

No one voiced any response, not that one had been solicited.

Shaw was next. "We need to get enhanced radiological imaging and detection to Manhattan. That's likely their target. But what of Phoenix? It isn't a primary target—spread out, low rise. It doesn't make a good target. What's there that they would want to hit?"

Sarah replied, "Palo Verde Nuclear Generating Station is just west of Phoenix. Hit that with a nuke, and you radiate most of Arizona's population. Lake Mead and Hoover Dam are close."

"Well, that fits with the threat chatter against infrastructure. Shaw, you concentrate on New York and have overall field command. Who do we use in Arizona?" Franklin responded, knowing that with the FBI compromised, the terrorists had crippled any response.

"I know and trust a great deal of FBI agents, but they would have to work under the Agency's umbrella, and it would have to be unknown to Bureau hierarchy. The Bureau is not likely to sit back while the Agency engages in this sort of a domestic investigation. It would go public. We can't let operational strategy be known to the Bureau if there is a leak, or it could accelerate whatever schedule the bad guys have. It will have to come from the president," Shaw said. Franklin knew Shaw was right. Shaw continued,

"The president's inner circle would have to be informed, but it needs to stop there. Justice can't be in the loop; it's too filled by those who believe in full disclosure, transparency, and the primacy of the press—laudable expressions that emasculate counterintelligence."

Franklin stood, summarizing for everyone, "I'll brief the president. I'll speak to Director Harrence within the hour. We'll take over the third-floor action room. Get who you need, folks; it's going to be a long row. One more thing: call Ivy Ferris at NYPD. I need to speak with him as soon as possible and tell him to keep the request between us."

CHAPTER 29

NORTH MIAMI, FL

The hospital appeared quiet. Visiting hours had just closed at 10:00 p.m., and a handful of cars remained in the visitor lot. Lateef and Alex wore the blue uniforms of medical technicians they had purchase earlier at the All Uniform Supply Store near the airport. Lateef carried a nine-millimeter Beretta in her purse. Alex carried an AR15 in a duffel bag that Gustavo had somehow been able to acquire on one day's notice.

Walking in the staff entrance, they walked by one of the guards, who never looked up from his paper. Alex thought this was going to be too easy as he pulled out the map of the hospital floor plan he had printed off the hospital's website. There, circled on the map, was Wing E, Room 2100, Nuclear Medicine. They got in the elevator, went to the second floor, and followed the green corridor markings to Wing E.

The door to Room 2100 was locked with a digital keypad. Lateef unbuttoned the two top buttons of her uniform, with the stethoscope around her neck resting on her very visible tanned breasts. At the door, she rang the buzzer. A male technician came to the door and peered through the narrow vertical glass. Lateef waved a file in front of the door, and the man gave his head a quizzical slant. She then put the file under her arm and with one hand softly rubbed the stethoscope, making sure her fingers occasionally touched the surface of her taut breasts pushed up by her bra, all the while mouthing, "I have a file to be delivered for a procedure in the morning."

The technician entered a code, and the door unlatched. He opened it just enough for her to step in the doorway. His eyes were fixed on her chest. He saw her hand with the file sweep toward his chest with the knife briefly and was startled by her movement. The man went down with a look of surprise in his eyes.

They were in. "We needed him alive. We need to know where the materials are," Alex curtly said.

"I know. He turned as I struck. It wasn't supposed to hit his heart. There has to be someone else on duty," Lateef replied as they pulled the body into an exam room and locked the door.

Alex threw the empty duffel and AR15 over his shoulder. In one hand he held a nine- millimeter and in the other a Taser. As they went down the hall, they heard someone talking. A woman's voice: "I told him no three times, but you know him; he won't take no as an answer. My shift's over at one, and I know he is going to be waiting for me." She had to be on the phone; no other voices could be heard. They waited for what seemed like forever, and she still was not getting off the phone. Alex tapped a metal cart against the wall.

"Robert, is that you? I'll be there in a second. Robert? Robert?" She then spoke into the phone. "Pam, I need to get back to work here; I'll call you tomorrow." She hung up.

With that, Lateef walked around the corner, file in hand, and feigned surprise. "Oh, I didn't know anyone but Robert was here tonight. I'm Dr. Johnson," Lateef said.

"Dr. Johnson, I'm Ellen Hower, a tech. Can I help you?"

Lateef walked toward her. "Well, as a matter of fact, yes, you can," she said, pulling out the nine-millimeter.

"Where are the radionuclides kept? If you cooperate, you will live," Alex said, walking around the corner into her view.

The reply was immediate. "Room 2113A, two doors down. In the cabinet, but it's locked," the woman said.

Lateef grabbed her by the arm, and they walked to the room. Alex pulled out a small pry bar and wedged it in the cabinet door near the lock. With one movement, the door sprung open...and a silent alarm went off three floors down, in the hospital security center.

Alex swept all of the vials and canisters from the cabinet into the duffel and turned around. He nodded to Lateef and walked through the door into the interior hall as Lateef slit the woman's throat. The gurgling sound of air mixing with blood and their footsteps in the hall were all that could be heard. They had done it...it had gone smoothly.

They peered into the main hallway from the secure door to find the hall clear. Alex stuffed the AR15 back into the duffel, keeping the Taser and the nine-millimeter in his oversized uniform pockets. Lateef wiped the blood off her hands on paper towels and slid her nine-millimeter into the purse she strung over one shoulder. They walked to the elevator and then decided against it, instead taking the stairwell. The stairwell opened with a loud screech. The sounds of their steps on the concrete-and-steel steps were louder than they had expected. At the ground floor, Alex peered out the small door's window and saw no one. He took the nine-millimeter out of his pocket, taking its safety off. Lateef held her nine-millimeter down by her leg.

They opened the door and walked across the lobby to the exit doors.

"Stop. Police. Drop the bags down on the ground slowly," an officer yelled.

Alex swung to his right, firing on three officers, each with gun drawn. The barrage of semiautomatic weapons fire lasted only a few seconds. Alex, Lateef, and one officer lay dead. Another hospital security guard lay mortally wounded.

Across town, Gustavo listened to the twelve o'clock news report a shooting at the North Dade County Hospital. He listened to the report of an attempted robbery—the anchorman insinuated that narcotics were believed to have been taken. He sat still, walking everything through his mind. No, he didn't think anything was traceable to him. Besides picking

them up at the airport and taking them to their hotel, his only other contacts were calls to two disposable cell phones and one trip to their hotel,
but he had walked to the hotel and used a hat and dark glasses.

He turned off his light and sat in the still of his apartment thinking and
remembered he had booked the hotel room. In the morning, he would go,
collect their things, and check out. That would terminate any connection
between them and him, or so he hoped.

CHAPTER 30

DENVER, CO

"**M**ovement on the second floor, lights. Looks like they have light curtains, but there is definitely activity on the second floor, sixth window from the left," Carol said.

Josh was half asleep, suddenly woken, his eyes trying to focus. He rubbed his eyes and stared into the small spotting scope. There, even as the makeshift drape dampened the shadows, he could see that there was light around the perimeter of half the window and shadows. Movement. They were still there. He needed to get into the building. Or they needed to move. He needed to know their plan, target, leadership. Without technical and human backup, this was a standoff, and time was not on their side.

"What if we force them out? A fire, security cop, something to push them into the open?" Carol said.

He knew that something was needed, but a cop might cause them to go to ground, or worse, become martyrs. Josh replied, "Too risky. A cop might spook them into detonating in Denver. If we could—"

Carol interrupted. "A gang. We need a gang." Josh stared at her. Maybe they don't have gangs in Israel, Carol wondered, then continued. "A street gang. Denver has a few, but not in this neighborhood. I know someone who might be able to help." She dialed a number. "Danny, it's Agent Manning. No, we're good. I need a favor, one that will get a favorable recommendation for your mom's next parole hearing. Call me back after you round up a few of your friends. I'll meet you at the Paper Tiger off Mississippi and

Bannock, and be sure to bring three or four of your friends. I'll be there at ten."

She laid out her plan to Josh to have a few gangbangers go onto the property and inside the building. Not directly confront them, just make noise and flush them out. "These gangbangers—can you trust them?" Josh asked.

"Not at all, but I can trust them to make noise, cause trouble, and act menacing. It's what they do, and they can take care of themselves," Carol replied.

Josh nodded. It could work. The American street gangs were ever present, and it wouldn't seem staged in an abandoned warehouse setting. Being flushed at night might cause them to be careless, off guard. It was a plan.

CHAPTER 31

Sandy arrived back at the Park Service trailer a few minutes past seven. Greer walked out with his portable oxygen tank and climbed into the pickup. A faint smell of lotion told him that she took this dinner as something more than work. For his part, he had changed into loafers, jeans, and a Tommy Bahama three-button shirt. It felt good to be out of the FBI mold. He'd washed up in the sink, not having a shower in the trailer, but he was pretty sure he wasn't offensive.

They drove out of the Wahweap Resort along Lake Shore Drive, which overlooked the channel and lake. Navajo Mountain, some thirty miles distant, was a soft red at sunset, the warm-yellow desert light still illuminating its crest. The lights of Page flickered on the hill above as they passed the Visitor Center at the dam and crossed the bridge to the Page side of the river canyon. The river, seven hundred feet below, was dark, the canyon walls still radiating heat from the day into the cool evening. He was taken by the serenity, the beauty of the desert and lake.

She noticed him staring and commented, "I never get over its beauty. I never appreciated Georgia O'Keefe's paintings until I moved here."

"It's surreal, as if someone flooded a moonscape," he replied.

After a scorching day, the temperature over the canyon was cool as the rocks began to cool. "Without soil and vegetation, the rock captures and holds the heat. It stays warm well after the sun goes down as the rock bleeds off heat. The cold water and shade below keeps the canyon cool," Sandy said.

They drove up the hill into town. "You like Italian? There are good Italian restaurants here. The Italian marble and stonecutters who built the dam settled here. Best pizza in five hundred miles," she said.

"Sure, as long as they have a cold beer," he replied.

Pizza, beer, and a beautiful lady sounded pretty fine. He needed to regroup after everything that had happened in the last twenty-four hours. They pulled up to a white building with half a dozen wooden picnic benches outside. The place was crowded with people standing and milling around. Despite Sandy's protests, Zach resolved to leave the oxygen tank in the truck. An hour or two wouldn't kill him, he said.

Walking in, Sandy spoke to some while others gave him an inquisitorial look. Small towns—everyone knows what you are doing before you do, Zach thought. They pushed inside to the bar and ordered two Peroni. He took a sip of ice-cold beer. Few things tasted that good, he thought. Then his cell rang. He looked at the blocked number. He thought about letting it go to voice mail but, given the events of the past few days, answered it.

"Hey, Greer, Shaw Ellison here; remember me? It's important. Can I have ten minutes?"

Zach was surprised. He hadn't seen or talked with Shaw in several years. They had been pretty close in Afghanistan in 2002–2003. Shaw had been in the Special Activities Division for the CIA's National Clandestine Service. Greer had been a ranger. Those were heady times. Few Americans understood that the Taliban were defeated and run out of power by a force of fewer than 100 CIA operatives and 350 special forces soldiers from each branch of the military, guiding fewer than 15,000 indigenous Northern Alliance fighters on foot and horseback—450 against an army of 50,000, and it was done in less than two months, with few US casualties. The bonds between these "operatives" were immutable.

"Sure. I'm in a restaurant trying to get a pizza. Let me walk outside." He motioned to Sandy that he had to take the call and walked out. "OK, I can hear you now. What's up?" Greer said.

He listened to Shaw's explanation of the events—the Phoenix radiological detection, which he knew about, and the Newark one, which he didn't. When Shaw explained the details of the NSA intercept from outside the FBI Building in DC and the Mossad agent attack in Denver, he stiffened. Confirmation that the Bureau had been compromised was unbelievable. Shaw explained that the president was being briefed within the hour and that a special task team headed by the Agency would be complemented by a handful of carefully selected FBI personnel. Unbelievable—the CIA on US soil, displacing the Bureau. That would cause all kinds of turf battles. The liberals, libertarians, and right-wingers would *all* go nuts.

"If it were anyone else but you, buddy, I would tell you no way. I'm going to need some cover with my office, as they have ordered me back to LA in the morning," Greer added. Greer gave Shaw the condensed version of where he was, why he was in Page, and the CO incident.

Shaw was silent for a second before responding. "I'll get you the cover. We are briefing the president this evening, but this possible attack on you may be related. Stay where you are. I'll get back tonight after we hear what the White House says."

Shaw hung up, his mind trying to wrap around this new twist, what it was, and what it could mean.

Zach went back into the restaurant and found Sandy. It was crowded, and he stood inches away from her. She handed him the beer, clicked bottles, smiled, and toasted. "Nella bocca del lupo."

"What's that mean?" Zach asked.

"We're in an Italian restaurant. It means 'into the mouths of the wolves.' To those who live fully."

Greer drank a sip, feeling that was certainly the case this week.

The hostess took them to a table out on the porch. It had a perfect view of the high plateau and the sun setting to the west, with the lake in the foreground. The glare of the sun was blocked by a partially rolled-down porch shade. The sky was turning from the glare of day to a solid blue that seemed to only occur in the desert Southwest. Against the muted oranges of the rock, it was like nothing he had seen.

Sandy smiled, remarking, "You haven't spent much time in the desert, have you?"

"Only in Afghanistan and Kuwait," he replied.

"Hmm. Guess you weren't enjoying the scenery there," Sandy said, feeling there was far more to Agent Zach Greer than she had expected.

Zach felt as if he wasn't good company, his mind still trying to assimilate the conversation with Shaw.

"You seem distracted. Has something else taken place?" Sandy said.

Not sure how much to reveal, he knew that if something was occurring here, he needed her help. Perhaps he just needed her. He didn't know quite how to respond but started anyway. "What I'm going to tell you I probably shouldn't, but I'd like another set of eyes and perspectives on this." He explained some of the call with Shaw. The fact that Shaw had called him, that the Agency was involved and president was being briefed. He left out the Newark radiological detection, as that was not confirmed and not necessary to what Sandy needed to know. Then he asked, "Sandy, I feel I am involving you in something far more than you expected, but I need your knowledge. What infrastructure is here that might be a target within, say, fifty miles of us?"

Sandy took another sip of her beer and thought. "Well, there is the dam, of course, the electrical yard, the power lines, and the Navajo Generating Station. But that's just the tribe's coal-fired power plant, not something that is much of a target for a terrorist. We've already talked about securing the dam. Maybe it's a simple as the electrical transmission lines. Or maybe there is no local target."

"Do you know all the Reclamation guys who work the dam?" Zach asked.

"I know some, but no, it's not my agency, and I don't deal with it that much. But Rich—you recall you met him—would know everyone."

Greer made a mental note to check the service records and duration of employment of each Reclamation employee with access to the dam.

He knew he needed this information, but part of him wanted to get back to where they were standing in the crowded bar. He knew the best approach was to ask about her. "So how is it that you came to be a ranger here in Page and are still single? I hope that's not too out of line."

She visibly straightened in her chair. Wrong question—too personal, he thought.

"Your capacity to switch gears and throw someone off must be an interrogation technique. It just took me by surprise. No, it's not too personal. I always had a love of the outdoors, and my college was oriented toward the physical sciences. Most of what a park ranger does is in some ways tied to the land, the environment. I just fell into it, and in case you haven't looked around, the dating pool is pretty limited here. I just haven't found an excuse to be attached to anyone in that way," Sandy said, her eyes a bit more vulnerable now.

"I thought Dylan and you were a couple," Zach said, trying to catch himself midsentence from blurting that out.

"We don't live together; we have separate places. We enjoy each other's company, but there are...complications. He's a good man, a good father to his daughters. I just don't know, but I feel like there should be horns, trumpets, lights when someone connects with that certain person, and I don't think I've seen that yet. But let's change the subject a bit. How about you?"

He thought a moment how to answer that, knowing it would follow from his questions, but he didn't have a good answer. "My wife left me eighteen months ago, no kids. We were married for eight years, but I was in the service and away for part of that. That's why I joined the Bureau. That and the Bureau paid for me to get a grad degree. Seems I was gone for the army, gone for school, or absent for the Bureau most of the time. It had to be hard on her. I don't blame her."

They were silent for a few seconds, and then the pizza and two more beers arrived. Mercifully arrived, he thought.

Sandy warmed and felt more for him. He was vulnerable and human, not just the tough guy she knew he was.

CHAPTER 32

SOUTHERN CALIFORNIA

Pedro knelt and crossed himself, as had done so many times. This time, though, it meant more. When he first arrived as a teenager, he resented having to imitate the practice, the religion. He felt it was a betrayal of his true God. But after a decade, a family, and a good life, he was open to the Catholic faith. The practitioners and clergy were good people. He waited. After ten minutes, he heard the heavy door open behind him and the footsteps of one person. He turned to find a young man, a delivery man, who said, "Pedro Ramirez?"

"Yes, that's me," Pedro replied.

"First time I ever delivered a package to a someone attending church," the employee said, shaking his head and walking away.

The return address read:

University Travel Services
1004 Main Street
Blacksburg, VA 24060

Pedro sat back into a pew and opened the overnight envelope. A brochure for Palm Springs, CA, Yucca Palm Desert Resort, with a voucher for a two-night stay. The date was two days away. A map was included with the route laid out from El Cajon. Marked in blue ink on a yellow Post-it was a note that read:

Rose S.
Dinner 7:00 p.m.
Hotel Bar
She has your cell number and will call

He was supposed to meet a woman by the name of Rose? What was he going to tell his wife? What lie he would need to come up with to leave San Diego, and for how long? He wanted no part in this but knew that no was not an option.

CHAPTER 33

SCOTTSDALE, AZ

Ibrahim brought Hector tea. Vincent and Amante were asleep in the down-stairs bedrooms. Ibrahim had rented the home online. It was a typical southwestern adobe home on two acres, hardly visible from any road in an area of North Scottsdale, where affluent families and retirees lived. Many of the homes were rented for parts of the year, so the goings and comings of rental cars and tenants drew little interest. The home was just off the busy Pima Road, near fine restaurants and golf courses. Tall saguaro cacti and cedars shielded the mostly one-story homes, all of which blended in with muted desert colors.

"Why did you involve your wife?" Hector bluntly asked.

"Relax. She is not really my wife. *You* sent her; she is my wife only as cover. Emilia is indeed well trained. Now, can you tell me what is in the luggage or the target?" Ibrahim asked.

Hector looked at him carefully and replied, "This is good. Emilia as your wife was creative. It will be good to see her again. She is a warrior. But for now, it is better that you not know, not just yet. It has taken a dozen years and many martyrs to bring the package and us to this place and this time. The one true God has been good to us. We will gut the beast and punish the fallen, those who have oppressed us. We will deliver a fatal strike upon the unbelievers. And there are others here—we are not alone, praise Allah."

Ibrahim knew he was in the presence of a master, a man who had devoted his life to serving. Emilia had never mentioned him by name, only reputation. His scars were visible proof of his commitment. "What is the timing of our work, and what can I do to be of service?" Ibrahim asked.

"We will stay two nights here, then we will deliver our enemies to Satan. You will assist us. You know this country and its people. You demonstrated that earlier with the police quite well. We will be in your hands to deliver us to the target," Hector said. Ibrahim beamed with pride.

Hector was weary from the stress of the day, of the past two weeks. He needed to sleep but knew he couldn't for two more hours, when Amante would take his place as watch. The doorbell rang, and Hector jumped up as Ibrahim walked quickly into the foyer. Hector shot him a glance to open the door. Ibrahim slowly opened the door, half expecting police or the American counterintelligence teams to race in.

Instead, a woman with large red lips and structural hair was at the door. "Well, hi there. I'm Annie Bellows, the property manager. I just wanted to welcome you to the home and see if I can be of any assistance." She was already halfway inside the door, her leashed white Bichon Frise dog leading the way, before Ibrahim could block her entry.

Seeing the woman's entry, Hector drew his knife to his side. The woman saw the bags, including the metal cases on wheels, and five pairs of shoes in the foyer. "Mr. Akapa, the terms of the lease state that no more than three people can occupy the premises without an additional fee. Are there more guests? The owner requires me to register the names of everyone who is staying in the house."

Hector put the knife in the back of his belt and came into the foyer. "I'm Hector Dominguez. I'm sorry; my two sons are students at Arizona State, and they aren't staying with us. They are merely visiting. I haven't seen them in over four months. Only my brother, his wife, and I are staying here."

The woman visibly relaxed but continued to stare at Hector's scars. Scars that pervasive must have been painful—a tragic accident? she wondered. "Oh, I understand. My apologies, but as the owner's agent, I had to inquire. The owner is very cautious. Do you have any questions about the house? Is there anything you need?" she asked.

Hector was amazed that the woman was concerned about one or two additional people in the home when her dog roamed unchecked. He was not used to dogs being pets and allowed in the home. The dog sniffed at the luggage, paying particular attention to the metal case.

Despite his insisting that he had no questions, the woman proceeded to show the outdoor range, hot tub, and pool filtration equipment to Ibrahim, which she remarked was what made the home "special." After nearly twenty minutes of insisting he had no questions, they made it back to the foyer and found her dog asleep on top of the rolling metal case, chewing on the bag's strap. "Come, Arthur. What a lazy dog you are. Get off of that suitcase," she nervously said, hoping the others hadn't noticed Arthur's chewing.

The dog straightened and jumped to the ground. As quickly as they arrived, Arthur and she were out the door, a deadbolt latching behind her.

Hector had been standing in the stairwell to keep her from walking down to where Vincent and Amante were sleeping. Ibrahim remarked, "We should have killed her. Do you think she suspects anything?"

"No, we did the right thing. She could have been missed by someone, told someone where she was going. It would have led to us. She won't be back," Hector said, rubbing he back of his neck. "Besides, we will push things up a day and be gone tomorrow. If you rented the home for a week, she won't return till the end of the week."

CHAPTER 34

WASHINGTON, DC

Franklin had been in the White House four times, each time because of events threatening the nation. This was his third president to brief. He had never met him, only heard reports that this president was different. He viewed foreign affairs as a distraction to his mandate, which was his domestic agenda. There would be no domestic agenda if Franklin's fears became reality. There hadn't been an attack on the homeland since 9/11, and this threatened to make that look insignificant.

He was greeted by National Security Advisor Kate Helmsworth. "The president will see you, Mr. Harbour. Please come in."

He had spoken to her several times since she had come on. He was impressed. Her credentials concealed her years. Barely forty, she was an Air Force Academy graduate, had been on the International Space Station for a stint, obtained a master's in science in foreign service from Georgetown, and had taught at the army's War College in Carlisle, Pennsylvania. Never having married, she was said to sleep only four hours a night. She didn't hide her political aspirations.

Franklin walked into the Oval Office to find the president, two of his national security advisors, the DHS, FBI Director Tankerfell, and the Agency's director, Harrence. "Franklin, what do you have for us?" the president said, motioning for him to sit.

"Thank you, sir. Mr. President, six weeks ago, a Mossad agent was following members of an Islamist cell in Marseille. A member of that cell is believed to have met with a former FSB agent now believed to be working as an independent selling arms in the Middle East, primarily in Lebanon and Syria. The Mossad operative was ambushed but able to evade his attackers after killing one of them, who, under duress, mentioned a previously unknown terrorist organization.

"The Israelis acted on the French cell and a related Italian cell within twenty-four hours, only to find that both cells had vanished within that twenty-four hours. The same Mossad agent tracked two persons thought to be members of the Italian cell to Denver, where he was ambushed once again. You are all familiar with the shooting in Denver yesterday. The Mossad agent believes his identification of the FSB agent and the person he was meeting with was the reason they tried to kill him in France and Denver.

"Mossad indicates there may be a new player in the region, a group called the Twelfth Gulf Sheik's Service. No one has anything on this group, but there is intelligence they may have some relationship or dealing with the Sinaloa Cartel in Mexico. Last night there was an unconfirmed radiological detection in Newark near the airport. Today we had a confirmed radiological detection in Phoenix." Franklin stopped to give all a moment to digest the information. The room was silent, everyone waiting for the president to speak.

The president rose and walked toward the window, head down, and finally spoke. "Do we know if the radiological threat flew from Newark to Phoenix or whether there are two separate sources?"

Franklin responded, "We do not, but given that the monitor that had the hit was along the highway and those installed at Newark International didn't go off, and given the time elapsed between the two detections, we feel there is a better than sixty percent chance we are dealing with two separate sources. But it gets worse, Mr. President." All eyes fell upon him; only the DCIA knew what was about to be said. "Mr. President, Director Tankerfell, we have reason to believe the Bureau has been compromised and may have a mole."

Director Tankerfell's gray brow narrowed, and he spoke slowly, each word deliberate. "Mr. Harbour, I have questions. First, exactly what information supports this assumption? Second, how widespread or contained do you believe this breach is? Thirdly, why haven't I been briefed on this before now, in this room, at this time?"

Franklin responded, "Sir, NSA confirmed an encrypted cell phone call was made to one of the two subjects the Mossad agent was following minutes before the Denver restaurant attack happened today. NSA was able to get around the encryption. That phone call gave a description of the Mossad agent. Only the Strategic Action Office of the Bureau and my group were informed that the Mossad agent was in Denver. Less than two hours ago, NSA confirmed that the transmission originated from across the street, from the J. Edgar Hoover Building. And yesterday, an FBI agent I have known for many years was the subject of a suspected attempted murder while conducting an investigation of a threat to the grid in Arizona, four hours from Phoenix. Only the FBI knew he was conducting that task and his whereabouts. It is by no way concrete or confirmed...but it suggests a breach."

Everyone looked at Director Tankerfell. His bushy brow deepened as he spoke. "Ordinarily I would say those facts are weak, less than convincing, but given the events of the past forty-eight hours and the gravity of the potential consequences, I concur. There is too much risk to argue with or ignore the coincidences."

Franklin—and he was sure the others—was impressed by the professionalism and decisiveness of Director Tankerfell. In DC, everything is about self-perceived image and turf; he had expected the normal interagency response and pushback. Instead, here was an objective response. Tankerfell's stock had just gone up.

The president nodded his agreement. "Gentlemen, Kate, what are the scenarios, options, and recommendations?"

Zignew Karlinski, Ziggy for short, Kate's fellow national security advisor, spoke. "Mr. President, we have to assume New York City—likely Manhattan—is a target. As for Phoenix, that is less clear. Phoenix isn't a large enough population, not a symbol of America. We have to assume it is another target, perhaps Las Vegas, Los Angeles, or perhaps an infrastructure target."

Kate spoke next. "If there is a mole in the FBI, we can't keep our knowledge of the investigation and countermeasures quiet. If the mole learns that we know something is in the works, it could accelerate the timeline. That means that either the Bureau will be hamstrung or the lead agency has to shift to CIA, and we all know what happens when the CIA is perceived to act within the States. We may need an AG opinion of whether the CIA can conduct investigations inside the US."

Franklin responded, "The Agency can, and has, conducted investigations within the US. It just cannot do so against US citizens. I think that gives us some latitude here. Besides, we could select a core group of FBI personnel we know are clean, whom we have personal relationships with, vet them, polygraph them, and label this an FBI-directed operation assisted by the Agency. We can run all digital comms through the Agency so there is no digital Bureau access."

"Do it. We can't have a nuclear strike in this country. It would crash the economy for a decade and would compel an unconventional response. Have we any idea whether a nation-state is behind this?" the president asked.

"Nothing for certain, Mr. President. The Israelis believe that one person in one of the cells may have been an Iraqi with connections to Hezbollah, but it's thin. The contact with Hezbollah is over fifteen years old. Thrown into the mix is that the Israelis also suspect that a former FSB operative who has gone out on his own may be the connection for the devices. There are still a number of nukes unaccounted for after the Soviet bloc fell apart in the early nineties. The price of a nuke on the market would limit the players and likely dictate some state assistance. An operation on US soil also means years of planning and coordination, which is outside the capabilities of most terror groups," Franklin said.

"Hezbollah points to Iran," Ziggy said.

"Or Russia," Kate added, sending a chill through everyone. The Russians had been overly aggressive lately under Putin. His conduct in Crimea, Ukraine, and Estonia was reminiscent of Soviet Bloc Cold War expansionism. The Russian economy had suffered greatly after the sanctions increased when the evidence pointed to a Russian contractor participating in the shootdown of Malaysian Airline 17. An economy not much larger than Italy, the Russian economy was fragile, deriving nearly 30 percent of its revenue from oil and gas exports, over half of that with Europe, which had begun plans to wean itself from the Russian spigot. The fear of Putin's militarism and the resulting sanctions had shrunk foreign investment in Russia. It was not outside the realm of Machiavellian thought to assume that Russia saw a need to level the playing field by upsetting the West's economy.

"That would be irrational on Russia's part. Their economy would only suffer more if the West fell into recession. Putin serves at the discretion of the oligarchs. If they suffer, Putin's history," Ziggy said.

"I disagree. Russia would have a strongman at the helm free of the puppet strings of the oligarchs. Remember, Putin has publicly stated that the downfall of communism and the Soviet Bloc was a great tragedy," Kate replied. Yet it was too much to imagine, too risky even for Putin, she thought.

During the course of this discussion, the president sat down behind his desk. He was visibly stunned. He hadn't wanted his administration to be mired in foreign affairs. His agenda was domestic. His disdain for matters of foreign affairs had been evident. He hadn't been afraid to act, but he did not feel comfortable in the arena. It was a distraction. Now he faced the largest crisis since another president had been elected on the basis of his domestic economic agenda. FDR had risen to the challenge when the world had gone to war; he prayed he would handle this challenge as well.

As the meeting broke up, Director Tankerfell leaned over to his aide. "I want every Bureau employee in the DC office polygraphed, no exceptions. Start with those in strategic action, antiterrorism. Top down. I want the son of a bitch found. Polygraphs begin within the hour."

CHAPTER 35

PAGE, AZ

Dinner went far too fast. A couple of beers apiece and good conversation. Greer was surprised by how much he had talked, wanted to talk, to Sandy. Her tanned skin had a subtle sheen from the heat—she seemed to glow. He found himself wanting to touch her. She must have sensed as much, as when the bill came, she reached as if she were going for the check, her hand on top of his, not withdrawing. "Let me pay half," she said.

Zach kept his hand in place, feeling her touch. "I'm sorry, but that would emasculate me. Something about the thought of a woman paying a check that just doesn't seem right," Greer said. He knew this had turned out to be something more than a business meal chargeable to Uncle Sam.

"Am I intruding?" Dylan seemed to appear out of nowhere in time to see the exchange and hands held.

"No, we were just fighting over the bill," Sandy replied somewhat nervously but with a look to Zach that left little doubt of her disappointment.

"I should get back to my motel, or wherever they have me now. I need to update my office and find out what's been happening. I haven't checked in since this afternoon," Greer said.

"I had your belongings transferred to the Marriott Courtyard. It has a government rate, central entry, and pretty much the only lobby with a webcam. No chance of someone coming in undetected in case your little incident last night was intentional," Dylan said.

"Thank you; I appreciate that," Greer said to Dylan. Greer put some cash with the check, and they were beginning to walk out when his phone rang. He looked at the caller ID: Shaw Ellis. "I'm sorry; I need to take this. I'll take a taxi to the motel, and thanks again to both of you."

Sandy and Dylan looked at each other and laughed. "We'll wait for you. There's only one taxi in town, and he's visiting his sister this week," Sandy said.

Greer listened to Shaw's short version of the meeting with the president. "Stay where you are. We believe this may be a coordinated attack. Do you have one or two friends at the Bureau in California who can assist under these circumstances, without alerting the Bureau chain of command?" Shaw asked.

"Yes, Robert Davies in LA and Phil Jackson in San Francisco. I trust both of them with my life. Davies and I go back to our service days. I'd also like to tap a local park ranger here, very bright, and I'm going to need access to the local facilities here," Greer replied.

Shaw continued, explaining that oversight and intel would all be through the Agency; nothing would be through the Bureau. Absolutely no digital intel, reports, or action orders would be entered through the Bureau's database. Franklin told him to expect a FEDEX package tomorrow with a return address from Amazon in Stillwater, OK. Of course, there was no such address or Amazon distribution center in Stillwater. Instead, he would receive a fingerprint-encrypted tablet that would be the foundation for all further communications between the Agency and him. Landlines, unencrypted cell phones, and traditional Internet no longer would be used. Franklin asked him to give the direct-dial numbers for Davies and Jackson to him. He would call both tomorrow at 08:00 Pacific time. Greer was to call Jackson and Davies tonight. Shaw signed off.

Greer exhaled a large breath and turned to walk back to where Dylan and Sandy had been waiting and, from what it looked like, arguing.

"I'm sorry to keep you waiting and to be such a burden. That was work, and it seems I have quite a lot to do yet tonight," Greer said.

"I'll give you a ride," Dylan said. It wasn't lost on either Greer or Sandy what Dylan was thinking and why.

Dylan and Greer drove the mile or so to the motel in silence. They pulled up to the front door, and Zach thanked Dylan and said, "Dylan, I need to ask you something."

Dylan thought, oh boy, here it comes. He's going to ask me about Sandy and our relationship. Dylan knew what he was going to say. He was going to be blunt and tell him to stay clear of her. He'd suffered enough infidelity with his former wife.

Zach thought about each word he would use. "This is a small town. Pretty much everyone should know what most locals are doing, don't you think?" Zach asked.

"Yes, and any indiscretion becomes common knowledge," Dylan responded.

"Well, then, have you seen anyone new come through here, perhaps a couple of people together, in the past month? Anyone staying longer than a tourist, not looking like a tourist?" Zach asked.

Dylan relaxed. The question wasn't what he had expected. Perhaps he hadn't read Greer right. "No, not that I've seen. I'll ask the other officers, but can you give me something more? Is there something the department should be aware of?"

Zach felt he may have said too much but needed Dylan's support. He didn't have to know the broader picture. He'd tell a partial truth that would sound more like a general criminal investigation. "The Bureau is looking for a suspect under investigation in California who may be traveling with one or more accomplices. There's reason to believe they may be in Arizona or Nevada," Zach said. It was all he could say.

Dylan knew there was more unsaid but also knew it would be point-less asking more questions if the Bureau wasn't going to be reciprocal and reveal more.

Greer got out, closing the door behind him. He turned and put his hands on the rolled-down window and said, "Thanks again, and let me know if you see anything out of the ordinary or something out of place," Zach said.

Dylan thought the only thing that fit that description was Greer him-self but replied, "Sure thing, Agent Greer. Good night."

CHAPTER 36

NEW JERSEY

Javier couldn't sleep. The gravity of what the day would bring excited him. It had been thirteen long years. America's consciousness had moved beyond the events of 9/11. America had fought two wars since then, and most Americans under thirty didn't understand the connection between 9/11 and those wars. Well, at least those who hadn't fought in them.

His early years in this country at Cal Tech had been difficult. Seeing the opportunities and excesses that this country offered had been conflicting. His roots in the Middle Eastern neighborhoods of Madrid had steeled his faith and commitment. He spent time with the new immigrants from North Africa and had lived a year with an uncle in Damascus. That was before the explosive influence of handheld Internet devices had launched the so-called Arab Spring. He felt the empowerment of democracy was a cancer against his religion. Allah's dictates were not subject to discussion, not subject to challenge. Exposure to Western ways corrupted. Those who accepted those customs were no different from the kafirs who had imposed secular rulers on his people. There could only be one God, one world.

He found himself boiling, raging internally. He needed to calm. He needed sleep. The next three days were his last on this earth, and he needed to be perfect in his execution. He looked at the hard-sided case. It had cost so many lives, so many martyrs. How ironic it was that the godless Soviets, who had invaded and been vanquished in Afghanistan, who had lost their empire, would now supply the means for the destruction of the remaining superpower. Allah did work in mysterious and deliberate ways.

Eduardo was on guard upstairs. He had been one of the original team, commencing this operation over sixteen years ago. He had lived in Mexico for over three years and had "legally immigrated" to the United States nearly a decade ago. The Americans needed their workforce; their own citizens were too lazy to do the work. Eduardo had actually begun to respect the Hispanics he emulated. They were virtuous, hardworking, family oriented. First-generation immigrants, their lives washed by new-found opportunities, they had always been the hardest-working class in America's history.

Phillipe and Marza were soldiers. He had not been around Chechens before. Their light skin and European features hid their religious commitment. They had delivered the treasure, killing three Russians who demanded more than had been agreed upon. They had honed their fighting skills in Grozny against these same Russians.

Tomorrow they would scout the targets as tourists. The next day, he would assemble the explosives he had secured from his "coal mining buddies" he had worked to develop. They had laughed when he purchased enough to bring down a mountainside, explaining he needed to get rid of beaver dams on a friend's property. Javier's expertise would enhance the destructive effect.

With these thoughts racing through him, sleep was impossible. He lay staring up at the water stained ceiling.

CHAPTER 37

CALIFORNIA

Robert Davies sat alone in his small apartment's kitchen listening to Greer's story. That was what it sounded like: a story. Had he not known Greer, he would assume a call like this, at this hour, was the product of too many drinks, but he could hear in Greer's voice that this was no delusional story. "Jeez, the Bureau compromised. The president authorizing Agency oversight," he interjected. The fact that the director would be calling him to confirm sealed its authenticity. Director Tankerfell didn't call field agents.

Greer conferenced in Jackson. They all three hadn't talked together since their last night in Kabul. It was almost surreal. "Jackson, it's Greer, and Davies is on the line. Sorry to call you so late. How are Anne and the baby?"

"You gotta be kidding. What's this? A reunion call?" Jackson's spirits soared as he laughed into the phone. It was great hearing his old buddies' voices.

"Afraid this is not a social call. Is the line secure?" Greer asked.

"As secure as any landline. This can't be good," Jackson responded. He toggled the remote to turn the TV down, the mood sobering. They listened without a word as Greer explained for the second time the events of the last forty-eight hours, the presidential directive, and the director's instructions. There would be no more than a dozen Bureau personnel involved. They would take their remaining "vacation time," starting tomorrow. The required three-week advance notice form to take vacation time, together with its stamped approval, had been already logged in for each of them "months ago" and approved by the regional office shortly thereafter. The Agency and NSA had somehow accomplished that.

"I'd like to bring in Matt Jalencia. He's an analyst. The best we have. He's a Stanford grad. Designed his first software program when he was in junior high in East LA. He'd be useful on many levels. He is without question not a risk," Jackson said.

"I'm not comfortable and would need to have director approval. Let's say we hold off on him until we need him," Greer replied.

"Roger that," Jackson responded. Just like the old days, Zach was in charge.

"Let's each work up a potential target list and reconvene *on our vacation* at 08:00. Concentrate on infrastructure targets, power, transportation, communications, that sort of thing. And, of course, we can't discount population centers and public venues in the western US. Other teams are handling the Eastern Seaboard," Greer said. They all knew this was an impossibly long list. Without more, they could never hope to preempt an attack. If the elements were all in place for an attack, it would happen.

Like Greer, Davies was divorced. His kids never spoke with him after the lies the ex-wife put in their heads. He didn't have the energy anymore to compete with her, to try to "win the kids over," as his shrink had told him. He couldn't compete, wouldn't engage in that manipulation. He'd just left an on-again, off-again girlfriend for what he hoped was the last time. No one would miss him. As for Jackson, it was a different story. He'd tell Anne that a potential job opening had opened up, a good promotion with the new baby, that he needed to go back east for the interview. Anne would love that. She hadn't really adapted to California well; her Atlanta roots were too distant.

CHAPTER 38

LANGLEY, VA

The Operations Room was full, even though it was nearly 23:00. All heads turned as Elle walked through the room to where Franklin was standing. Even after a seven-hour flight, Elle commanded the room's attention. Her form-fitting Italian suits were legendary. It gave "pantsuits" a whole different meaning. At nearly six feet in flats, she still towered over most. She preferred five-inch heels, but work demanded less. She wasn't unaware of the attention. At times it was an unwanted distraction, a label of less than she was. But most of the time, she confidently used her presence to command a level of intimidation she enjoyed.

"Elle, good to see you. How was the flight?" Shaw asked, coming over to her.

"Uneventful; I slept most of it. Got an upgrade, which was nice," she responded.

There was a palpable tension. The last time they had seen each other, they had nearly slept together in Beirut. He still blamed the Israelis for that intrusion. After dinner at La Petite Maison and a few drinks at the hotel bar, the mission behind them, something sparked. It was not to be. As they were nearing her room, an Israeli air attack on a building two blocks away brought them back to reality. The Israelis had been given a tip by a Sunni imam in Qatar that a Hezbollah commander was meeting with two of his field commanders a block away. The Hezbollah commander had been directing rocket strikes into the northern Israeli towns of Avdon and Betzet. The Israelis attempted further communication with the imam but were never able to communicate or learn of his true identity after the successful strike. Shaw had never forgiven the Israelis for literally blowing that opportunity with Elle.

Elle removed a sheet of paper from her portfolio and began to explain the document. NSA pieced together two telephone calls made to the cells in Europe the night they disbanded. Partial communications, but the transcript reads: "Mahdi shall return inside Satan's home at the Twelver next hour." Elle then highlighted missing words in the recorded transmission. "'The time' something is 'upon each of the three apostles to its wakening.'"

"This message was delivered to both cells and is believed to have been sent from Tbilisi, Georgia, but that could have been a relay point and not the point of origin. And there's more. The person who rented both apartments the cells were using was a man named Helmut Pjorsky, former East German Stasi. He was found decapitated the day after the cells disappeared. GSG-9 investigators from Germany have been working with us on this. They were able to salvage part of the hard drive in a computer that was smashed at the crime scene. The drive reveals a large cash transaction that was made through an account at UBS Bank in London to a Cayman company. All looks perfectly legit except that it was for 175 million pounds, and Mr. Pjorsky's annual salary was just under 110,000 pounds a year. We came up with a dead end in Grand Cayman, but we are working it. The funds deposited into the UBS London account came from Zurich. The bank's policies are that they do not share information as to their depositors absent good cause or a Swiss order, but a comptroller we have in place believes funds may have originated in either Qatar or Bahrain."

"How much is a nuke going for these days?" Shaw asked.

Sarah spoke first. "It depends. Of the ten 'missing' units, all but three came from the former Soviet Republics, and only three are believed to be easily transportable. The others are simply too large. Here is a rundown on all known missing units." She projected a slide on the screen reading:

Origin	ID/Yield	LK Date	Wt./ W/D Dimensions
USSR	RDS3/42 Kt	10/62	2,890 kg 2.9x1.3 m
USSR	RDS3/42 Kt	12/1991	1,054 kg 3.1x1.3 m
USSR	RDS37/3 Mt	12/1991	1,054 kg 3.1x1.3 m
USSR	15F42/1.2 Kt	12/1991	2,459 kg 1.8x1.3 m
USSR	RT20/500 Kt	01/1992	1,901 kg 1.2x1.1 m
USSR	RA115/?	01/1992	29 kg 0.86x0.04 m
USSR	RA115/?	01/1992	29 kg 0.86x0.04 m
USSR	RA115/?	01/1992	29 kg 0.86x0.04 m
USA	B53/9Mt	11/1961	4,010 kg 3.3x1.4 m
USA	M7/32Kt	04/1964	764 kg 4.6x0.8 m
Pakistan	Ghaznavi/?	03/1998	1,055 kg (?)

Franklin spoke first. "What am I looking at?"

"Sir, the first initials are the country of origin, followed by type or model identifier, and the yield. Then, the initials 'LK' designate the last-known date the weapon was accounted for, and the 'W/D' stands for weight and dimensions. Where we do not know the answer, a question mark designates that," Sarah replied.

Everyone sat in silence as it sank in. Fourteen missing nuclear warheads? Eleven still unaccounted for?

Franklin spoke. "What is the yield of the three Soviet lightweight weapons? By their size, I assume these are so-called suitcase nukes?"

Sarah replied, "Yes, sir. Their existence has never been confirmed, but we have anecdotal evidence that up to three dozen were developed by the Soviets between 1979 and 1986. Stanislav Lunev, the highest-ranking GRU defector, is a source that these weapons exist. His testimony was confirmed by two KGB officers who came over to us after the Soviet Union imploded. Their yield is unknown, but we developed similar-sized weapons in the five-kiloton range, about a third the yield of the Hiroshima bomb. The same sources indicated that they believed that three of these units were unaccounted for when the Soviet bloc disbanded in December 1991."

"How the hell did we lose two?" Shaw asked.

Again, Sarah replied, "Both the 1961 US unit and the 1962 Soviet unit were lost over the Arctic, presumed in fifteen to seventeen thousand feet of water, when the planes that were carrying them were lost. You'll recall we each flew the Arctic as a part of strategic readiness in those days. We located two and could not locate the third. The Soviets admitted to losing one. The other one was pretty much a stupid mistake. We placed two underground nukes at a testing site and detonated one milliseconds before the other, but number two was a dud. We know it's buried now under nine hundred feet of radioactive rubble. It's not really missing, just not properly disposed of.

"The list doesn't account for potential units that could have been built by Pakistan's A. Q. Khan, North Korea, or terrorists using manuals scattered across the Internet, but we have ninety percent confidence that the list is accurate." Sarah let the last qualifier trail off, which wasn't lost on anyone in the room. Sarah continued, "We don't believe this is a dirty bomb, as they ordinarily would not trip the radiological detectors unless it was right next to it. And there is likely a leak in the containment shield, or we wouldn't be getting a reading for the same reason."

"Does that mean whoever is transporting this around may be exposing themselves to lethal doses?" Franklin asked.

"Yes, that's a distinct possibility," Sarah replied.

"Let's have a hospital alert go out from CDC to report any radiation sickness symptoms to CDC and for CDC to notify us," Shaw interjected.

"I suggest we have prepositioned action teams, three NEST teams, on twenty-four-hour alert. One can be prepositioned to handle LA, Vegas, and Phoenix. Another to handle Chicago. And one to handle New York, Philly, Boston, and DC. I think we can do that quietly through DOE. We can tell them no action bulletins, to avoid panic. That should keep it under the radar at the Bureau," Shaw suggested.

"Agreed. Handle it," Franklin said to Elle.

"There's one other item that I hesitate to mention, as its connection is weak, but it might be related. We just received a DHS notice that there was a shooting at a hospital in Miami. The perpetrators—one man, one woman—were killed along with two medical staff, two officers and a security guard. They broke into a locker with radioactive isotopes used in nuclear medicine. Very weak materials. DHS says they couldn't have constituted a dirty bomb," Elle reported.

"See if there is a black market on such for medical reasons. It might not be related. These people look serious. I don't see them making a mistake like that," Shaw said.

Shaw knew that they needed to catch the mole in the Bureau sooner than later. It hamstrung the one agency they needed the most. What he was about to suggest would occupy the minds and libraries of every journalism and law school in the nation for decades to come. "We are ignoring the elephant in the room. We need authority for NSA to domestically wiretap and search every computer of every FBI employee in DC. The president and directors of the Agency, Bureau, and NSA all need to be onboard with it. We may need a FISA warrant, but as I recall, we can avoid making anything public for seventy-two hours. Justice might need to be involved, but I believe Bureau employees sign a waiver as an employment condition. I suspect whoever it is will have his or her tracks covered, but we might get lucky."

Everyone knew Shaw was right. The search of personal computers and phones would later result in an outcry, but not a big one. After all, all Bureau employees knowingly consented to Fourth Amendment incursions when they accepted employment. "Agreed, and whoever it is will likely go dark once the event occurs. If we don't act now to find him, we may never get another chance. I'll brief the president and directors. Elle, get with the Agency legal department to work this up ASAP," Franklin said.

CHAPTER 39

DENVER, CO

Ever since she returned from her meeting at the Paper Tiger, Josh had been sleeping—actually snoring—for close to two hours. Carol had been sitting in the dark looking at the old factory and sipping on a now-cold mug of tea for nearly as long. A single light was on in the factory, and every once in a while, a shadow appeared, undoubtedly someone keeping watch. She'd received a call from Shaw Ellis informing her over an hour ago that a NEST chopper had overflown the position and detected no radiation emissions. That was at least one bit of good news. Backup support from Langley had arrived about ten minutes before at Buckley Air Base, the Air Force's Space Command facility just outside Denver. ETA was another thirty minutes. She'd feel a lot better when the cavalry arrived.

A second light, a flashlight, was suddenly visible, but only for a moment. Had she imagined it? Staring, she thought she saw a shadow move. The binoculars were not night vision, but they were strong. She'd sprung for them herself at Cabela's and kept them in her car. Until today, she had only used them twice, both at Bronco games. There. Yes. There was movement. "Josh, wake up," she said firmly.

He was up instantly, hand on his weapon. He cleared sleep from his eyes and tried to focus. "What is it? What time is it?"

"Quarter till midnight. There's movement on the west stairwell. I think it's our gang friends. Our backup isn't due for thirty minutes but at this time of night, we have to assume the targets will start moving," Carol replied.

"Your gang members for sure," Josh said.

"Not sure. I'll call it in. We need an air asset, something that looks like a police chopper but high altitude so they don't feel as if they are being pursued."

She was right. The chances of following without blowing the surveillance with only two people and two cars was not good. She made the call to Shaw.

Carol listened to Shaw explain what was in place. She was impressed. The Bureau would not have such assets and definitely wouldn't react as fast. She discontinued the call and matter-of-factly said to Josh, "Seems we already have air assets, have had for over an hour. They have two drones hovering over station. Small ones, but real-time feed to Langley. The drones have a top speed of thirty-eight miles per hour, but that should be fast enough to pursue in the city line of sight."

"I have seen variants of these. This is good. They are quiet mini-helicopters around one meter in size and have a long battery life. We've used them over Gaza and the Sinai. We should get ready to go," Josh said. He packed up the duffel, straightened the room, and wiped prints from the surfaces they could have touched in the room. Chances were the owners would suspect someone had been there, but with nothing taken and no damage, the police weren't likely to dust for prints. That said, prints from an FBI agent and a Mossad operative would send a few alarms off.

Carol watched as a dark form appeared at the base of the stairwell twenty feet or so away from the parked panel truck. Then she saw two more forms, one appearing smaller, perhaps a female, load several duffel bags in the back. The third person appeared from within the open factory bay on what appeared to be a forklift carrying two pallets with something shiny were being loaded along with what appeared to be three drums. She adjusted the binoculars and saw what appeared to be a shrink-wrapped carton or box on the one pallet, perhaps three feet by two feet. The pallets were loaded into the back of the panel truck. The three got in and drove quietly out of the lot. Carol and Josh had miked up with headsets by this time so they could communicate easily with Shaw's group and each other.

"Subjects moving east on Mississippi, now north on South Broadway. Air coverage, take over; we are getting to vehicles," Carol said.

Carol and Josh briskly left, checking for anyone who might have seen their departure. It was late, and the halls and streets were all quiet. Carol got to her car, got in, and connected her phone to the car charger. "Shaw, Manning here, rolling. Do you have eyes on?"

"Yes, subjects now on the interstate, I-25 northbound. On the interstate, they may outrun the drones. We are bringing up traffic cams on I-25 and I-70, both east- and westbound," Shaw said.

"Josh here, Shaw. Rolling now. Proceeding to I-25."

The decision by Shaw to not bring them down now, when they had them, wasn't shared by Sarah and Kathy at Langley. They argued for an immediate takedown and interrogation. At least stopping one possible set of attackers was assured. Shaw knew that it was more likely that the cells would be separate, with no contact or knowledge of each other. That weighed in favor of an immediate takedown. But the time to extract information was limited. On the other hand, taking this cell down would be known to the FBI and potentially the mole, and it was almost certainly assured they wouldn't talk or cooperate. No, the best move was to follow this group in the hopes of observing what type of target they were after, which might narrow the target list of the other cells. They would never let them out of sight, never let them execute their plan.

"Subjects exiting I-25 at Sixth Avenue westbound." Sarah was now reading out the drone surveillance.

"Roger that. West on Sixth Avenue; I am exiting in one minute," Carol said.

"Looks like I am a bit behind you, Carol. What make, model, and color vehicle are you in?" Josh asked.

"I'm in an Audi A-4, 2012, silver," Carol replied.

"Nice. I'm in a Dollar Rental car, white, Nissan something or other, with New Mexico plates," Josh replied.

Carol could see the panel truck about a half mile ahead. At this hour, few cars were on the road, more trucks. She didn't want to be too close. "Subjects in sight, about half mile in front of me," Carol reported.

"I have Carol in sight now, about one kilometer ahead of my position," Josh continued after a brief pause. "There are two trucks between Carol and the panel truck. She's staying behind both, and I am five hundred meters behind her." With I-70 being one of the three primary transcontinental interstates, Shaw began to wonder if the highway itself was a target. Shut down I-70, and it would disrupt, not stop, commerce. No, there had to be a target other than the highway itself. "I want a list of all potential infrastructure targets within two hundred miles of the I-70 corridor west of Denver," he ordered.

The drones were too slow, falling behind. They wouldn't be able to keep up with the vehicle on the interstate and were questionable at high altitude. "Get me the Joint Chiefs. We need them to task a drone out of Creech Air Force Base in Nevada. I don't know if they have any there, but their command authority is there," Shaw ordered. Had they been overseas, the Agency had its own platforms, but on US soil, well, the Agency never considered it a possibility.

There was more traffic on I-70. That was good and bad. They would need to tail a bit closer, but the presence of more lights in the panel truck's rearview mirror made detection of the tail at night less likely.

The operation-command duty officer listened to Shaw's request for immediate air assets and drone coverage incredulously. "Sir, the United States Air Force is not in the domestic spy business. Your request is unorthodox. I will get back with you after talking to my commander."

Shaw's reply was immediate. "I'll hold, but while you are getting your commander on the line, I'll conference in the situation room at the White

House. I'll let you speak directly with the president's national security advisor, Kate Helmsworth."

"Yes, sir. One minute, sir," the young duty officer's tone was suddenly all professional.

Shaw could only imagine the number of groggy generals being woken up in the next minutes.

The sound of clicks identifying who was on the line and the verification that all lines were secure was lengthy. Shaw counted twelve. He started the discussion. "Gentlemen, ladies, my name is Shaw Elliott. I'm with the Agency in Langley. We have been tracking a truck with a possible WMD westbound out of Denver. We need to clandestinely track this vehicle, and we need your help. We have two agents following the truck, but we need air support. What can you give us in the next fifteen minutes?"

He heard voices, papers rusting. "General Williams here, Mr. Elliott. I'm at the Pentagon. We can help you as long as the White House or Justice gives us a green light under the John Warner National Defense Act. That authorizes limited military activities in the homeland during times of imminent terrorist attack, overriding the Posse Comitatus Act.

"My folks tell me we have a HAATS command in Gypsum, Colorado, about a hundred miles west of Denver. HAATS is a high-altitude army training facility for our chopper pilots. We set it up to deal with the terrain we were faced with in Afghanistan. The closest drones we have are at Creech in Nevada. We can scramble a Blackhawk that can track your target, but it will be visible at dawn. At that point, we'll have a Triton 4C on station. DHS may also have some units operating with Border Patrol you can access out of Texas or Arizona. But this all hinges upon the approval from the White House or Justice." The general was thorough and smart enough to make sure that when all was brought to light, as it would someday be, he would have his "get out of hot water" note in his back pocket.

"General, Kate Helmsworth here, national security advisor. We will transmit confirmation of the order from the White House within thirty minutes. Please give these folks everything they need. And one more thing I need to stress to everyone: This doesn't go beyond those on this call. We have a true national security crisis unfolding. No leaks." Shaw was pretty sure the generals were bristling at this comment. Leaks historically came out of the White House and the politicians, not the Pentagon.

After being given the duty officer's name and number at both Creech Air Base and the training facility in Colorado, Shaw hung up and dialed the Colorado facility. "HAATS Colorado, Corporal Miller here."

"Corporal, my name is Elliott at CIA. Write down my caller ID number. You will be receiving a call from the Pentagon shortly. I need you to scramble a Blackhawk crew with full fuel for a night-ops surveillance mission now. Take down my number and connect me with your comms so we can interface all communications with the flight crew and my team."

The young corporal, undoubtedly a National Guardsman, was shocked yet professional, replying, "Yes, sir. We'll need some time. This is a Guard facility, and we have no one on the field. We have two crews training that are staying in a local motel, which I'll raise, but ETA to be fueled and airborne is likely forty-five minutes."

"Tell them it's a national emergency, not a drill. I want them airborne in thirty," Shaw said.

"Sir, I've got another call, likely the call from the Pentagon. I have your number. I'll get back to you." The corporal hung up.

Shaw walked over to where Sarah was directing communications with Josh and Carol. "What's the status?" he asked.

"Still westbound on I-70 at about the Georgetown Exit 226 marker. Looks like they will be in the tunnel in a few minutes. We will lose aerial surveillance in the tunnel. I've told Carol to tighten up the trail through the tunnel. The drones can't get over the mountains and are laboring now at that altitude. Will we have coverage on the other side?" Sarah asked.

"Tunnel? What tunnel?" Shaw asked.

"The Eisenhower Tunnel. It goes under the Continental Divide," Sarah replied.

"Jeez, get me design schematics of that tunnel. If they don't blow it up, it's a perfect place to lose aerial surveillance." Shaw was worried now, continuing, "Tell Agent Manning to close it up...maintain direct eye contact through the tunnel."

Inside the panel truck, Estaval yelled back to the passengers, "Get ready to open the side door. Throw the drums out. They have to go out in order but right after each other....the one marked one, and then the one marked two, and last the one marked three in the tunnel when I say."

"What is in them?" Rose asked. She had not trusted him but was gaining more respect now.

Estaval explained, "It's actually quite simple. Two barrels, eighty-four gallons, of synthetic engine oil, with one barrel of molybdenum disulfide in the barrel marked two. In the two-lane tunnel, this concoction will create an impossibly slick environment no vehicle can operate within. It should create a devastating accident when the vehicles swerve to avoid the barrels themselves. All we have to do is slow down in front of vehicles, causing a pileup."

It was brilliant. A later traffic investigation would reveal motor oil and barrels that could have fallen off of any truck, with nothing to trace the event to them. The altitude of the tunnel and the night precluded satellite detection. And Estaval's "maintenance" of the four traffic cameras the week before when he installed a cable interrupter on the common camera feed ensured that as they entered the tunnel, all camera images would be interrupted. The interrupter would be found, but not for days.

"Cell coverage in the mountains is always a challenge. Verizon works best outside the major cities, but even that has challenges in the winding mountain valleys. In a tunnel with trapped cars, cell coverage won't exist. It should give us the time we need," Estaval proudly said.

Estaval looked in the rearview mirror, two trucks disappearing quickly due to the grade and about a half dozen cars. Ahead lay the tunnel, and in between, seven more big rigs all struggling to make the grade. Two cars, a Ford pickup and a Prius, were doing the speed limit. He knew that if he could time it right with the trucks, they would begin to pick up speed in the level tunnel. The vehicles would hit fifty-five to sixty in the tunnel. That would be enough.

"Get ready; the tunnel is ahead. Lift off the lids to the drums, but be careful not to spill them. When we get to the tunnel, open the side door but wait for my instructions to dump the contents of the barrels and then throw out the empty barrels themselves, They all must be dumped as close as possible to each other," Estaval said, nervous and excited.

"Carol and Josh, we'll probably lose you in the tunnel, but we'll have air coverage in about an hour. Keep your eyes open; the tunnel makes me nervous," Shaw remarked.

Carol could see the tunnel ahead and the lights of the panel truck, now not more than a quarter mile ahead. Josh was maintaining a visual on Carol's car lights.

The panel truck entered the tunnel with its gray lighting and dingy white tiles seasoned by decades of emissions. It had strained up to the tunnel's portal, but as the grade leveled out, it picked up speed. Carol couldn't see the side door to the panel truck open as she entered the tunnel. There were two big rigs in the tunnel building speed, a pickup and a compact between the panel truck and her. Out of the side of the truck, she saw something fall, then another, and another. Dear God, this was the target. She yelled into her mike, "They're throwing objects from the truck; it's—"

The effect was immediate. The fluids hit the pavement and washed across the two narrow lanes, with the three barrels now spinning and rolling across the lanes. The pickup swerved to avoid the first barrel and hit the slick mix, losing all traction, crashing sideways into the side of the tunnel immediately in front of the red Peterbilt, which by this time was jackknifing across both lanes. The compact slid under the sideways truck as the second rig tried to brake, hitting the blackish liquid surface. Without decreasing any speed at all, the second semi crashed headlong into the other big rig, vaulting up to the tunnel's ceiling and pinning one truck under the other.

"Shaw, Josh, the tunnel's blocked, all lanes. Stay out" was all she was able to say before her airbag deployed as she slid into the side of the tunnel fifty feet from the wreckage, which was beginning to smolder.

"Say again, Carol; you're breaking up," Sarah said. "Carol? Come in, Carol?"

Static was all that came over the headset and the speakers in the room. "Josh, do you read? Stop where you are," Shaw yelled into the mike.

"I'm here, stopped just inside the tunnel. There's smoke coming from inside the tunnel. An accident. I lost comms with Carol, but I saw her car go sideways before the accident. Tell whoever you need to signal the tunnel is closed, or people will begin piling up," Josh yelled. He could see the traffic slowing behind him. A big rig had evidently seen the smoke and Josh's stopped car and was blocking both lanes with its flashers on.

He ran into the tunnel toward the smoke. He got to Carol's car, where she was pinned between the collapsed steering wheel and the seat. "Are you OK? Are you hurt?" he asked.

"No, shaken up. I think I'm OK. Where's the truck?" She asked, clearing the powder from the airbag from her eyes.

Josh yanked on the steering wheel enough to dislodge it sideways from the stem, and she was free. He pulled her out and crawled up the three feet to the walkway above the road surface. Looking around the accident, he saw no cars and no panel truck.

He leaped down, grabbed her, and ran back to his car. "Shaw, Josh, we lost them. They created an accident to get our tail off them. The westbound tunnel's closed. Get them to close a lane of the eastbound tunnel. That's the only way through. Carol's shaken up but OK. I have her."

"Roger that," Shaw said, pointing to Sarah to get it done.

They had lost them. Unless they were made and came up with this plan on the run, they likely had another vehicle waiting for them on the other side. "Notify the Colorado Highway Patrol. Tell them there's an accident in the westbound tunnel and that we have a vehicle that is leaving the scene of the accident and give them a description of the truck. But tell them not—I repeat, *not*—to apprehend it. They need to follow it, and let them know this is a matter of national security. And tell them to shut down one lane of the eastbound tunnel for two-way traffic," Shaw said, thinking that sooner or later, all this national security stuff was going to be known by the Bureau mole, press, or both.

"Josh, Shaw here. Two-way traffic will be set up for the eastbound tunnel, but it will take a while. Do you think you can get through the other tunnel without killing anyone?"

"We'll try. We will be flashing lights and hoping all the way. Once through, where can we get back into the westbound lanes? Shaw, they set this up. They have to have another car waiting for them," Josh said.

"I know. I've brought in the Colorado Highway Patrol. They should be able to locate the truck. I have not alerted them to you and have advised them to follow but not apprehend the vehicle. But they're a sovereign and might decide to pull them over," Shaw replied.

The panel truck exited the interstate at the next exit, pulling into the parking lot of a LaQuinta Motel in Silverthorne. The parking lot was shared by two other motels and a restaurant, reducing the chances that a car parked by someone not registered at any of the lodgings would get towed. Estaval had parked the Jeep Laredo three nights ago and gotten a ride with one of his former classmates at the Colorado School of Mines after telling him his car had broken down. The classmate never hesitated to help.

A light snow fell, illuminated by the parking-lot lights as they pulled next to the 2012 gold Laredo. It had been purchased from a used-car dealer just weeks ago on the condition that the back window and side rear passenger windows be tinted as dark as the law allowed. He had told the dealer he was thinking of camping in it on his way across country.

They loaded the duffels and the carton into the back of the Laredo after folding down one of the back two seats. Rose would ride up front, making for a perfect couple appearance on a cross-country road trip. Savano was in the rear split seat, intent on getting some sleep, out of view by the heavily tinted rear windows. They pulled away from the van after wiping it down for prints and got back on the interstate. At this time of the morning, no one had seen them. The soft snow was stopping, and the stars were appearing. The crunch of the tires on the snow and sirens racing up to the tunnel in the distance were the only sounds.

CHAPTER 40

PAGE, AZ

Greer wasn't able to sleep. The dinner with Sandy was still on his mind, competing against his thoughts of the attempt on his life, the mole in the Bureau, and what "they" could do to his country. Sliding his legs over to the edge of the bed, he sat up and felt the usual scratchy three-star motel carpet under his feet. No cushion and the feel of sand paper...the stuff had to last forever, he thought. He turned on the light and was reaching for his laptop when the phone rang. It was 4:15 a.m., and it was the Agency's Virginia area code.

"Zach, its Elle Hardwicke. I work with Shaw. There have been some developments you need to be briefed on. At approximately three o'clock mountain time, our tail of the three Denver subjects was lost. The subjects planned and executed an accident that took out and blocked the westbound interstate over the Rockies, I-70, behind them. The search so far has not turned up anything. There's not much between I-70 and a town called St. George in Utah. From that point, they could go south to you; west to Phoenix, Las Vegas and LA; or northwest to San Francisco. Not much to go on, but you should be aware. I understand you are working with two Bureau agents in California. They should be notified. We have personnel en route now to Los Angeles and San Francisco who should arrive by noon local time. I need you to brief your people with the latest developments. We are setting up surveillance at the major choke points. We estimate that *if* they are headed that way, the Denver group could be to you by eleven a.m. local time and the West Coast by early afternoon."

Greer was now wide awake. He wouldn't have been able to sleep anyway. "Send me what you can on the subjects and vehicle. There's only one road in and out of here, so they shouldn't get past me. I'd suggest using the local police here to look for the car. I have a contact in the Page Police Department and believe they'd cooperate without knowing the full story," he said, one had on the phone and the other grabbing sweat pants.

"Will have that information to you shortly. Your contact here will be Sarah Tashkent. She's brilliant with data and information; use her. Shaw has called a meeting that he'd like you on the phone for at six a.m. Pacific... Sarah will patch you in. Your agents in California need to be on the line as well. Any questions?"

"No, other than, do we have any idea yet on what they are after or what their origins are?" asked Greer.

"Unfortunately, no on both counts. Later." The phone went dead.

In-room motel coffee. My kingdom for Starbucks, he mused. He knew he and the West Coast were grossly understaffed to counter a threat, or threats. Without the resources of the Bureau and coordination with local police departments, they were unprepared, as they were before 9/11. Even if the mole wasn't privy to information, his presence emasculated the Bureau and any response. Whoever was behind this had developed a plan far beyond the capabilities of a terrorist organization. This had to be state sponsored. The timing, depth, length of the operation were logistically too great. Russia was his first choice, then Iran, maybe China. It was a short list. After Crimea, the Russian appetite had been whetted, and Iran had been a thorn for nearly four decades. He called Davies first...he'd wait until closer to 5:30 to call the family man. He'd call Sandy at 5:30 as well. She and Dylan needed to be brought in on this.

CHAPTER 41

COLORADO

The Jeep crested Vail Pass. Estaval needed to piss. "I'm getting off here; there's a rest stop. I need to relieve myself and stretch. We can't stop in the towns ahead," he said.

"I agree. I need to stretch," Rose replied.

He pulled off and drove by what looked like a maintenance facility with idling snowplows with two men milling around. Even though it was May, snow still fell in the Rockies. That wasn't a place to stop. He took a left turn over the interstate to a rest stop. A sign read Elevation 10,662 Feet. It was deserted; one empty pickup with snowmobiles on a trailer was parked next to a brown hut marked Restrooms. Savano and Rose opened their doors and got out. They were awestruck by the cold stillness, the stars so bright they lit the parking lot without a moon. It was beautiful. It reminded both of the Urals and home.

A sound in the distance, the unmistakable signature of a helicopter. They ran to the eave of the hut, watching the sky. From the west came a sole black helicopter, very high. It looked military but could have been a medical chopper. As it passed, they ran to the car.

Estaval, winded, said, "It might be a search helicopter. Helicopters usually don't fly at night. But it didn't slow or take notice. They are looking for a panel truck; we should be all right."

Rose was beginning to respect Estaval more. He had proven himself with selecting the factory in Denver, the tunnel plan, and prepositioned car. He had done well and was a valuable member of the team.

Their car accelerated back on to the interstate. Estaval keep the speed slow, no more than fifty to fifty-five, to avoid an accident. Even though the skies had cleared, there was still an inch or so of snow on the road. In a few minutes, they finished the descent into the town of Vail, lit with the lights of buildings crowded in the narrow valley and bright lights high on the mountain. "Those are snowcats on the ski area. They work at night to groom the ski trails. Next week, this ski area closes. Most other resorts are closed already," Estaval said.

How decadent, Rose thought, to make sure ski trails were smoothed. It was unheard of in her Urals, where people took the mountains in their natural state.

The Blackhawk had been searching the interstate, both back to Vail and then back to Silverthorne and north on the highway toward Wyoming, with no luck. Coming back from his northern search out of Silverthorne, the pilot saw it. There, next to an eighteen-wheeler in a motel parking lot. "HAATS One to Ground One. We think we may have your vehicle in a motel parking lot in Silverthorne near an Old Chicago Restaurant. Northeast of the interchange."

Josh was behind the wheel randomly searching the parking lots of Silverthorne and nearby Dillon with Carol covering her side of the road from the passenger seat. "Roger, HAATS One, en route. We are fifteen minutes away. Stay on station until we arrive. Ground One out," Carol acknowledged.

"Roger, Ground One. Staying on station. Be advised that we have fuel for only another twenty-five minutes on station. HAATS One out."

Shaw broke in. "Josh, Carol, without that chopper, you will have no backup for another two hours. We have a team en route from Los Angeles. We will inform the highway patrol we've located the vehicle but to stay clear while you canvass that motel."

"Shaw, this is Josh. It doesn't make sense to pull over and check into a motel at the very next exit after going to all the trouble of losing the tail and closing the tunnel. We may need a forensics team at that van if we don't have them at the motel."

"Agreed. I'll take care of that with the highway patrol," Shaw replied.

As Josh drove into the parking lot, he saw there were three motels, not just one. He pulled up to the first, and Carol went into the office. She rang a bell, undoubtedly getting someone out of bed. It was just past four in the morning. The groggy employee mustered a pleasant greeting, which was cut short by Carol's FBI ID being held up for her to see. That and Carol's bruised eye and the air-bag abrasions on her cheek made the attendant's eyes go wide. "Ma'am, Agent Manning, FBI. Do you register vehicles when you book rooms?" she asked.

"Yes, we do," was the reply.

"Can I see your bookings for the last two hours?" Carol asked.

The reply was immediate. "We haven't had anyone since eleven."

Carol thanked her and went out, leaned into the car window, and told Josh the news. She walked across the parking lot to the next motel. The answer was the same there—no check-ins in the last two hours. She got in the car, and Josh drove down the lot to the far end and last motel. Carol asked the employee the same question.

"Yes, Agent, we've had two parties check in in the last hour or so. Room 213 and Room 311," the wide-eyed front deskman said.

"Can you describe the guests?" Carol asked.

"Well, yes. I put two college-age men in Room 213. Said they wanted to skin-up Breckenridge early and left a wake-up call for six o'clock. Room 311 is a single lady. Young, maybe thirty," the deskman said.

"Did she register a car with you?" Carol asked.

The deskman pulled out a loose-leaf notepad with the last two check-ins. "Yes, Room 311 has a silver 2010 Range Rover, Arizona license plate. Room 213 is a 1993 Saab, Colorado plate," the attendant said.

Carol thanked the employee and walked out and over to first the Saab and then the Range Rover. Both vehicles' hoods were still warm, making their stories check out.

With no target in the motels, Josh and Carol carefully checked the restaurant and adjacent convenience store. Both were closed, dark, with no signs of entry. With no target identified, there was no other option than to approach the vehicle. The truck was parked midway between the two security lights, the darkest part of the lot. The closest vehicle was an eighteen-wheeler about thirty feet north, along the edge of the lot. Carol made her way behind the eighteen-wheeler while Josh approached from the opposite direction, crossing the lot toward a parked car as if it were his. They nodded to each other and slowly approached, weapons drawn. No matter how lightly they tried to step, the crunch of the snow and ice seemed deafening. Carol approached the back of the truck on the driver's side, searching into the rearview mirror for any sign of movement. The only sounds were her footsteps on the snow, the distant interstate, the faraway thump-thump of the chopper, and her heartbeat.

Josh approached the passenger side from an angle near the front, staring for any movement of the vehicle frame or shadow in the windshield. Inches from the driver's side window, Carol used the side mirror to view the interior. Nothing. Making sure Josh had been on the other side long enough to be prepared, she thought, "Here goes," and lit up the inside with her flashlight, her finger on the trigger.

"Clear! It's empty," Josh yelled.

Carol walked around to Josh, and then she saw it.

"Stop! Don't move," she said in a low firm voice. He froze. A trip wire? An IED?

"Look. Footprints in the snow, and there, a tire imprint. They parked next to a parked car and unloaded the rear of the truck to the rear of the other vehicle. You can see the footprints all stop just behind where the rear of the vehicle would have ended. One set of tire tracks in one direction, meaning the car was there before the snow."

She was right. Josh could clearly see it, envision what had transpired.

"We need a forensic team before sunrise, or we'll lose the tracks, imprints. Sunrise is less than two hours away," Carol said.

Josh was on the comms to Langley, relaying what they had found. After a few minutes, Sarah was on the line. "CBI, Colorado Bureau of Investigations, will dispatch a unit in thirty minutes, but driving time is sixty to ninety minutes."

Carol knew that might be too late and replied, "And thank the HAATS crew. We don't need them on station any longer."

"Find out what hotel that truck's driver is in. We can use his rig to block the sun," Josh said.

"Excellent," she replied.

They both sprinted to different hotels. The hotel attendant Carol had woken minutes before was awakened for the second time in an hour, this time by Josh, who announced himself as a fellow "agent." Looking at the screen, she scrolled down, and there it was: "Room 215, Mr. Blain."

Josh thanked her and dialed Carol. "He's here, the Hampton Inn. He isn't going to react well to be woken by me. You have the badge," Josh said.

"Be right there," she replied.

They walked down the hall to the door and knocked firmly. They could hear coughing and a few four-letter words before the door was opened. Carol's FBI ID was already out and at eye level when the door opened. The man started to yell and then stopped and stared at the ID. He calmed, mustering a "What's this about?"

"FBI, sir. We need your help. You are the driver of the rig outside, right?" she asked.

"Yeah, the green Kenworth," he replied.

"Sir, we have a crime scene outside and need your truck to preserve it. There is evidence in the snow and ice that will be lost when the sun comes up without your trailer to shade the scene," Carol said.

The reply was firm. "Give me a second to get some clothes on; I'll be right out. But I need to be on the road by nine o'clock to make it to Lincoln this evening," he said.

"Shouldn't be a problem sir. Thank you," Josh said.

The man closed the door.

He was outside quickly. Carol used an app on her iPhone to determine the exact direction at which the sun would rise and cross the early morning sky. She had used the Planets app for fun on her balcony, to identify constellations and stars. What did people do before smartphones? she wondered. She directed the trucker where she wanted the trailer, and he fired up the diesel. The trucker put the rig exactly where directed. It was perfect.

CHAPTER 42

JERSEY CITY, NJ

They were out early, as any other commuter would be. Javier and Eduardo dropped off Ellise, Phillipe, and Marza at the Paulus Hook Ferry Terminal, then headed north to Fort Lee and I-95. At opposite ends, they would explore the city's weaknesses.

Marza gazed out at the *new* World Trade Center. Even though she had been young, only in grade school, she remembered watching the twin towers fall. The imam had told everyone that Satan had been struck a great blow. Her parents had never again attended that mosque, but for her, she knew the imam spoke truth. Now she saw the new building that seemed to defy the blows struck not long ago. She was amazed by the resiliency of America. She had been told the Americans were weak, just technologically advanced, but the sheer power and will to replace the towers so quickly told her the Americans were not the weak, self-indulgent people she had been taught about.

The city's size, skyline, and wealth viewed from sea level were unlike anything she had ever seen. Its density would be its weakness. At the announcement, the passengers, most in business attire, walked as a herd toward the ferry's rear. The ferry slowed as it approached its destination, Pier 11. From there, the map showed Wall Street was a short walk.

As people began disembarking, Ellise remarked to Marza, "No security, no guards, no police."

Marza replied, "Unlike Europe and the Middle East, which have been forced to accept the presence of security, America still believes it is immune, an island of safety. Did you know that fewer than a quarter of the people in America know who was behind the attacks of 9/11? I read that most below the age of thirty, 9/11 never touched them. They have no knowledge of the reason for America's war in Afghanistan."

The walk to the intersection of Wall Street and William Street took just a few minutes. Here, beautiful shops were intermixed with financial institutions. At this hour, 8:00 a.m., other than a few tourists, all were dressed in the attire of business people. Walking as if theirs were the only purpose.

Phillipe and Marza took pictures of buildings, trash cans, dumpsters, and stairwells. Only in America would such actions be tolerated or seen as harmless. Following their tourist's maps, they walked to the Fulton Street Station and took the subway to Fifty-Seventh Street. Walking up into the air, they emerged into a crowd so dense that Marza had trouble not bumping into people. They turned the corner and walked up Fifth Street. "What is that line of people surrounding that large glass box?" Marza asked.

Nearly everyone in line had a backpack, briefcase, or purse. "That's our target," Phillipe answered.

They took pictures of Marza in front of the building's entrance and moved to their third destination. At Eighth Street, they went south three blocks to the metro station. As they walked down the stairs, few people were in the stairwell. Once alone, Phillipe withdrew a small set of bolt cutters from under his raincoat.

Phillipe used the cutters to cut the flimsy padlock on the chain link door. They ran in, careful to pick up the chain and close the fenced door behind her. Marza led with a flashlight toward the hum of equipment. They rounded a corridor to the transformers. They were huge, two of them with a control panel behind a sturdy reinforced barrier. That would not be cut by bolt cutters and would stop any intruder. It wouldn't, however, stop the shaped blast.

Marza lifted the bomb out of the reinforced shopping bag while Philippe placed a tube of PL adhesive in the caulk gun and spread a thick square, one foot by one foot, onto the wall at eye level facing the control panel. Phillipe pressed the bomb against the adhesive and held it for thirty seconds. He pulled his hands away. Perfect. The box had "Con Ed Part 0036701" stenciled on it. The day before, they had painted the aluminum box gray and rubbed it with dirt after it was dry. It looked as if it had been there for years. Marza placed the bolt cutters, glue gun, and broken lock into the shopping bag and walked back to the entrance. They waited several minutes until they could hear no footsteps and walked out, replacing the chain with a new padlock. Once outside, she turned down an alley and threw the shopping bag into an open Dumpster while Phillipe found the next location marked on the tourist map.

CHAPTER 43

SCOTTSDALE, AZ

Hector stood amazed at the American desert. When compared to the deso-lation of Iraq and Egypt, the American desert was filled with vegetation and life, even with the absence of water. The tall Saguaro cactus, barrel cactus, and cedars were as far as the eye could see. He had seen American western movies. The landscape looked like a movie.

"Let's go. We have cleaned the house of fingerprints. It's time," Amante yelled. They loaded the heavy luggage into the trunk and set out. Ibrahim had rented another car, a large SUV, a Yukon, it said on its side. Vincent sat in the back of the SUV with the cargo, with Hector and Emilia in the front. They had paid a large sum of money to obtain false identification, but it matched Ibrahim's identification completely except the picture. If they were pulled over, his driver license would match the rental car registration. He looked like any other tourist.

Ibrahim went to Emilia's open window and leaned in. "You have been my friend, my brethren, for the past five years. We have lived as man and wife, even if it was for Allah. I will see you again. Peace be with you."

Emilia leaned over and held his hands in hers, a tear visible in her eye. "Praise be to Allah. We will succeed and be in his kingdom together again."

With that, Amante got into Ibrahim's car. They each nodded and exchanged wishes, all cumulating in a common verse: "Praise be to Allah, Allah Akbar." They set out, several hundred feet of separation studiously maintained. At the I-17 exit, the Yukon went north. They never would speak again.

CHAPTER 44

SILVERTHORNE, CO

The CBI team had been at the parking lot for nearly two hours, meaning whatever vehicle the suspects were now in was at least four hours ahead, but in what direction? Josh wondered. They could have doubled back, but the odds were they were traveling west. The Utah State Police had been asked to look for a vehicle with three passengers, two men and a woman, but I-70 was one of the main cross-country interstates; the amount of traffic was too great without knowing a make or model.

One of the CBI agents came over to Carol. "Agent Manning, we have some preliminary results for you. Three persons. One an eleven shoe size, obviously male; another ten, likely a male; and a smaller size with less weight, odds are a female. The tread track matches a Goodyear Fortera tire, 245-70-17. That was original equipment on three vehicles. A 2011–2012 Jeep Laredo, a 2011–2012 Jeep Cherokee, and the 2014 GMC Acadia Crossover. It's preliminary, but our confidence level is high. The truck tests negative for explosives or radiological exposure, but if those were properly shielded, we might not pick up traces with the equipment we have here. We're going to transport the vehicle back to the lab, and we may have more for you later."

Carol thanked the officer and repeated the findings over the comms to Shaw.

"Excellent. We have air assets now. Two drones and two choppers. My gut tells me they didn't do all this to return to Denver. Too many traffic cams. We've analyzed possible targets, and they all point west, likely California. But it troubles me that they would stage out of Denver and risk detection along a thousand-mile road trip. It just doesn't add up," Shaw said.

"Shaw, Manning here. Since they have a four-hour head start, we need to go west by air. There's an airport an hour west of here. They call it Eagle Vail, but it's in Gypsum, a community closer to the town of Glenwood Springs than Vail. This time of year, flights are limited. Grand Junction is the nearest other airport with service west, but we need a destination—LA, Phoenix, Vegas, Frisco?"

"I'd rule out Phoenix. If they are in concert with whoever set off the radiological monitor in Phoenix, they wouldn't need another team to drive there all the way from Denver. Vegas would not disrupt the national economy, so I am leaning toward California. We've worked up a target list. They are in four categories: population, electrical grid, transportation, and IT. If it's nuclear, they would hit a population target. If it's conventional, it could be any of the category targets. The best chance we have is to find the vehicle. If California is the goal, we have twelve, maybe fifteen hours before they are in play," Shaw said. "At a town called Green River, they can go north to Salt Lake and eventually west to San Francisco or west and south to Vegas and LA. There are only two primary routes; with what we now know, we should be able to intercept them..." Shaw's last words trailed off. He wasn't too sure. They had proven they were smart and elusive so far. He sensed they would continue to be unpredictable. He needed every available asset to be out there searching. "Agent Manning, recommend you proceed at high rate of speed west toward Green River. I'll have further instructions later," Shaw instructed.

Savano was glad they were off the interstate. The idea of one westbound highway was far too dangerous. He knew that by now, the authorities probably had located the truck. Would there be roadblocks on the interstate? He guessed there would be. They hadn't stopped for gas or food, and it had been nearly five hours. He saw two signs along the highway that advertised Mountain Bike Capital. What was a mountain bike? He assumed it was a motorized dirt bike but wasn't sure. Nearly every other car had a bicycle on its roof. A bicycle? These Americans—to drive into a desert and ride a bicycle was not understandable.

"We need to stop. We need bathrooms, fuel, and food. The next town is Moab. It seems to be a tourist town; strangers won't be noticed," Rose said.

"I have been here once before. It is a beautiful town. The cliffs and rock formations are what they call slick rock. People ride bicycles, drive off-road vehicles, and hike on the rocks. Large rock formations cut by wind and water that attract tourists. There are many places to eat, get petrol, and check the news," Estaval added.

Captain E. J. Hart sat in the terminal—actually little more than a double-wide trailer in Nevada, just north of the Strip. From here, he had been flying missions this week in Afghanistan, Yemen, Iraq, and Sudan. He had joined the air force hoping to be a fighter pilot, but his size, over six feet four, prevented that, and he had opted for a new type of training rather than fly military transports, which he knew was likely his only other career option. The idea had seemed odd. Sit in a desert building and literally fly missions all over the world. At times it felt like a video game, but he knew lives depended on and were taken by this game.

He had "flown" missions throughout Afghanistan, Iraq, the northern territories of Pakistan, North Africa, and even eastern Ukraine, the latter to monitor Russian troop movements. But this was new, and far more disturbing. He was flying an unarmed Phantom Eye, the latest in unmanned aerial vehicles (UAV), able to stay airborne for up to four days. The UAV was bulbous, ugly, and powered by two Ford Fusion engines that Ford Motor Company and Boeing had joined forces to modify as a liquid-hydrogen propulsion platform. Cruising at 150–170 mph, it was an easy target for ground fire but for its capability of flying at up to sixty-five thousand feet. This mission would be below commercial air traffic, at ten thousand feet, just five to six thousand feet above the ground. It was unlikely it would encounter antiaircraft fire over Utah.

Taking off from Edwards, it had taken nearly two hours to come into the theater of operations, which had been defined in his orders as Utah, southern Nevada, and northern Arizona. It was a large area to cover, but he knew the target vehicle types, and the number of highways was limited. Still, he had never heard of a mission over US soil. And the urgency with which this one was launched told him the threat level posed by the target vehicle was great.

He communicated with the AWACS aircraft. "Night Eye One, this is Phantom Eye One. Am beginning my search at Mesquite, Nevada, and proceeding northeast on Interstate 15 to a position over St. George, Utah. There I'll climb to twenty thousand to avoid ground recognition. Advise of any civilian air traffic along my route." It was daylight now, and the threat of visual recognition from a small plane was real. To minimize exposure, an A-3 Sentry airborne early-warning and control-radar plane had been launched from Tinker Air Force Base outside of Oklahoma City. It would loiter over Utah outside of commercial corridors and advise him if traffic was in visual range. Or at least that was the plan.

The AWACS replied, "Phantom Eye One, this is Night Eye One, received transmission. You are clear of other traffic; proceed your route. Good day, sir. Night Eye One out."

Traversing along the interstate was quick. It took far more time scanning metropolitan areas to make sure the vehicle had not pulled off the main route for gas, food, or rest. The software had been programmed with the vehicle types, but in a congested area, many IDs were showing up, each having to be checked out. Thermal imaging allowed him to look for a vehicle with three occupants. It was tedious.

His plan was to search I-15 to I-70 and then eastbound on I-70 to Grand Junction, CO. It would take him over the sparsely populated towns of St. George, Hurricane, Cedar City, and Green River. At Grand Junction, he would have to break off the coverage; there was a major airport there, and any hope of locating one particular Jeep in a Colorado town of sixty thousand would be impossible. There likely would be hundreds of late-model Jeeps. He planned to sweep back south along Highway 191, which would be the only highway south other than I-15. It led to Monument Valley, with the towns of Moab and Blanding being the only large towns until the sprawling Navajo reservation. If they went north to Salt Lake, the two primary routes west led along I-80 to Sacramento and Frisco, with I-84 to the Pacific Northwest. Matt, in the "cockpit" next to him, was tasked with that theater. Somehow the term "theater" now had more meaning as the deadly play unfolded.

CHAPTER 45

The Utah Highway Department had placed signs at Hurricane off I-70 and Tuba City north from Phoenix announcing all truck traffic larger than pickup trucks was prohibited over the Highway 89 Bridge at Page. The sudden closure had forced some truckers to backtrack a full day, bringing an outcry from Page businesses and truckers alike. When this was followed by the closure of the channel from the dam to Antelope Island, a distance of almost two miles, it drew howls from fishermen and locals alike. Most blamed overly cautious federal bureaucrats; the idea that boat or truck motor vibrations could trigger a spall was universally labeled stupid.

Greer didn't care. It was a cover story and the only thing on short notice they could dream up. With Sandy's and Rich Stanway's help, he had accessed the security cameras at the Visitor Center and pointed two at the adjacent bridge. They would record all cars traveling over the bridge on a twelve-hour loop. Reclamation had also agreed to suspend dam tours at the Visitor Center, ensuring that the dam and turbine area, 528 feet below, was inaccessible. The dam itself was nearly impregnable, composed of 9.6 million tons of concrete, nearly three hundred feet wide at its base and twenty-five wide at its crest. Even so, Greer didn't want to see if it was actually *impregnable*.

"Sandy, what would happen if the dam failed?" Zach asked.

The statistics she calmly recited were chilling. "At capacity, the dam holds back twenty-four million acre-feet, nearly eight trillion gallons, of water. A possible scenario is the so-called domino effect, where a wall of water surges through the Grand Canyon, flowing into Lake Mead and damaging the Hoover Dam. If Hoover were to fail, it could trigger the loss of downstream dams at Davis, Parker, Imperial, Palo Verde, Laguna, and Morelos. The resulting loss of electricity and water to nearly fifty million people would probably disrupt the national economy for decades..." Sandy's words trailed off.

Without the FBI's involvement and with the need to preserve operational security, inter-agency cooperation was stifled out of fear that counterterrorist actions would be discovered by the FBI mole. It had forced strange partnerships acting in strange locales. The CIA, NSA, DHS, and military intelligence were now running the operation inside the country, with the FBI in the dark save for select FBI personnel. Greer knew it was dysfunctional and destined to fail. The brilliance of running a mole in the FBI was impressive. Whether they found the mole or not, it muzzled a response.

Greer knew he needed backup. He was alone here, backed up only by Sandy and possibly Dylan. Shaw had advised he would try to send an operative to Page, but they were overwhelmed and undermanned across the board. He had resolved to place Page PD on a rotational basis for oversight of the dam. Placed on the crest, they would be able to see any approach to the dam from above on the bridge or down below on the lake.

"You look lost in thought," Sandy said, walking in the door.

"I am. I'm trying to think what the bad guys' end game is and trying not to think about an attack on that dam," Zach replied.

"I just came from the office, and the locals have already contacted their state and federal elected representatives. I don't know how much longer we can keep things shut down. If anyone looks deep enough, they'll know we made the story up and start asking why," Sandy said.

Zach sighed, closed his eyes, and said, "This thing will be over in seventy-two hours. I'll ask Shaw to intervene with the White House. Maybe they can keep the elected officials at bay for that long."

"Zach, have you told me everything? Do you know what we are looking at or who we are looking for?" Sandy asked.

The look on his face told her the answer: he didn't, and it scared him. She sat down next to him, and they looked at each other. He started to speak, and she touched his lips, leaning into them. He didn't know if it was nerves, the years of being alone, or her scent, but he circled her waist with his forearm and brought her tight to him, as if tomorrow would be taken from them.

CHAPTER 46

SCOTTSDALE, AZ

She called the vet twice before 8:30. Her little Arthur was so sick. He had thrown up constantly and had sores along his gums. Patches of his fur had come out, making her fear he had the mange. But the dog was sicker than that, appearing to slip in and out of consciousness. She feared he had gotten into poison put down by someone. She reached her vet at his after-hours emergency number and met him at the animal hospital before office hours. She carried Arthur into the room as Scott opened the door—she never called him by his last name or Doctor.

Arthur's temperature was burning up, not indicative of poison. After the dog had thrown up a small bit of blood, Scott drew blood. He called his lab technician to meet him at the office. The lab would have the preliminary results momentarily.

Dr. Scott Hall tried to calm her, telling her, "Annie, I'm sure it is just a virus. Dogs are no different than people. They catch a disease, run temperatures, and recover."

The intercom summoned him, and he took the call from the lab. He couldn't believe what he was hearing. "Scott, you're not going to believe this, but the dog has aplastic anemia, a severe loss of red blood cells," the lab tech said. The symptoms pointed to one thing the vet couldn't accept: acute radiation poisoning. The Mayo Clinic was only four miles away. He knew they had facilities to confirm or refute his diagnosis.

"Annie, I need to know where the dog has been in the past twenty-four hours. Has Arthur been around any industrial sites or hospitals?" he asked.

"No, he's been with me. We were at my office and inspected some homes, and then back to my home. Why?" she asked.

"Annie, we need to take some samples from Arthur to the Mayo Clinic. Just some blood and stool samples. I will be back within the hour; I want you to stay here with him. He is a sick little guy," Scott said.

She nodded her head OK, thinking she never knew the Mayo saw animals.

Scott walked out of the treatment room and to his office. He called Edgar Garvin, a doctor he played golf with, at the Mayo. Dr. Garvin treated endocrine diseases with nuclear medicine and had facilities that could confirm the presence of a radiological link to the dog. While Dr. Garvin balked at the thought of conducting tests on the dog's samples, he heard the urgency in Scott's voice. "Ed, please. It should only take a few minutes," Scott implored.

Scott sat in the Mayo's waiting room thinking of the implications of his diagnosis and whether there were alternatives. He knew he would look pretty silly if he was wrong, and he so hoped he was wrong.

Dr. Edgar Garvin walked out of the lab and motioned him to follow him. They walked into an examining room and closed the door. "The blood, tissue, and stool samples all confirm acute radiation poisoning. A large dose, I would say, for this sort of a reaction. Where did the owner say the dog had been?" asked Edgar.

"Nowhere. She said she had been with the dog the full time, and she appears fine," Scott responded.

"We need to call CDC, and we need to place the dog in a safe quarantine and have the lady tested," Edgar said. He dialed CDC while Scott dialed his office to advise them that full protections should be used in treating and being around the dog and its master.

Dr. Garvin delivered the information to the CDC Office of Preparedness and Response. Dr. Jules Gitlow listened to the information and replied,

"Stay on the line. I will be back in less than thirty seconds." She searched her e-mail for the action bulletin she had seen yesterday. There it was. She dialed the number for Elle Hardwicke, agency unknown.

Elle ran into the response center. "Shaw, line four. I have a doctor at CDC on the line with another doctor from the Mayo Clinic in Phoenix. They have a radiation patient."

Everyone scrambled as the line was placed on speaker. "Shaw Ellis here, Doctor. What do you have?"

Shaw listened as the CDC physician relayed what had been told to her from the Mayo Clinic. "Conference us in with the doctor, please," Shaw instructed. Several beeps occurred, and Shaw spoke. "Dr. Garvin, you are on the line with the CDC and members of a joint terrorism task force. We need to know everything about this patient and where he or she has been in the last forty-eight hours."

"Uh, Mr. Ellis, this is Scott Hall. I'm a veterinarian in Scottsdale. The patient is a four-year-old small dog brought in to me by Annie Bellows, an area realtor. The owner is experiencing no symptoms, but the dog exhibited all of the symptoms of acute radiation exposure. I'm not equipped to test for that, as you can imagine, so I brought samples to the Mayo and Dr. Garvin."

"Mr. Ellis, this is Dr. Garvin at the Mayo Hospital in Phoenix. Our lab confirmed exposure of the samples to a radiation source. We don't have information on the source or dose, as the literature is pretty sparse for exposure to domestic animals."

"Doctors, you were directed to me because our office is tracking several threats that make this report of great interest to us right now. I need to ask you to keep this as quiet and confidential as you can. A diagnosis of acute radiation exposure could start a panic and interfere with our investigation. This could be a big break in our investigation, but we need to isolate the owner and dog and whoever else has become exposed. We need to interview the owner as soon as possible," Shaw said.

Dr. Garvin spoke first. "Sir, the Mayo has isolation rooms. One in my wing is somewhat shielded since we use radioactive medicines. We can bring the dog and its owner to the Mayo and isolate them and test Dr. Hall and his staff for exposure. I'll have a Skype interview set up with the owner in the isolation room and call you back when we are ready."

"Thank you, Dr. Garvin, and excellent job, Dr. Hall. My bet is that diagnosing the dog would have slipped by most others," Shaw commented and hung up.

Scott Hall felt a mixture of pride and fear thinking about his friend's words, "test Dr. Hall and his staff for exposure."

Elle had already made the necessary call to NEST to have the emergency teams arrive at the animal hospital. They were on call. It would be a fifteen-minute chopper ride to Scottsdale Airport. From there, it was only a few blocks from the clinic. Elle dialed. "Dr. Hall, my name is Elle Hardwick. I'm going to walk you through this and will be interviewing the dog's owner. We want you to meet one of our elite response teams. They will be brought over to your clinic by the local hazmat team. They will pick up the dog and its owner and take them to the Mayo. Call your office and let them know what to expect and what to do. They are going to be visited by men in suits, suits to protect the men *from them*. They are to let the NEST team explain 'the why' to Annie Bellows. No one is to enter or leave. No one is to touch or clean up anything. And most importantly, no one is to get near the dog."

This was a nightmare. He feared for his employees and his future. Who would want to bring their pets to a clinic that had been exposed to a radiation hazard? Dear God, he remembered his receptionist, Heidi, was pregnant.

An hour south, Vincent was feeling bad, tired. He hadn't kept his breakfast down. He attributed it to the food these people ate. He had stopped at a convenience store to get gas and had bought a "turnover." It had said it had apples inside it, but he couldn't tell.

Ibrahim saw his discomfort. "Vincent, try to get some sleep. The nausea should pass with rest. We have a four-and-a-half-hour drive ahead of us." They would spend the day in Las Vegas scouting two locations and leave the next morning at sunrise for Los Angeles. They needed everything in place by midday the next day. Everything was planned for 1:00 p.m. Pacific time.

CHAPTER 47

YONKERS, NY

Javier and Ellise drove north out of Fort Lee on Interstate 87, the New York State Thruway. Traffic was light. Their plan was to find a suitable location to park the vehicle while they set the bomb. Ellise and Javier talked about what they would need and decided that a stroll along the reservoir banks would tell them where they should stage from. They would look like a couple on a stroll on a beautiful May morning. "We will park at the edge of the Yonkers Raceway parking lot, adjacent to Hillview Reservoir," Javier said.

The reservoir didn't look like much, a dual cell impoundment. Javier had studied the facility, explaining to Ellise, "The reservoir is small by reservoir standards, only 2,761 acre-feet in volume, about 90 surface acres. But its location is strategic. It receives water as a terminal storage reservoir from New York's Catskill and Delaware Aqueducts and delivers water from multiple reservoirs in upstate New York and the Delaware collection system to the city. It was built in the early 1900s. It regulates deliveries into Tunnels One, Two, and the new Tunnel Three of the New York City delivery system. Some of the tunnels are up to twenty-eight feet in diameter. They furnish a billion gallons a day to the New York's eight million inhabitants." Javier had studied the reservoir, which few had ever given any thought to. Hillview Reservoir had never attracted much attention other than the ill-conceived and failed attempt by EPA to require a $200 million to $1 billion cover to protect the water from bird droppings.

Javier asked, "Is this background boring?"

Ellise replied, "No. It is a little technical to follow but interesting. I wish to know everything, please."

The professor in Javier was pleased, and he continued. "The advent of municipal water delivery systems spawned urban growth. Before the rise of municipal delivery systems, urban density was prohibited by a lack of adequate sanitation and the availability of drinking water. Waterborne disease and poor sanitation kept urban densities naturally low. New York was no different. In the 1700s, private wells were the source of water to the city's population of nearly twenty thousand. As population increased, the city built the Collect Pond near what is now Central Park and drilled wells for public consumption. The problem was that the Collect Pond was adjacent to a tannery and unrestrained sanitary sewers. Sickness, dysentery and cholera swept the city in the late eighteenth century. In response, the city began plans to construct an aqueduct from the Croton River. Later, the system expanded by tapping the pristine waters of the Catskills. And more recently, the city diverted flows from the Delaware River and its tributaries. The planning and development of the New York supply system was ahead of its time and a model of utility planning, providing excellent quality water to its inhabitants. But all that is about to change...the city will revert back to eighteenth-century conditions."

CHAPTER 48

BLANDING, UTAH

The meal in Moab recharged them, though taking this route placed them far behind schedule. They weren't going to make it. They came up over a hill, and Savano saw it. "Turn there—the airport," he said, seeing the sign.

"It's just a municipal airport. There'll be no scheduled service anywhere. All the planes are small and private. It's probably not even manned," Estaval said.

Savano shot Estaval a glare that made him understand that questioning orders could be very dangerous.

They drove to the field and circled the tower. It didn't look manned. There were a few single-engine planes, a glider parked near the tarmac, and only one vehicle, a pickup with a bumper sticker that read, "BYU Cougars." No one was in sight. They parked the Jeep and walked toward a small hanger. The door opened with a loud screech of metal. Inside, they saw two twin-engine planes, a Cessna 310 and a King Air.

"Can I help you?" said a voice from behind the Cessna.

"Ah, we were looking for the person who runs the airport. Is anyone in the tower?" Rose asked.

"Ma'am, the tower isn't manned. This is a small operation. Ed Fink manages the field, but he's on the lake this week. Is there anything I can help you with?" the man said.

"We were looking for one of the pilots to these planes," Savano said.

The man put a tool down, wiped his hands with a rag, and crawled out from beneath the nose gear. "There are no charter services here, if that's what you are looking for. These planes are private. I'm Matthew Killiam. I own them both, but I sold the 310 here last week and was just doing some last-minute cleaning on it before it's picked up," he said.

Rose stepped forward. "Do you fly them yourself?" she asked, trying to sound impressionable.

"Well, yes. We're pretty removed from things here. Flying affords the freedom to live here, although this King Air is probably more than I need. She's a beauty. Only nine years old. The engines only have..." He stopped when Estaval pulled the nine-millimeter from his jacket.

"We are going to need to borrow you and your plane for a few hours. You will be fine if you do as we say," Savano said.

Matthew knew that was probably not true. He asked, "Where are we going? I need to file a flight plan and fuel it for the trip," he asked.

"You won't need a flight plan. We will be VFR. Top the fuel off, and we'll let you know the destination when we are airborne," Savano said.

At that, Matthew knew they would not let him go. He figured them for criminals—likely narcos. One man and the woman were Caucasian and spoke with what sounded like a European accent. The other, silent one, he figured to be Hispanic. They loaded heavy duffels and a large metal dry box. Drugs or cash, he surmised.

The King Air, fully loaded, took nearly three-quarters of the six-thousand-foot runway to get off the ground at this altitude. With four, a full luggage load, and full fuel, he figured he could make most airports in northern Mexico if that was the destination.

Estaval called Pedro to tell him of the change in plans. Pedro said he would get back with him with a destination. At only five thousand feet above the terrain, they were below air traffic control and in cell phone coverage.

As the plane neared the Nevada border, Estaval's phone rang. He listened, hung up, and leaned up to Matthew. "Thermal Airport, TRM, Jacquelin Cochran Regional Airport. Twenty-five miles southeast of Palm Springs International. That's your destination."

Matthew never figured these types for Palm Springs. They definitely weren't the golf set. It was less than an hour away; he knew he needed to think fast. There was a look in the European man's eyes that chilled him. He had flown to Palm Springs several times before for golf trips. If he could ever so slightly adjust his heading from 182 degrees to maybe 200 degrees, he might encroach on the edge of Twentynine Palms Marine Base's restricted airspace. If he turned the radio to only his headset and failed to respond to warnings, he would either be forced down or met by authorities wherever he landed. He was hoping for the second option.

Pedro had driven to Palm Springs, as directed. He was now on his way to the Regional Airport. He hoped that by tomorrow, his tasks would be done and he could go back to his life, his family. How long ago he had thought of the cause, jihad, and those angry times. It wasn't him anymore; perhaps it never was. He had come to appreciate this country and its people. He wanted no part in this.

CHAPTER 49

SCOTTSDALE, AZ

Elle phoned the clinic. "Ms. Bellows, my name is Elle Hardwick. I work for the government. I need to ask you some questions about your dog. Can you tell me whether the dog has been within your sight the past forty-eight hours?"

Annie struggled to hold back tears and tried to compose herself before responding. "Yes, Arthur always is with me. We go everywhere together. Is he going to be OK?" she asked.

"First, we would like your permission to search your home to determine if there is anything there that could have sickened Arthur. Second, can you recall exactly where you went and who you talked with starting with two days ago?" Elle asked.

"Yes, of course, you can search my house. Let's see...Yesterday, I went to Kierland Commons for some shopping. I had lunch there at Zinc Bistro with my friend Marge Hellerman. We were getting our hair fixed, nails done. Then I had two real-estate showings and two rental inspections." She gave the details and locations of each.

Elle then asked, "Ms. Bellows, tell me a little more about the inspection of the two homes that were rentals. I believe you said one was rented by a single male. Can you describe him for me?"

Annie could. She knew him from the club. "His name is Phillip Trundel. He's a lawyer going through a divorce. I've known his wife and him for about ten years; they are nice people. They have two daughters, preteens. Such a shame," she said.

"Can you tell me about the other rental and describe who was at the property?" Elle continued.

Annie thought and began, "Well, the home is a three-bedroom just off Pima near the Pinnacle Peak Golf Club. It's owned by a couple in Utah who winter there and lease it out in the off-season. It was rented to a gentlemen by the name of Akapa. I can't recall his first name, but I have the paperwork at the office. There was an awkward moment, I recall. The lease restricted tenants to three, and I noticed more than three sets of shoes at the door. I thought how nice it was they had removed their shoes but then recalled they weren't allowed more than three tenants. The other man—I think he was Hispanic—said his two sons were at Arizona State and just visiting and weren't staying overnight. So I guess that meant that there would only be three people sleeping in the home. I mean, his kids were only just visiting. Come to think about it, it was a bit strange, as the place was rented for three weeks, as I recall, and the luggage was still in the foyer. Very expensive luggage—you know, metal sided," she said.

Elle knew that was it and closed with, "Thank you, Ms. Bellows. That's very helpful. Can you have your office send me the address of the rental? Some people will be there shortly who will ask you a few questions. Please give them that address for me. I'll also send someone to do some sketches of the tenants with you. Thank you, and again, I do hope your little Arthur is better."

Elle then called Shaw. "I think we have something on the Phoenix radiological exposure. The lady remembers visiting a home with four men and one woman, metal luggage. The men looked Hispanic to her. Chances are they weren't Hispanic. We need a FISA warrant and the NEST team to move on this."

"Do it. I'll take care of the warrant; I have them standing by," Shaw responded.

CHAPTER 50

Amante was feeling worse. He was tired, and whatever he had eaten earlier wasn't sitting with him. He cursed himself for becoming sick when he had so much to do in the next twenty-four hours. "We are behind schedule. We need to split up. You need to drop me off in Las Vegas and continue on to LA alone. I am sick—the flu or something. We run the risk of me getting worse or you getting sick. Besides, there is less chance the packages will be discovered if they are not set out too far in advance. If I stay in Las Vegas and you continue on, we won't need to set out the Las Vegas packages too early," Amante said.

Ibrahim didn't like it; it wasn't the plan. But Amante did look sick, and he could be more of a burden than a help if he worsened. If he left him to take care of the Vegas part of the operation, he could continue on and make LA tonight, giving him ample time to do his part. "Yes, that makes sense. I have reserved a room at the Rivers Hotel. It's an older hotel on the Strip. It's prepaid—here's the voucher. I'll give you a credit card and my school ID as a picture ID. We all look alike to these people. Destroy the ID and credit card after you check in so nothing comes back to me," Ibrahim said.

Amante just nodded. He was feeling worse by the minute. He was flushed, and the rash on his face burned.

They drove on in silence, making their way to the Strip. It was midafternoon, and the streets and sidewalks were filled with people. Amante had never seen anything like it. Buildings with large signs, huge buildings looking like pyramids, Greek temples, an Eiffel tower, and temples of glass. The people walking were equally disturbing. Overweight men with tank tops, women wearing very little, everywhere people drinking. Decadence and weakness...the America he had been taught.

They pulled up to the front door of the hotel. Amante took two duffel bags, one on wheels, the other thrown over his shoulder. His eyes blurred, his body weak, he turned and willed himself through the revolving door, where he was overpowered by a chorus of sound from slot machines and an assault of stale cigarette smoke. A collage of purple, bright-orange, and red carpet with lines directed him to the front desk, where he presented his voucher and credit card. "Thank you, Mr. Shastani. We have two guests for one night in one of our standard rooms with two queen beds. If I can just get your signature here on the bottom...yes, thank you. Here is your room key. You will be in 2134. The elevators are behind you to the right. Thank you for staying at the Rivers," the front desk woman said as if in a trance. Walking out of the elevator, he found his room, opened the door, and fell back on the bed. It was all he could do to not sleep.

Amante knew there was work to do. He struggled to open the wheeled duffel. Inside, he took both backpacks out. He opened the first, a blue Sierra Designs backpack. He carefully attached the three wires, red, white, and black, to the small plastic box's color-coded terminals. He opened the lid to the plastic box and set the digital timer to 12:45. He then did the same for the gray backpack, setting the timer again for 12:45. He had a moment of panic, checking his digital watch: it showed 15:35. He relaxed. It wouldn't be good to blow himself up by setting the timer more than twenty-four hours beforehand.

Amante knew he had plenty of time tomorrow to place the charges. Now, he needed rest. He leaned back on the pillow, assuring himself that he would only rest for an hour before going out in search of locations.

CHAPTER 51

EDWARDS AFB, CA

After over six hours, the drone had discovered nothing. He'd searched all of I-70 and the secondary highways. Teams were scouring the cities of Grand Junction, St. George, and Moab. "Night Eye One, Phantom Eye One. Negative location on the vehicle. No joy on the suspects." He had overflown all parking lots, airports, and motels. Nothing; they had slipped through. He exchanged looks with his "wingman" sitting next to him, who had the same exhausted and disheartened look.

Less than two hundred miles away, Matthew had been adjusting the heading of the King Air one degree at a time for the past twenty minutes. At any minute, he expected air-traffic control to warn him of restricted airspace ahead. The European man was behind and asleep. The Hispanic-looking one was staring out the window. The woman sat in the copilot's seat. Matthew wondered if she had flying experience. He thought not, or he wouldn't still be alive.

"King Air N339011, come in. Restricted airspace sixty miles ahead. Adjust heading to 165 degrees, climb to thirteen thousand, and check in with TRM approach, over."

Matthew held his breath and didn't answer. The warning came again. Again he didn't respond.

A few minutes later, a woman's stern voice came over his headset. "King Air N339011, this is Twentynine Palms Station. You are directed to immediately turn to 165 degrees and respond. If your mike is not respond-ing, flip responder off and on twice to acknowledge."

Matthew wondered whether interceptors were being scrambled. Cold drips of sweat began to crawl down his back. He knew he had just a few minutes. His options were to not respond or to do something unexplainable to the controller. An act that would demand a ground response upon landing.

Matthew clicked the mike button on the stick. "TRM Control, this is King Air N339011, seventy miles out. Request VFR approach from the north to Runway Seventeen, over," he broadcasted.

His communication sparked Rose to wake Savano. He needed to be ready. Estaval took his phone out and began to dial Pedro.

After several minutes, Matthew's headset blared, "King Air N339011, you are in restricted airspace. Your comm with TRM Control was copied. Your comms are active. Respond immediately and divert course to 160 degrees. Authorities have been notified." The female controller's voice was barbed, threatening.

With that he changed his heading to 160 degrees, exiting the airspace, maintaining silence.

"King Air N339011, TRM Control here. You are cleared for landing Runway Seventeen, winds Northeast at ten knots gusting to twenty knots, no traffic. Cleared to land. Upon landing, taxi to west hanger at the far end of the runway, where you will be met. You are instructed to stay onboard until advised, over," the TRM controller broadcast.

Matthew's heart pounded as he managed, "Roger, TRM Control."

"Folks, we are about five miles out, on final. We've been instructed to taxi to the far hanger after landing. I don't know why. Perhaps they just want to check why we didn't file a flight plan," Matthew said into the onboard intercom.

The three exchanged looks. Savano pushed the nine millimeter into Matthew's ribs, hissing, "What have you done? Who did you call?"

"Nobody. Ask her. She's been listening the whole time," he said, looking over at Rose. "I radioed no one. After 9/11, sometimes the FAA does this when a flight plan isn't filed. It's no big deal. They'll lecture us on the dangers of not filing a flight plan, but that's all. I'll just say that time didn't allow it," Matthew said.

It seemed to calm Estaval and the woman, but the European man seethed. Matthew was betting that as the pilot, he would be ordered to disembark alone.

The plane touched down and taxied to the hanger. He could see a sign at the hanger, Airport Security, and two tan government vehicles, each with occupants. He taxied and was met with a ground controller, who directed him to a pad and crossed the orange wands, signaling him to cut the engines. Both shuddered to a stop. Matthew turned the volume on so that it was audible in the cabin.

"Pilot, you are instructed to disembark. Your passengers are directed to remain onboard. Bring your registration and license with you," the intercom menacingly sounded.

"What should I do?" he asked his captors.

Savano spoke first. "Give me your license and materials. I'll go. You stay here."

"But they'll know you're not a pilot, not me," Matthew pleaded.

"That's not important. Rose, get ready to move, be ready to come out," Savano instructed.

Rose pulled her nine-millimeter Beretta and took the safety off. Estaval instructed Matthew to climb out of the cockpit into the back. Savano took the light jacket he was wearing and opened the door. He walked down the three stairs, a bundle of papers in his left hand, his right hand ready to grab the weapon from his back.

A uniformed TSA agent stood next to a man in an open white shirt and trousers while another TSA agent stood off to his left. Savano walked toward them and went down on a knee, reaching for his weapon. Before the three could react, he fired six rounds, five hitting the targets. All went down without exchanging fire. A TSA officer in an idling car jumped out, firing wide. Savano cut him down. He walked calmly to where the remaining officer stood, his hands raised. Savano shot him in the face. Rose was out, her gun drawn but devoid of targets. Matthew felt sick. He'd gotten all of these people killed, and now he would most certainly die as well.

The gunfire had attracted the attention of several maintenance men working on a hanger door and several men standing around their planes. It was only a matter of time until they were engaged by others.

"Where's Pedro?" yelled Savano.

"He's on his way. He's been waiting at the FBO on the other side of the runway. He has to go out and come back in another entrance to get here," said Estaval.

"You, pilot, open the luggage compartment and pull the luggage out," Savano ordered.

Estaval went over to the plane to help with the luggage while Savano and Rose took up positions next to the vehicles. As he opened the cargo door panel, Matthew saw it. A wrench for manually operating the luggage compartment door. He felt frozen with fear but knew he had to act. He swung the wrench across Estaval's back. Estaval yelled, slumping to the tarmac. Matthew began to run, but at fifty-five and with a few extra pounds, it was more of a lumber. Rose fired three rounds and Matthew fell, dead before he touched the pavement.

"Tell Pedro to pick a place outside the airport to meet. We'll take one of these vehicles and meet him. Too many witnesses here for his car to be seen," Savano yelled to Estaval.

CHAPTER 52

PAGE, AZ

Hector reached over and shook Emilia's arm, waking her. The sign said Page, 8 Miles. They were there. Vincent had also been asleep but in a different way. He was nauseous, feeling he must have caught whatever Amante had come down with in Phoenix. His tongue felt swollen, his throat glands enlarged. He was sweaty yet cold. As the muscle, he knew he didn't have the luxury of being sick. He had the heavy luggage behind him to contend with and might be called on to do a great deal more. Looking out, he could see nothing but rock and sand and an occasional trailer, which for some reason had tires laid across the roof. Nearly every home was a trailer, and nearly all had tires on the roof. Why? he puzzled. Did they need to be weighted down?

They had traveled through the "RES" for nearly an hour. The sprawling Navajo Indian Nation occupied over twenty-seven thousand acres surrounding the Hopi Reservation, which had been a source of contention since its establishment. Technically independent nations, they provided a glimpse into the failed relationship between the United States and its aboriginal roots. Hector stared out at the magnificent, desolate landscape.

They pulled into the Holiday Inn parking lot. It was nearly a hundred degrees; when Hector opened the door, the heat took his breath away. He could only imagine what it would be like in the later months of the summer.

They checked into two rooms next to each other. "Vincent, unload the luggage. Put the package in your room and the rest of the luggage in the other room. Emilia and I will stay in the other room so that we appear the part of just another tourist couple.

"Vincent, prepare the packages. We'll need the satchel package done before nightfall and the primary to be ready for our meeting at 19:00. Emilia and I will go find some dinner and bring it back. We are meeting the contact at 19:00," Hector instructed.

Vincent nodded and closed the door to his room. He felt horrible but would get his tasks done. It was almost done. The *times* were finally upon them.

CHAPTER 53

SCOTTSDALE, AZ

The NEST team confirmed the presence of radiation. "Mr. Shaw, we have a fairly strong signature here. It's enough to sicken anyone exposed for very long. The dog died. Given the dog's weight, length of the time since it was exposed, and the levels detected in the home, initial estimates are between three hundred and five hundred rads, enough to bring the onset of hematopoietic and gastrointestinal symptoms within twenty-four hours. The concentration was greatest in the downstairs bedroom and the foyer closet."

Shaw stared at the report on the screen. Dear God, he thought. They have materials that are breached. That could mean they intend to deploy a dirty bomb, or bombs, or worse, they have an unstable fissionable weapon. "Thank you, Nest One," Shaw replied.

Elle broke in on the line. "Shaw, preliminary DOE tests confirm plutonium, not uranium, and its signature shows it likely came from the Chelyabinsk enriching facilities. Soviet made during the period 1972 to 1988." The pieces were coming together, and they formed the worst-case scenario.

The CDC had put out a bulletin to all hospitals and clinics in the country to send an NOI, Notice of Inquiry, of anyone seeking treatment for symptoms compatible with acute radiation exposure. Whoever was transporting the material would likely die within thirty-six to forty-eight hours if they were in an enclosed vehicle or room with the material.

Shaw felt relatively certain an attack would come within the next twenty-four hours. And he feared a coordinated attack would occur at several sites. It was no coincidence that radiological detections had occurred in New Jersey and Arizona within the same day. He needed to brief the president. Shaw dialed Franklin.

Franklin listened to Shaw's report and responded with a simple "Understood. I'm going to need you on the line when we brief the president."

Franklin motioned for Elle to come into his office and dialed the White House. The line came on. "Mr. Harbour, this is the president's secretary. The president is on his way from the residence. It will be sixty seconds."

Franklin tried to use that time to collect his thoughts. The president was going to want retaliatory recommendations. There was a multitude of models and game plans already drawn up, but selecting which to use was the key. Staging and planning could save thousands, if not millions, of lives.

"Franklin, what do you have for us?" the familiar voice of the president resounded in his ear.

Franklin started, "Sir, it's not good. In fact, it appears evident that we will be attacked within the next twenty-four to forty-eight hours. The attack will be WMD-nuclear. We believe the attack will be coordinated in several, at least two, locations in the US. One will be on the Eastern Seaboard; our best assessment is New York.

"The other is more perplexing. Everything we have points to Arizona, but if they have a nuke, it would be a waste to attack a smaller city. I would have expected LA or San Francisco. We have confirmed the nuclear signature origin is Russia, Cold War era. The source is exposed in Arizona, and we have exposure confirmed by both the Mayo and NEST. Since it appears exposed, we don't believe they can transport the materials to California by vehicle before they succumb to its effects. We have orbiting detection platforms over California to intercept any attempts to bring it west undetected.

"I think we may have a third threat, which was under surveillance in Denver and was lost westbound earlier today. We have had drones looking for that threat, but we have not been able to locate it. By now, that threat could be in the Southwest also. We believe we know the type of vehicle and have teams at pinch points on all major arteries west.

"Sir, I believe we need Homeland Security to issue a Level-One Alert. We now have TSA's multimodal VIPR teams in place, but we haven't issued the alert, given that it would be immediately known by the Bureau leak we think we have. But given the timing, I don't think we have a choice, sir."

The president was silent and then slowly spoke. "My God. Do we know who is behind this?"

Franklin answered, "The intel we have is that the nuclear materials may have come from a former FSB agent who has turned independent. We believe he met with representatives of two Islamic cells in Europe that the Israelis were shadowing. Those cells we know had one link to Hezbollah, but I caution that connection is decades old."

"Iran? Do we think this is state sponsored?" the president asked.

"We just don't know at this time, sir. The evidence the Israelis have to link the cells with Hezbollah—it's weak, a sole picture of a meeting with a senior member of the Hezbollah action group in Lebanon in the nineties. Nothing current. But sir, an operation of this size, this coordinated, could only have been planned and executed by a state, and then, only three or four have the logistical sophistication to pull this off: Iran, Syria, Russia, possibly China."

Franklin continued, "Given the state of Syria, I think that can probably be ruled out. Ordinarily, I would say that Russia would never try something so brazen, particularly since we would know the source of the material came from them, but after Putin's recent actions, I'm not so certain anymore. This isn't China's MO. China's not reluctant to engage in cyberattacks, but nuclear terrorism would damage their economy as badly as ours. And then there is Iran. Iran's relationship with Hezbollah and the fact that we have documented several ventures abroad, including one in Texas that killed a vocal opponent of the regime and the bizarre attempt by Iran's Quds Brigade to pay the Mexican cartel Los Zetas $1.5 million to bomb the Israeli Embassy in DC, indicates Iran is a potential actor."

"I need a definitive answer. If an attack with a WMD occurs on US soil, we are going to need to act and act in similar measure, and we damn well not act against the wrong player," the president said. The tone and look of the president focused everyone in the room and those on the line. This president had always thought first of the political implications of his acts, always solicited political advice before making his decisions. Not now. The president's resolve was unquestionable.

Admiral Heller of the Joint Chiefs was about to speak when Elle broke into the conversation. "Gentlemen, turn on CNN. Something's happened in California," she said.

They turned to the screens and listened to Wolf Blitzer talk with a reporter from KMIR, a NBC affiliate in Palm Springs. "For those who have just turned in, CNN is reporting a gun battle that has left three federal police officials and at least one civilian dead at the private air terminal at the Jacquelin Cochran Regional Airport just outside Palm Springs, California. Witnesses reported two men and a woman exited a twin-engine plane and immediately began firing on TSA officers. Three TSA employees were gunned down and killed. At least one civilian—an unconfirmed report was that the civilian was the pilot of the plane—was also murdered. The tail numbers of the plane, a Beechcraft King Air, show it's registered to a Killiam Investment Company in Blanding, Utah. Witnesses reported that the three fled in one of the TSA vehicles. We'll have more on this breaking story after a short break."

Admiral Heller asked the obvious question: "How is this event linked?"

Shaw spoke up. "Sir, this is Shaw Ellis. This could be the missing group that was behind the Denver attack yesterday. We lost them last night westbound out of Denver and have been unsuccessful reacquiring them. This could explain why we were unable to locate their vehicle. It could mean this group is bound for Los Angeles or a target in Southern California. If we locate their vehicle where this plane took off from, it will confirm that suspicion. We'll ask the Utah authorities to help with that."

"Gentlemen, I think we are beyond the point where we care whether the mole, if there is one inside the Bureau, is a concern. We need to involve the full resources of the Joint Task Force, including the Bureau," FBI Director Tankerfell interrupted.

"I agree, Mr. President," echoed Franklin.

"All right, make it so. Find these people, gentlemen, before they send this country into the dark ages," the president said.

The lines disconnected.

CHAPTER 54

OUTSIDE OF LAS VEGAS, NV

Carol and Josh listened to the report from the Denver FBI Center. She had been ducking calls all day from her superiors, claiming she needed to take an unexpected personal day. She had slept most of the way from Green River, Utah, to Mesquite, Nevada. About all they could say was that they had been heading west. They had had no leads until the news came on describing the incident in Palm Springs. When the Utah State Troopers confirmed that a Jeep Laredo was parked in the hangar where the King Air had taken off in Blanding, Utah, Shaw's assessment was confirmed. After sixteen hours in a car, they needed to stop, if even for a decent meal.

They were forty-five minutes outside of Las Vegas, where the Bureau had a field office. Carol decided she needed to tell her office where she was and what she had been doing. The call from Sarah explaining that the Bureau was back in the game had actually been a welcome relief. Carol dialed the Denver office, expecting Frank Holland, her boss, to be more than a little upset. She'd lied to him. Despite the circumstances, that would not be forgiven quickly.

"Agent Manning, I understand you've been busy, and not with a personal day." He let the words sit, not expecting a reply, and then continued. "All's not forgiven, but it's understood. It's not been the Bureau's finest hour. Bring me up to speed on how we can support you and what's been going on that the action reports don't say," Frank Holland said.

Carol was relieved. Frank was all business and hadn't let ego get involved. "I'm with Joshua Marcus, a Mossad operative operating under the wing of Shaw Ellis, from CIA. You are on a speakerphone. Josh was the target of the attack in Denver. He and I followed the attackers to the old Gates Factory in Denver and later tailed them into the Eisenhower Tunnel, where they staged an elaborate and successful elimination of our tail. We had a description of a car they switched into that was just found at an airstrip in Utah. They flew from there to Palm Springs, where they evidently landed and killed local TSA employees and the pilot. We are just north of Las Vegas. I'm not sure what we can do at this point but would like the Vegas Field Office as a base until you have an assignment for us," Carol reported.

"I suggest you get into Vegas and check in with Jack Wills there. He's the agent in charge of that office. And get some food and rest. If we need you two, we'll need you fresh. I suspect tomorrow is going to bring a full day. The LA office is in charge of the California threat, but we are in the dark about the threat that originated in Phoenix. If the target isn't in Arizona, then it might be Vegas," Frank said.

When Carol disconnected the phone, Josh quipped, "Great. Rest in Las Vegas just in case a nuclear bomb goes off there."

Carol laughed. "Yeah. There are more than a few people who would call that urban renewal."

CHAPTER 55

JERSEY CITY, NJ

Javier and Eduardo had spent the past hour shaving, washing, and preparing themselves for the next life, repeating in unison, "Martyrdom is not only the path to life—it is the door to life. Martyrdom is life. Praise be to Allah." Javier established the software protocols that would be downloaded into the iPad, which would manage the detonation. A few decades earlier, a mainframe computer would have been required; today, that computing power was carried in your back pocket, briefcase, or purse.

Ellise had been in the kitchen preparing the backpacks. Her time in Milan had trained her in cloud-sharing techniques that would allow her to commence a set of sequenced charges. The effects would ripple through the lives of every American and bring the US economy to its knees. She knew that the technologically dependent West was powerful only because it could amass superior technology. But its dependency on energy, upon communications and technology, made it fragile.

She had studied how on August 14, 2003, a few small, seemingly insignificant physical events had caused a series of rolling blackouts that culminated in two Canadian provinces and eight US states losing power. Twelve airports were shut down, over one hundred power plants went offline, and fifty million people were affected, with a loss of over $5 billion to the US economy. It would happen now on a grander scale. Without power, water, sewage, and traffic, commerce wouldn't flow. Within days, millions of people who were once comfortable would become scavengers, unable to locate food, water, or shelter. Most would be unable to fend for themselves and die; others would prey upon the weak. Chaos would ensue.

What they were about to do would eliminate the United States as a superpower. A fifth of its population would perish in the next three months.

CHAPTER 56

Hector met the contact. A Syrian who had come into the country through the porous Mexico border a little more than a dozen years ago, passing himself off initially as a Nicaraguan refugee. He had forged a past and citizenship papers. His engineering degree from Colorado State had been real, and it opened the doors he had been told to access. After six years, he had become shift supervisor for the Bureau of Reclamation's Glen Canyon Dam. Mannie Calamos was a model federal employee.

"The shift changes at 08:00, 16:00, and midnight. Only the 16:00 shift is manned with supervisors and a full staff, and that is only during the first four hours of that shift. I'll process one of you as an intern to come in with me. With the tours stopped, there will only be two security personnel with access to the control level, two technicians, and one or two maintenance personnel. The control level can be locked off from access from above," Mannie explained.

"Do you have the type of charges that were specified? The reservoir is nearly at full pool, the first time in thirty years. We'll be spilling through the eastern spillway, as the snowpack in Wyoming and Colorado are well above average again this year. The west spillway is shut down for a new concrete lining. If the eastern spillway is inoperable, there is no way the dam will hold, even if the detonation doesn't take it down. The pool is already at 3,692 feet elevation, just 8 feet below full capacity," Mannie explained.

"Won't the water just go over the top of the dam if it gets too full?" asked Hector.

"No. There is nearly twenty-one million acre-feet of active capacity behind the dam and another six million in what we call dead storage. The dam is only twenty-five feet thick at the crest, far less than the three-hundred-foot thickness at its base. Dams are curved toward the waters they hold back, to direct the pressure of the water behind the dam toward the walls of the canyon. If water goes over the dam, that pressure is exerted vertically against the dam. It simply will be too much. The dam will collapse. This almost happened in 1983, when cavitation damage shut down the spillways and the Bureau actually had to install plywood at the top of the dam to keep water from overtopping, and that was with some spillway releases and the power turbines releasing water at their full capacity. I've already taken three turbines offline for maintenance. No, without any releases from the spillways or turbines, a catastrophic failure will result," Mannie explained.

"Emilia, you need to set the charges by 06:00. The charges should damage the spillway tunnel once the rotary mechanism keeping the spillway closed is opened at precisely 07:00. The rotary mechanism is a giant wheeled cog that raises and lowers concrete block panels, allowing water into the forty-eight-foot-diameter spillway tunnel. At full capacity, the spillway can release 138,000 cubic feet of water per second, over a million gallons every second. The suction will sweep the charges into the spillway. The spillway elevation is 3,710 feet above sea level; the discharge at the bottom of the dam is 3,180 feet above sea level. Set the altimeter detonators to trigger the charges at 3,500 feet, half-way down the tunnel," Mannie instructed.

Hector remembered listening to the engineers in Beirut. Now he listened intently to Mannie explain. "In an underwater detonation, the gas bubble from the explosion remains confined by water on all sides. During the initial expansion of the gas bubble after shock-wave formation, the inertia of the outflowing water causes the expansion to persist. The bubble then collapses in a high internal pressure and expands again. The initial shock wave is followed by a further series of bubble oscillations that gradually diminish. Each of these bubble oscillations transmits a secondary pressure pulse, which, inside the rigid surface reflections of the tunnel, generates a series of compression waves. This cavitation erodes the lining of the tunnel. If the lining is degraded to the soft sandstone, the anchoring of the dam to the walls of the canyon will be undermined. Reclamation will be forced to shut the spillway down, and the waters will rise behind the dam."

Mannie continued, "The problem now is accessing the spillways. The channel in front of them has been off limits as of a few days ago. No boat traffic is allowed within a mile of the dam. Emilia will have to access the dam from a jeep road the locals use for fishing. She will have to slip into the water and make her way a hundred meters downstream to the spillway entrance. She needs to set the charges and be back on dry land at least thirty minutes before the spillway opens. That will give her time to make it back into Page before the charge goes off.

"It has to be done from the water, as surface access to the site itself is monitored by cameras that record any movement, transmitting an alarm at the dam and back in Salt Lake. Emilia, you have trained for this for a decade. You will be shallow, less than twenty feet below the surface, to maximize your air supply and take advantage of ambient light. You won't be able to use a dive light," Mannie instructed.

"She will do as you say. She is well trained. You need not worry; Emilia has been in far worse and more dangerous conditions," Hector said to Mannie, looking over to Emilia, smiling, and then continuing, "Here, at least there will be no river crocodiles or Chinese troops."

Emilia showed no emotion, nodding back to Hector.

Less than three blocks away, Greer disconnected the call. The Bureau was back in the game, and that meant the threat had become so imminent that detection by the mole was inevitable. The Los Angeles office was taking over strategic oversight to keep DC as much removed from counterterrorism details as possible. An attack, perhaps two, was imminent, and he was here in Page, Arizona...out of the loop. His orders were to prevent an infrastructure attack at Glen Canyon, which was a second-tier-infrastructure listed target. But he knew the real target would be a metropolitan area, and that was anywhere but here.

He'd spent most of the day with Sandy, inspecting the boat closure of the channel, precautions at the dam, visitor center, and electrical yard. His guilt was palpable. He had enjoyed his day with her. Several times during the day, their eyes had caught each other's, and their hands had touched or brushed, sending a sensation both experienced. He felt like a damn kid on a date, and all the while, terrorists were plotting the worst attack on his country it had ever faced. She'd be at his room any time now. The call had changed everything. He could now explain the threat, leaving the nuclear element out, to the local police, and to Dylan.

CHAPTER 57

PALM SPRINGS, CA

The forensic team canvassed the sites of both the abandoned, bullet-riddled TSA pickup and the grisly scene at the airport, rattling off their findings to the local police and FBI. "All three TSA officers were killed by nine-millimeter rounds; from the look of it, by the same gun. The pilot was shot in the back, fleeing, by a .380 ACP, a European variant of the nine-millimeter. Cartridges were everywhere and were taken for fingerprint analysis. We will have those results within the hour. No radiological detection either in the plane or the pickup, but initial results show traces of HMX, an incredibly powerful, military-grade conventional explosive."

Davies interjected, "We are checking available security and traffic cams in the vicinity, but the location was outside the more densely congested Palm Springs area, and traffic cameras are scarce. We have a description of the three on the plane from several witnesses who were on the tarmac—two males and a female. One Hispanic or Middle Eastern and one Anglo male; the woman was Anglo. All in their late twenties, early thirties. The Hispanic or Middle Eastern male was in jeans, blue shirt, and brown jacket. The Anglo male had light-brown hair; wore jeans and dark gray T-shirt. Both average height and weight. The woman was short, brown hair, above the shoulder in length; in jeans and black fleece top. Not much to go on."

One of the Palm Springs detectives chimed in, "Witnesses say they observed the Anglo male on one knee firing all rounds. A trained shooter." Most handgun stances were erect, the Weaver or Isosceles stances. This shooter had fired from a distances of thirty feet or so with two rounds designated to each victim, all placed in the torso. The victim in the vehicle was struck with two rounds from a distance of fifty feet or so, both head shots.

Davies added, "We are dealing with a highly trained group. There aren't many people in the world who could have made those shots in succession."

Pedro thought the choice of hotels was perfect. A two-bedroom unit with kitchen, accessible through a hallway leading from the parking lot. No security cameras or front desk attendant to deal with. He unloaded the luggage into the room and asked, "Is there more for me to do? Should I come back tomorrow?"

The three stared at him. Savano spoke first. "You're not going anywhere. Go get us dinner, coffee, and cigarettes."

Pedro nodded and walked out. He got in his van and stared at the other cars in the lot. He knew he would never survive this. He started the engine, and the radio came on. As he pulled out of the lot, he heard the CNN account of what had happened at the airport. He hadn't heard. He came to a stop—he felt sick, almost passing out. If he left now, turned himself in, turned the others in, would they let him escape with his family? He was in the country illegally. Whatever happened, his life was over. He would never see his family again. His wife and children uncared for. His mind raced, his body shook. He tried to catch his breath...to think. One certainty kept cascading: He would die tomorrow, his family hounded, his children traumatized by the knowledge their father was a terrorist. If he left, there was a chance his family could be protected.

But how? Should he run now? Call the FBI? Should he call his wife first? Give her time to get safe? Without realizing it, he found he had driven to a supermarket, a Vons. He parked and sat. Looking into the mirror on the visor, he saw himself. Years before, he had seen a warrior. More recently, he saw the reflection of a man. At this moment, he saw only a shadow. Perhaps he could put something in their food, something to make them sleep. Could he kill them and escape home, no one to link him to them? No, he had given the hotel the make and license of his van. His identity would be known. Maybe drug them and leave with the luggage; it had to contain explosives.

The phone jarred him to reality. It was the same number calling. "Pedro, where are you? Get some large garbage bags. And don't think about leaving.

Your family is being watched," the familiar voice of Savano seethed, bringing Pedro back to his reality.

Watched? Did they have other people in the country? Was it a bluff? He couldn't take that chance. He knew it was stupid, but he knew he needed to warn his wife, and he knew he needed to make the call. He would tell her a half-truth, that men had threatened his family if he didn't meet them.

He called. "Anna, it's me. I only have a few seconds. I can't explain, but the kids and you are in danger. I'm in danger...I'll explain later. Take the kids to your girlfriend's in Escondido, and tell no one, absolutely no one. Now. You must leave *now*! I'm sorry, I'll explain later. I'm in trouble. I'm sorry. So sorry." He didn't mention his past, and she cried, asking "Why?" over and over.

He hung up after telling her, "I have to go. Remember, don't tell anyone. I love you."

He then dialed information and was connected to the FBI in Los Angeles. "Federal Bureau of Investigation; how can I assist you?"

He had expected an electronic message; more time to think. He blurted out, "I have information on the people who were involved in the attack at the airport today."

"One minute, sir. Stay on the line; I'm transferring you to Agent Davies," came the reply.

"This is Agent Davies. Can you identify yourself, please?" the voice said.

Pedro took a deep breath and spoke excitedly. "My name is Pedro Ramirez. I have a, ugh, irrigation business in Chula Vista and a family. I was forced into helping these people. They said they would kill my family. I don't know what to do; I—"

Davies broke in. "Pedro, calm down and take this slowly. First, where are you now, and are they nearby?"

"I'm in a Vons parking lot on Palm Canyon Road. I'm in a white utility van that has my business name, All-California Irrigation Systems & Supply, on the sides. They are a couple of miles away, in a hotel," Pedro replied.

"Pedro, why did they let you go? Do they have people with your family?" Davies asked.

By this time, several agents were listening to the speakerphone while the call trace was coming up. It confirmed a cell call coming from the parking lot as the triangulated address.

"Yes. They asked me to go get them dinner and supplies. I don't think they have anyone with my family, but I don't know," Pedro replied.

The agents exchanged looks. The unspoken thought on everyone's mind was that terrorists would never allow someone to leave alone unless they trusted the person, unless he was one of them. Davies asked, "Pedro, are you telling us everything here? When did you first *meet* them?" The word "meet" was intentional.

"I was told yesterday over the phone to meet them in Palm Springs today, or they'd kill my family. Today, a man named Estaval called me from a plane, the one that landed at the Regional Airport. He told me to meet them at the airport, but when I went there, they told me to meet them outside the airport at a gas station. I just heard what happened at the airport. I wasn't there. I had nothing to do with that. You've got to help my family. You've got to help me," Pedro pleaded.

Something more was going on; it was apparent to everyone in the room. "Where did you leave the others, and when do they expect you back?" Davies asked.

"I left them at a Comfort Inn on Palm Canyon Drive. They expect me back any minute," replied Pedro.

Davies knew the suspects had military-grade explosives and were hardened terrorists. They would detonate a city block rather than be apprehended.

They needed time; they needed to know what the target was and whether they knew the targets for the other cells.

"Pedro, listen to me carefully. Go into the grocery store and get the items they asked you to get. Keep your cell phone charged, and keep it on. We can track where you are by your phone. If you don't go back, they may harm your family. We'll get your family under protection. I know I can't tell you to do this, but I'll ask. We need you to go back to them. If there is a chance and they are talking, I'll give you a dedicated line to call so we can eavesdrop. But only do that if you are absolutely certain no one will see you doing it. I can assure you that whatever you've done up until now, if you had no part in what occurred at the airport, it can be undone if you help us. Can you do this?" asked Davies.

"I don't know. I don't know if I can do this. They are very dangerous people. One who calls himself Estaval says he is Hispanic, but I think he is Syrian or Iraqi. The other two are Eastern European or Russian. The one who calls himself Savano is the leader. They are very, very dangerous. I'll do what you say, but please protect my family," Pedro pleaded.

"I give you my word, Pedro. Stay calm, and you'll get through this," Davies replied.

The room erupted into action. Davies directed a team to Palm Springs and briefed Ellis at CIA. This was the break they needed. A professional team would never be taken alive, and if taken, they would lawyer up and never divulge the plan in time to stop it. This wasn't a TV show where some simple "enhanced interrogation" techniques could be employed.

Davies ordered, "Our only play is to contain this team and hope that information is divulged as to the other teams' plans. Access Pedro's van and bug it, audio and directional. I want listening devices on the hotel room's windows. And I want an explosive device on the undercarriage of Pedro's van."

The last order brought a silence in the room. The Bureau didn't assassinate, it arrested, brought criminals to justice. To Davies' amazement, there was silence, no argument.

A few hours after eating, Savano and Estaval were both asleep, leaving Rose to arm the weapons, with Pedro sitting across the room staring in silence. Rose carefully had installed what appeared to Pedro to be small black plastic boxes inside four separate Velcro bags. Each bag was about two feet by three feet, rectangular in shape. Blue Velcro covered each bag. Separate were two small computer tablets, not much larger than iPads. After she typed for several minutes, one of the blue Velcro covered bags chirped a single tone, then the second bag chirped. Rose then repeated her typing with the other tablet, and the third and fourth bag let out the same tone.

Pedro sat, trying to gather courage to reach into his pocket and turn his phone on, dial the preset number. All he needed to do was slide the phone on and hit send, and it would dial. He sat frozen. As Rose picked one bag up and walked it over to the larger wheeled black duffel, she turned her back. Pedro slid his hand into his front pocket, withdrew the phone, hit Send, and slid it back. He made sure the speaker was muted before coming back but checked it once more. He slid the phone into the front pocket of his cargo pants just as Rose turned around.

He felt Rose staring at him. Felt she knew. Pedro tried to relieve the pressure of silence, "What are you doing? Are those bombs?" he asked.

She looked at him; he felt she was looking for any sign he was not allied with them. "You don't need to know. And don't touch anything," she replied. She entered information in the tablet and then closed the unit down and set it aside. "Set the clock for two a.m. We need to leave here by two thirty. We have a lot of driving to do," she said.

"Where are we going?" Pedro asked.

Again, Rose glared and responded with a frown, replying, "We are going to slowly kill California and America's power."

CHAPTER 58

WASHINGTON, DC

Having heard from Ellis and Tankerfell, the president and Joint Task Force had a decision to make: take down the California cell, which had announced in the intercept's chilling words that they would "slowly kill California" or risk allowing them movement in the hope they'd reveal a connection or some insight into the intentions of the other cells. The window was closing. They had no information on the other cells. The terrorists likely would succeed, and that sense of failure was on everyone in the room.

Shaw spoke first. "Mr. President, as I see it, we have three options. One, we allow the California cell to operate on the slim chance the informant, whose veracity is unknown, solicits some information on the other cells. Two, we take down the California cell, stopping a known attack, and suffer one or more additional attacks. Or, third, we take down the California cell now and subject them to overwhelming enhanced interrogation for the next few hours in the hope of obtaining information as to the location and details of the other attacks, which we believe will come tomorrow."

The president spoke. "Shaw, I appreciate your assessment, but we live in a nation of laws. The third option is off the table."

Tankerfell spoke next. "Even, sir, if that means several million Americans die tomorrow?"

The comment resonated not due to its truth, but because of the man delivering it. Tankerfell had been a federal prosecutor in New York and professor of constitutional law at Columbia. No one understood the constitutional implications of the statement more. Suddenly the lines between principle and humanity, law and holocaust, compelled once-taboo questions. There was precedent. America had interned those of Japanese descent in WWII, Lincoln had suspended the writ of habeas corpus in the Civil War, and the nation had established GITMO after 9/11.

Kate added, "The people will chastise but forgive a breach of laws. They will never forgive a nuclear Armageddon at the expense of legalese. And how does one come to terms with themselves and their God if they elevate the pronouncements of man, however principled, above the dictate of the protection of the innocents found in nearly every religion? For lawyers, the dilemma can be debated, but for others, the choice is clear."

"What has been the success rate of such interrogations?" the president asked.

The fact that he asked surprised everyone. Franklin responded, "Sir, there are three types of enhanced interrogation used to solicit information in a finite time frame: Pain, fear, and drugs—cocktails of what can be called truth serums. The first two have high success rates, but only on untrained subjects, which is not what we have here. I would rule them out. Medications have mixed results, perhaps a fifty-fifty success rate."

The president turned to his chief of staff, who had run his successful campaign for him, and asked, "Frank, what will the people say or do if I authorize interrogation?"

Knowing the political ramifications, the chief of staff responded, "Mr. President, they will forgive you temporarily, but over time, they will only recall that you authorized torture. You can forget a second term. Worse, both parties might impeach you before the election."

"OK, I'm ruling it out. Give me other options, people," the president said.

Shaw spoke next. "Mr. President, that leaves us two potentials: One, they voluntarily reveal a connection, a communication, or description of the overall attack plan before we are forced to take them down. Or two, we take them down now and use whatever sanctioned efforts we can to have them talk. Neither is a good option, and I fear neither will be successful."

Tankerfell spoke next. "Sir, these are highly trained operatives. They won't break and tell us anything in time to stop the other attacks. The only play is to hope the informant, reluctant participant, or whatever we are calling him, solicits the information."

"I agree. It's the only option. But DO NOT lose this cell. I want them dead or captured if they even look like they are getting close to executing their attack," ordered the president.

CHAPTER 59

3:00 A.M., PALM SPRINGS, CA

"We've got movement. One female, one male loading the vehicle. No lights in the hotel room or van; we can't make out what they are loading," Agent Sam Perrin said into his mike.

"Roger that. The tracker on the van is operational. Verify all subjects are in the van as they leave," Agent Davies ordered.

Sam strained, trying to make out the subjects. These guys were good. They had parked the van at the only location in the lot that had bad light. Despite those precautions, the Zeiss low-light binoculars were effective. He could clearly make out the woman and two men getting into the van. There should be a fourth, he thought. "Bill, Sam here. Can you locate the fourth suspect?"

"Negative, Sam, not from my position. I'll try to get a better angle. Wait one," came Bill Ritter's response.

A few minutes passed, and the van continued to idle. "Sam, Bill here. I have a better line of sight now. I make out two in the van, over."

Static, no reply. "Sam, Ritter here, come in." There was no reply. Ritter scanned his binoculars over to where Sam was concealed, and he saw him, sprawled on the ground. "Central, this is Ritter. We have an agent down. Repeat, Agent Perrin is down. Proceeding to—" His communication was cut by the silenced nine-millimeter round that tore through his temple.

"Ritter, this is Davies. Come in. Ritter, say your status," Davies repeated. He knew, feared, there wouldn't be a reply. "All agents, suspects on the move, multiple agents down." Davies didn't want to make the call to detonate the van without first clearing it. He called the Joint Task Force line and detailed the suspects' movement and loss of the agents, requesting authority to remotely detonate the van. *Detonate* wasn't the right word; *incinerate* was more accurate. The charge under the vehicle was phosphorous, nicknamed a Willie Pete charge. It burned with intensity and very high heat, instantly incinerating everything, even metal. Davies had seen it used in Fallujah in 2004. Its use on US soil demonstrated that no chances would be taken with these terrorists.

The tracker still showed the van stationary. They had to know others would descend on them. "Agent Davies, you have a green light for WP use; take them down," came the order. Davies relayed the approval to the field team five blocks away from the hotel, which detonated the charge. The parking lot erupted in a blinding white light. The van and all of its contents were incinerated in seconds. The agents watched as the van melted in on itself.

People poured out of their hotel rooms. All but room 214. Its occupants were dead, their car gone.

CHAPTER 60

NEW YORK CITY

A crisp breeze came across the port side of the ferry as it turned north and eased into the ferry dock. The sound of the waves lapping against the wakeless ferry was a lull from the drone the ferry's diesels as it made its way from Jersey. The weather called for nearly eighty degrees and sun later. A short walk under the FDR Expressway, and they were on Wall Street. At Williams, they separated. Phillipe walked north. Marza continued west to Trinity Park to sit among the tourists until the time approached. Phillipe's subway ride would take several minutes to reach midtown.

Even though it was midday, Eduardo and Javier had battled traffic for nearly two hours to get back to the racetrack in Yonkers. Everything had to occur at the same time, precisely 15:00 on the East Coast, noon on the West. The time had been chosen for maximum effect—early enough to catch the commute in New England and at the height of the power demand in the West on a hot May day. It would be late enough in the spring to make the heat in the Southwest work for them but early enough to avoid the summer exodus from New York. They had become smarter. They understood their adversary.

Phillipe and Marza both carried packages. Phillipe's in a backpack, Marza's in the fashionable rolling Tumi briefcase so often seen in the Financial District.

Peter and Jim were on East Fifty-Seventh Street in their squad car, nearly halfway through their shift. "What do you make of the sergeant's briefing this morning?" Jim asked. The sergeant's briefing that morning had been somber. The NYPD was on a heightened state of alert for a terrorist event.

Pete shook his head, responding, "It sounds like the Big Apple is back in the crosshairs by these assholes. Makes me wonder why we don't just either bomb them back to the Dark Ages or stop buying oil from them and let them go back to herding."

Jim laughed at Pete, who always had a way with words.

CHAPTER 61

PAGE, AZ

Emilia turned off the pavement onto the sand-packed road, turning her lights off and being careful not to touch her brakes. She could barely make out the road as it wound down to the lake. She parked the SUV about twenty feet from the water's edge. She removed a white cooler and lawn chair and sat both by the water's edge. Mannie had told her it would make her appear to be just another fisherman. In the predawn twilight, the lake was glass, the moon casting long shadows across the sandstone surface. The only sounds were the almost-imperceptible, soft lapping of the water against the stone and a faraway bullfrog. Emilia was amazed by this place. No grass, just stone. An occasional patch of sand on the rock gave birth to an occasional cactus, fine tan grasses, and the scratchy, invasive, nonnative tamarisk along the bank.

She slipped out of her clothes to reveal a one-piece bathing suit in the cold air, shivering as she pulled the wetsuit on. She knew it would be far harder getting out of it when wet. She gently tightened the regulator's O-ring connection against the tank, which was already attached to the buoyancy vest. She stood the tank up on the tailgate, turned the tank's air on, and backed into the vest, slipping her arms in and then buckling the heavy vest's cummerbund in place. In one hand she carried her fins and mask; in the other, the dry sack. She lumbered carefully under the weight to the water's edge.

Mannie told her the sandstone was known as slick rock, so she approached the water carefully. With her first step, her feet swept down the slick surface, and she fell into the water. The cold water flooded into her wetsuit. She froze, scanning around to see if anyone had heard the splash. After a few seconds, she knelt in about three feet of water and put her fins on over her booties, spit into her mask to keep it from fogging, and put her regulator in her mouth. When she dipped down, it was pitch black—she couldn't see three feet. Slowly her eyes adjusted, and she could see the surface light a few feet above, and she looked at her illuminated compass. Without a dive light, she needed to break the surface and take a bearing of her destination a few hundred yards away. She again descended just under the surface and followed the soft-green, illuminated compass dial.

She reached the spillway forebay and kicked toward the steel gate. It was imposing, unnerving to be this close to it in darkness. If it opened now, she would be swept through the forty-one-foot diameter pipe and killed by the turbulence and bomb she carried. She clipped the dry sack line to the extra weight she carried in her vest pocket and set the weight down on a shallow ledge. With most of the air out of the dry sack, it floated up from the bottom a few feet and hung motionless not far from the closed spillway gate. She started the swim back. Six twenty; it had taken much longer than planned, and she was nearly though her air—only 1,100 PSI left. She needed to be back to the car in ten minutes and knew that wasn't going to happen.

She kicked long, straight strokes, with her arms as close to her sides as possible to minimize resistance, and she fought to return to the vehicle. The light was coming up. In a few minutes, the sun would rise over Navajo Mountain and expose her. She was exhausted. Her legs burned. The last hundred feet, she had been on the surface, trying to avoid sound, her air depleted. At the bank, she desperately wanted to rest but knew she had only minutes. She struggled out of her fins. She tried twice to scale the bank, but each time, the fine mud on the slick rock caused her to slide back into the water.

Getting out of the BC vest, she let her fins and mask drift away. They were designed to be neutrally buoyant, and she didn't know whether they would float or sink from sight. There was nothing anyone could do anyway. The spillway gate was set to open in minutes. She clawed her way onto shore. With her remaining strength, she lifted the tank and attached vest into the back of the SUV, peeled off the wetsuit, pulled on sweat pants and a fleece jacket, and crawled in.

Inside the dam Control Room, no one heard or felt the explosion. Paul, a maintenance tech, was bringing a box of cleaning supplies from the central corridor to a storage area when he felt a shudder. Then another. In eleven years, he had never felt anything like it. He went to a wall panel and pulled out the phone. "Paul here. I'm on 56W near the end of the corridor. I just felt two vibrations."

"Well, we just opened the W Spillway, so that was probably it," came the reply.

Paul shook his head. "No, Mike, this was different. I know what it feels like when the gates are opened, and this wasn't it," Paul insisted.

"All right, I'll go down to the outlet and see if there's anything unusual. Thanks," Mike said.

The explosion of six kilos of HMX inside the concrete spillway tunnel had been silent. Deep inside the dam and shielded by a hundred thousand cubic feet of water each second, sound wasn't a factor. But the explosion had seriously damaged the tunnel. A five-meter length of the meter-thick concrete tunnel wall had been blown out. This in turn allowed the rushing current to begin damaging the lower portions of the tunnel, the process known as cavitation. Mannie had explained that when water runs down a smooth surface pipe under pressure, resistance along the pipe surface is minimal, the water slipping by unimpeded. When water passes through a constricted rough area, vapor cavities, bubbles, form. The rapid collapse of these bubbles causes shock waves, eroding surrounding surfaces at an accelerating pace. If erosion reached the porous sandstone, the anchoring of the dam to the cliff wall could fail, with devastating results. A silent and hidden process had commenced.

CHAPTER 62

YONKERS, NY

Javier pulled the car into the racetrack parking lot. A few empty buses and cars littered the empty lot. The reservoir was a mere thirty meters away. Javier and Eduardo got out of the car and walked back to the trunk. The reservoir was built up on all sides, more of a large man-made pool than a lake. Small by reservoir standards, less than three thousand acre-feet in capacity, roughly nine hundred million gallons. Scores of birds sat on its surface, ironic given the EPA's unsuccessful attempts to compel installation of a multi-million-dollar "bird cover," which the Agency felt was necessary to protect New York City's water supply. Ironic, Javier thought. Millions to protect the installation from bird crap but a modest fence to keep the real threats out.

Javier had studied the reservoir's unique multicell design. It was here that two of New York's three aqueducts delivered water from distant sources in the Catskills and Delaware River Basin to the city. From here, water was pumped via two massive tunnels south to serve over eight million people in America's economic hub.

Javier, the professor, knew the blast effects of a one-kiloton ground burst. "It will vaporize everything within a kilometer, leaving a crater a hundred meters wide and fifteen feet deep. Here in New York, that means a steam event, given the shallow water table. A ground burst would result in more fallout, but that would be mitigated, given the proximity to the Atlantic. New Rochelle and Long Island would bear the brunt of the fallout, but the effects on Manhattan and the US would be multiplied hundreds of times over. The metropolitan area will be rendered uninhabitable. That's only possible by eliminating an essential element of life—water. New York can never be evacuated. It is simply too large, too dense, too unprepared. Without water for drinking, sanitation, and fire protection, the city will be reduced to unimaginable chaos. The death, destruction, and disruption will be far greater than a detonation in Manhattan would be."

Eduardo smiled, even though he had heard it several times before from the "Javier the professor."

Eduardo's smile, though, was in his knowledge that America would react swiftly and with overwhelming force against its enemies and *his*.

They wheeled the large duffel from the parking lot up the grassy hill to a middle-class residential neighborhood and then along the perimeter fence of the reservoir. Dressed in one-piece blue service overalls, they looked the part of utility maintenance men. Javier wheeled the duffel while Eduardo carried a tool belt and extension cord over one shoulder. They walked the two blocks to the southern end of the reservoir, past women walking strollers, a jogger, and several residents working in their yards. No one paid them much attention.

Walking up to the intersection of Kimball and Hillview Avenues, they approached a utility panel. "That will do. We will set up here as if we are work-ing on this panel," Javier said. After a few minutes, Eduardo affixed the duffel to the panel post with police plasticuff ties. Then he strung yellow tape marked Utility Maintenance around the panel in a ten-foot perimeter. "Set the timer, and let's go," Eduardo said under his breath. They turned and began walking back the way they had come.

They'd walked about fifty feet when a police car turned onto Kimball Avenue and stopped alongside them. The young officer asked, "I saw you working on that panel. What company are you working for?"

"Con Edison," replied Eduardo.

"Kind of unusual not to have a truck. Where'd you park?" asked the officer in a strong Bronx accent.

It wasn't the answer that gave them away; it was Javier's eyes, which darted between Eduardo and seemed to look down the street as if to see if the officer was alone on patrol.

The officer gunned the squad car at the sudden movement of Eduardo toward his utility belt. That reflex saved the officer's life as nine-millimeter rounds struck the back door.

"Dispatch, Unit 304, Kimball and Hillview, shots fired, request backup. Two suspects on foot, northbound on Kimball. Request backup," officer Hernandez yelled. Eight years on the force, this was the first time he had been shot at. He gunned the car, accelerating and putting fifty yards between his assailants and him before turning the wheel sharply and hitting the brakes, wheeling the car into a 180-degree skid. He was instantly out behind the door, his gun out, opening fire on the two.

At this range, hitting the subjects would be more luck than marksmanship. Eduardo separated to flank the officer. Hernandez was surprised by this. Criminals seldom had wits, much less tactical training. This was not good. "Dispatch, Hernandez Unit 304, where's my backup? I'm taking fire. Subjects appear well trained and—" his words were cut short as the round struck him in the shoulder. "I'm hit, I'm hit. Repeat, officer down," he yelled into his shoulder mike. Eduardo walked up and fired two quick shots, ending Officer Hernandez's life.

They could hear the sirens and knew it was only a matter of time. They ran through the yard of the closest home, into the backyard and into the next block. They ripped off the overalls behind a hedge, ran into the parking lot, and jumped into the car, which they slowly drove toward the exit.

"Get down. They are looking for two men together," Eduardo instructed.

They made it to the exit and had just started over the Clark Street Bridge when a patrol car blocked the street in front of them. "There's another police car behind us. Its lights are flashing," Javier said. Two officers, guns drawn, approached the vehicle from the rear, one on each side. The officers could see the two men sitting still, talking straight ahead, their heads nodding as if in a trance. As one officer got close enough to the open driver's-side window, he heard the words "Allah Akbar." The car exploded, sending a shock wave that vaporized everything in a two-hundred-foot radius.

People heard and felt the blast for blocks, staring as the plume of smoke erupting into the sky. The residents across from the duffel bag and reservoir watched the plume of smoke rise in the distance.

CHAPTER 63

NEAR CATHEDRAL CITY, CA

Pedro was in a panic. He knew he should never have gone back. Now he would most certainly be compelled to kill or be killed. He thought only of his children and wife, knowing their lives were over as well. The only thing he could hope for was the tracking of his cell phone. They must be doing that.

"Davies, Shaw here. The van was a feint. NSA is tracking the informant's phone. North and west of the incident. Looks like it is on I-10 eastbound."

"Eastbound? Can you confirm that? Subject is moving east, *away* from Los Angeles?" Davies asked incredulously.

"Roger that. The signal is moving east," Shaw replied.

Pedro was driving, and Estaval was in the front seat using an iPad navigational program that every few seconds ticked off directions and distance from inputted coordinates. Savano and Rose had three of the four backpacks left, having just set one at what looked to Pedro to be an electrical yard of some sort.

Rose kept asking, "How is it we were tailed? Pedro here must have talked to someone on his trip to the store."

Estaval had thought the same thing and earlier demanded to see his phone. A check of received and sent calls showed only one call. Pedro would never have thought to delete them from the phone logs if the FBI agent hadn't told him to do so. Rose hit redial for the one number and received an electronic message:

"You have reached the Verizon wireless support line. Your call will be answered in the order in which it was received. Please do not hang up or dial again. If you wish, you can access your account or support at www.verizonwireless.com/supportcenter." The call seemed harmless, but Rose wasn't sure.

They came upon another fenced-in, deserted electrical yard. Savano told Rose, "I'll set this charge. I'll put it next to the largest transformer. Help me cut the fence."

Savano ran toward a large gray metal box with massive black terminals coming out of it. It reminded Pedro of a metal beehive, or the arms of Robbie the Robot in the 1956 movie *Forbidden Planet*, which he had watched with his kids. This one was huge, over thirty feet in height, and was in the middle of three similar but smaller transformers.

"Agent Davies, this is Sarah at Mr. Ellis's office. The tracking either stopped or slowed near the intersection of State Highway 62 and I-10. It resumed eastbound on I-10."

Davies yelled out, "Get me maps, anything that looks like a target within a forty-mile distance east of Desert Hot Springs, particularly along the I-10 corridor."

After the last backpack was set, Savano curled his upper lip in an attempt to smile or perhaps sneer, telling Pedro, "Our job here is finished. We need another car. Check-out time at that hotel is eleven. They've probably found the car's owners. This one by now will have been reported. Take the Indio exit and look for a neighborhood with large homes, a rich area."

Pedro did as instructed, and in a few minutes, they were driving down a residential street with manicured lawns, flowers on porches, and cars in driveways. "There. Pull in that driveway but stay in the car. Rose and I will go," Savano instructed, pointing to a house.

The home was a large, one-story ranch-style home with a two-car garage. A car was pulled up under a tree just to the right of the garage doors. In the heat, it meant that the garage had to be full already.

Savano and Rose went to the front door and rang the doorbell. The bark of a small dog began, followed by the sounds of someone coming to the door. The door unlatched, and an elderly lady in a faded yellow robe came to the door, opened it, and hoarsely whispered, "Yes, may I help you?"

Rose stepped forward one step, smiled, and said, "Good morning, ma'am. We are from the County Planning Office and are canvasing the neighborhood for opinions on a request to build a new office building in your neighborhood."

"Oh, my, an office building? Here? How large...I mean how tall would it be?" the lady asked.

Rose wiped her forehead as if she were hot and said, "Well, we have the plans we can show you. It *would* be visible from your house."

That did it. The frail lady invited them in and closed the door behind them. Savano put his knife to the woman's throat and hissed, "Who else is in the house?"

"No one. My daughter has gone for a run. No one is here besides me," the woman managed to get out, beginning to cry.

"When will your daughter be back?" Savano asked.

"Any minute," she sobbed.

Rose went out to the garage, half of which was filled with boxes. She found the keys and backed the car, an Audi A-8, out of the garage and motioned Pedro to pull the stolen car from the motel into the garage. Then she parked the Audi in the drive, walked into the garage, and touched the garage-door button. The door vibrated down. Nothing to do now but wait for the daughter.

Pedro walked into the kitchen and sat down, looking at the woman and knowing what was to come. He averted his eyes. Estaval walked in and saw the woman, whom Rose had already gagged with a dishtowel to stifle any attempts to warn the daughter. They moved into the living room, out of sight of the front door. Savano stayed in the foyer. He would close the door once the daughter walked in. It would be days before anyone noticed them missing.

"It's three and a half hours to Phoenix. See what food there is," Estaval said to Pedro.

CHAPTER 64

Mannie arrived at the Visitor Center and took the elevator down nearly five hundred feet to the Generator Floor. The new security protocol required employees to go through the two-mile tunnel leading to the parking lot at the base of the dam after a full vehicle and occupant search or access through the Visitor Center elevator with a key. Access across the dam crest was closed. There would be minimal security through the Visitor Center since only six people possessed keys. The elevator opened to a dark-gray concrete hallway, which then opened up to long, sterile, yellow-tiled hallways reminiscent of an old hospital's basement area. The labyrinth led to the Control Room overlooking the vast, open Generation Floor. Even through the sound-control windows, the hum and vibration of the eight massive red-and-black generators, each sitting atop turbines capable of generating over 155,000 horsepower, filled the room. They were immense. Each about thirty feet in diameter and thirty feet high, the turbines were many feet below the floor's surface, spinning by the force of water rushing through the penstocks.

With the tours discontinued, there would be fewer than a half dozen people to contend with in the Control Room and the halls leading to it. Mannie would assess the numbers to contend with and then introduce the engineer from Hamburg masquerading as his cousin, a professional photographer.

Two miles away, Hector knocked on the door to Vincent's room. There was no answer. He knocked harder; still nothing. The door was locked. His heart began to pound, only to feel as though it stopped when the door opened. In front of him was a dead man. "I'm sick; been throwing up all night," Vincent said in a half-whisper. His fit, hulking frame appeared smaller, weak, pale. A deep-red rash covered his arms, neck, and forehead. He wiped sweat from his forehead and caught a handful of his hair across his forehead. It came out in a clump.

Eyes wide, Hector said, "Sit down, my friend. Rest. There is only one more task for you to help with. We will leave in twenty minutes." Seeing Vincent, he knew he needed him to drive the package to the dam to minimize his exposure. He hoped the fifteen to twenty minutes of exposure would not be lethal, but that was in Allah's hands. He walked into the room briskly, set the timer for 13:00, and left.

He went to his room, vigorously washed his hands, showered, and left his clothes on the floor, changing into new clothes. He sat and thought how this changed the plan and what now must be done.

CHAPTER 65

LOS ANGELES, CA

Ibrahim turned off the Santa Monica Freeway to the address the navigation app directed him to. His phone gave him step-by-step directions to the industrial parking lot that sat directly under I-110. At this location, I-10 and I-110 intersected, with I-10 elevated over I-110. He parked the car next to the overpass support. He pulled two charges stuffed inside two black garbage bags from the trunk and placed one on one side of the support and one on the opposite side. A thin wire led to each from the car's trunk. Inside the trunk, a third charge affixed to the trunk floor would provide a vertical directional charge.

Looking around, he closed the trunk. No one was in sight. The closest people were the lucky ones in the cars and trucks who were passing now, ahead of the chaos that would ensue in a few hours. He walked the two blocks to the bus stop on Washington Street and got on the first bus. A simple bus connection, and he would board Amtrak's Southwest Chief back to Tempe to resume his studies. His hope was that Emilia would be waiting for him there.

CHAPTER 66

LAS VEGAS, NV

Carol had showered and put on the same clothes from yesterday, the only ones she had. She had at least been able to iron the blouse but made a mental note to pick up a change of clothes today. She was on her second Starbucks. Sleeping for six hours after thirty-six hours of the chase from Denver wasn't enough. But it had recharged her; the fog induced by lack of sleep and food had dissipated—she was thinking clearly. Yesterday was a blur. It seemed another life since she had left her townhouse in Denver for the office two days ago.

As she walked into the field office, she saw Josh wave her over. He was shaved and in a crisp, clean short-sleeve white shirt, the sleeves taut against his tan biceps. "Carol, I want you to meet someone. This is Anna Levy. She works with me and came in last night from Tel Aviv," Josh said.

Anna was short and fit, with large green eyes set off by her dark-olive skin. She extended a hand to Carol. "It's a pleasure to meet you, Agent Manning. I see you have kept my boss alive."

Carol instantly liked her. "Please, its Carol, and I'm not sure who kept whom alive," she replied. "Do we know anything more? It sounds like everything is happening in LA, and we are all here. Perhaps we should hit the casinos."

Josh said calmly, "Actually, a lot has happened this morning. There's been a suicide car bombing in New York, in the Bronx, I believe. And the vehicle that the FBI was watching in Palm Springs apparently contained the same group we followed out of Denver. It blew up with all occupants in Palm Springs...except that the cell phone of the informant who was with that group is apparently traveling east from Palm Springs into the desert."

Carol's eyes narrowed, staring at the floor, thinking. She said, more to herself than to Josh, "Traveling away from LA? What's in the desert? Why would they fly west to drive back east? They could have landed anywhere." After a pause, she continued, "And what did they hit in New York?"

"Nothing. They blew themselves up with high explosives when the police were apprehending them. First estimates are forty to fifty dead, including eight police officers, another seventy-five to a hundred injured. But with the amount of explosives they detonated, it could have been far worse," Josh replied.

"Shaw called about twenty minutes ago; they're assembling a list of possible targets east of Palm Springs, but none are high priority. Shaw's now in New York trying to piece together whether the threat in New York is over. The New York car bomb was conventional. So that begs the question of where the radiological is that set off the alarm two days ago in Newark. This is not over," Josh added, rubbing his temples.

Anna began, "We've been following two Islamic cells in Europe over the past four months. They disappeared overnight, and we believe they are the ones involved here. The nuance is that they were composed of engineering students. Electrical and mechanical engineering students. They aren't suicide-vest fodder. These are educated people who have trained for this for years."

A few miles away, Amante was struggling. He had awoken in the middle of the night. Nausea had turned to vomit, and that had turned to chills and fever unlike any he had ever experienced. Looking in the mirror, he saw the sores on his tongue and inside of his jaw. He had so little energy, he hadn't been able to get out early and canvass the area for locations to place the backpacks. He knew the likely targets, but a lone backpack would attract attention or theft. He had to find locations where they would not be detected.

He splashed water on his face and ran his fingers through his hair. His hands were covered with his hair. He had felt no tugging; the hair had just fallen out as he ran his hands through it. He opened one backpack and checked the timer. He closed the pack, threw it over his shoulder, and walked out of the room. He struggled to walk down the hall toward the elevator. Once in, he leaned against the wall as it descended.

The elevator stopped, and three college-age men got in. They looked at him, and one laughed, saying, "Hey, dude, you look like I feel," causing the other two to laugh.

Amante tried to glare but was too weak to offer anything back. The elevator door opened at the lobby to a pounding chorus of slot-machine bells.

Amante walked through the casino as best he could. In Vegas, odd behavior and an inability to walk a straight line didn't stand out. No one gave him a second look. He walked out the revolving door and was hit full force by the heat. He thought he would be sick again and lurched for a trash can. This time he only heaved, but the spittle was red. He had studied the effects of radiation. The knowledge and fear of his situation struck him. He would die today. If not today, tomorrow.

He walked along the Strip to Caesars Palace. He walked through the Forum Shopping Center, amazed by the ceiling's likeness to an evening sunset. Abruptly, he was in the casino, looking for the right spot. He knew every inch of the casino was monitored by cameras. He walked out, following a stream of people. Women dressed in provocative miniskirts; men in shorts and armless T-shirts carrying two-foot-long drinks. There...he saw it. An outdoor café with a large trash can immediately before an escalator that carried throngs up to a walkway and another hotel. He slipped the backpack off his shoulder, holding it with one hand as he leaned against the trash can with the other, looking into the crowd. He slipped the backpack into the trash can. He knew one or two people may have seen it, but the surging mass of people had carried them away. His legs felt like weights as he turned, knowing he needed to get back to the second backpack and repeat the task. He knew his other target; he had seen it last night. On a schedule, every thirty minutes on the hour and half hour, hundreds of people flocked to observe the fake pirate ship. Everyone stood shoulder to shoulder. He knew there would be no point to evasion. He knew the alternative was a slow and gruesome death. He would stay with the bomb.

CHAPTER 67

NEW YORK CITY

Both Peter and Jim knew cops who had been killed up in Yonkers. Word traveled fast in the ranks. The alert had described the event and been punctuated by a warning that more attacks were expected *today*. Suddenly, everyone became a suspect. Call it profiling, or just call it good police work. The attacks would be carried out by people between eighteen and thirty-five years of age. Likely male, although that wasn't a given. Definitely Middle Eastern. The two who had blown up half of Yonkers fit that profile, and the odds were the others would as well. The argument against profiling to them seemed naïve—plain stupid. Ignoring statistics is negligence. Time was limited; an attack was imminent. They weren't about to waste their time worrying about a fifty-year-old white guy in a business suit any more than they would worry about a sixteen-year-old gangbanger. They weren't the perpetrators, at least not today. A cop could sense—no, see—behavior linked with someone fitting the profile.

Peter and Jim had just had their shift extended and now were being directed to be on foot in the Financial District for the final shift segment. It actually felt good after they had been sitting for seven hours in a patrol car. Jim remarked, "Port Authority handles security at the World Trade Center. That's a likely target, particularly after all the shit they caught in the opening weeks. What was it, three security tests and three failures in the first week?"

"Yeah, but they beefed up security after those trespasses and called out that that private security firm, so I'm sure they have it back together by now," Pete replied.

"Anyway, we will be among fifty or so cops in the twelve-block Financial District. Someone would be a fool to try something with that coverage," Jim said. With the exchange and adjacent high-profile financial institutions, brokerage houses, and law firms, the area was a likely target.

Marza sat in the park reaching into her rolling luggage as if she were looking for a book or snack. She armed the timer to 15:00, zipped the bag, and rested against it in the sun. She felt at peace. She had planned, studied, and worried about this day for over three years. If it went as planned, her enemies would be struck on opposite sides of the world.

Philippe got off the subway at midtown. As he walked up Fifth Avenue, the sidewalk was full. He was amazed that people seemingly didn't watch where they were briskly walking and yet didn't crash into others. At five seven, he couldn't sense what was ahead or to the side. Looking at his watch, he could see he had just under two hours to get to the objectives and safely away. The sun was out now and beginning to bake the city. Last night's rain was turning to steam as the city began its first muggy day of the season.

He crossed Fifty-Fifth Street and walked past opulent shops—Harry Winston Jewelers, Armani, Zegna, Prada. He knew he was close; the crowds were thicker. At Fifty-Seventh, he stopped at the corner and waited alongside scores of shoppers for the light to change. Finely dressed women in high heels walked into Bergdorf's like ants to a picnic, with a singular focus. He wondered how they would feel after today.

Walking another block, he saw the crowd in line to walk into the glass cube gleaming in the warm sun. Scores of people stood patiently in line to enter the glass cube and wind their way down the stairway to the creative crypt beneath. First-timers peered with the same reverence as those entering St. Paul's Basilica.

Looking at his watch, he saw that it had taken nearly twenty minutes to get admitted to the store below. He walked to something called the Genius Bar and set his backpack down among purses, shopping bags, backpacks, and discarded jackets deposited by those waiting divine guidance. Walking to the next table, he looked casually at iPhones and iPads, then walked back up the staircase and out. With his fanny pack, he had one more objective.

He walked to the curb, hailed a cab, and instructed the cabbie to go to Times Square. It took ten minutes. He was still on schedule. He got out, handing the cabbie the fare, and walked across the street, where a large crowd had gathered to watch street performers. Sitting on a bench next to a trash can and watching the throngs, he unbuckled the fanny pack and let it drop between the bench and trash can. It might be found when they emptied the trash can, but it was hidden from view until the trash can was moved. His watch read 14:10—fifty minutes to go.

A few minutes earlier in Yonkers, Officer Ronnie Jacobs and his partner, DeShaun Johnson, were patrolling the perimeter of Hillview Reservoir. All infrastructure and public buildings were on lockdown following the explosion a few blocks away. DeShaun saw it—something that just didn't look right. A suitcase, duffel, leaning next to a utility panel. While there was Con Ed yellow utility tape around the area. It still didn't look right. "Ronnie, over there, pull over," she said.

Walking out of the patrol car, she ducked under the tape and saw the twist ties binding the luggage to the utility rack. "Get Con Edison on the horn. Ask them what's going on with this utility post," she yelled to Ronnie.

Ronnie called it in, and a few minutes later, he jumped out of the car and ran to DeShaun. "Con Ed said they don't have any utilities here. I called Bomb Disposal just to be on the safe side," he said.

Beads of sweat were forming on DeShaun's face as she bent down and slowly tried to unzip the luggage. All pockets and zippers were closed with twist cuffs. That was a bad sign. "Start getting these houses across the street evacuated," she ordered.

Sarah interrupted the task force room. "Elle, NYPD reports a bomb disposal team has been dispatched to a location near the site of the earlier suicide-bomb incident."

"Bring a map up on the screen with both locations, bring the audio live, and get Shaw on the line. He's in Manhattan," Elle replied.

The wall had multiple screens, one large and three smaller monitors. Sara brought up a map on the large screen. In between the two marked locations, it screamed at them: a lake. "What's that lake? It doesn't look natural. Find out everything you can about it, and get me Captain Miller at NYPD now," Elle snapped.

Sarah's fingers flew across the keyboard, and in less than a minute, she was relaying what she was seeing on her screen. "It's Hillview Reservoir. It belongs to the New York City Water Supply Agency. It supplies water to Manhattan, Bronx, Brooklyn, pretty much all of the city."

Franklin stared. "How can that be? It's so small."

Sarah responded, "Pipelines—aqueducts is what they call them—bring water there, and from there, water is piped to the city."

Franklin saw it clearly. He stood and said, "They're after the water. To deny water to New York would shut the city down, cause widespread panic, riots, fires. Eight million people without water or sanitation. How long can a person live without water? Three, maybe four days? Not enough time to evacuate a city the size of New York. It would be a thousand times worse than 9/11. Get it offshore!"

Sara interrupted. "Elle, I have Captain Miller on line two."

"Put him on speaker," Elle said. "Captain Miller, Elle Hardwick here at CIA. We met a few years ago at the Agency's training symposium in Langley. I'm afraid we have a crisis. We believe we have a WMD in Yonkers, a few blocks from the site of the earlier bombing, targeting the water supply infrastructure of the city. We can't risk not being able to disarm it. We need it removed to a safer location."

"By safer, what distance and direction are you suggesting?"

"East. We believe it may be nuclear. The prevailing winds are to the east. We need to get it offshore, and we don't know the timing," Elle responded.

"Then I better get off the phone, Ms. Hardwick. Find us a drop site," Captain Miller replied.

CHAPTER 68

Hector ripped the woman out of the car; detection was no longer an issue. He needed a car; he had only ten minutes to meet Vincent at the dam.

Vincent drove the SUV alone with the weapon. Driving down the hill from Page, Hector pulled into the Visitor Center parking lot and saw Victor, who was retching, bent over. The two of them pulled the heavy duffel bag out of the SUV. "Vincent—no, Sa'id—you have the right to now be called by your own name. You've served Allah well. You have one more task, brother. I need one hour. I will disable the two elevators, but you need to guard the stairs. No one can pass," Hector said.

"No one will pass, God willing," Vincent managed.

Hector rolled the duffel into the metal-floored elevator and hit the button to floor L. This was in the top third of the dam, about one hundred feet below the top. To maximize the effect of the weapon, it would be detonated at this level. Here, the estimated dam width was less than twenty meters. The plans they had studied showed the top of the dam was just eight meters thick, but at its base, it was nearly one hundred meters thick. While they believed that the nuke could take out the reinforced concrete, no chances would be taken. If the top portion of the dam was blown away, the pressure of the overtopping water would finish the job.

Mannie had killed three of his crew and taken over the Control Room on the generation floor, closing off access to the tunnel parking lot. There were still four employees somewhere in the dam. One, a contract security guard, had heard the gunfire and seen the others go down. He had made the right decision not to engage the gunman but to get clear and report the intrusion. One level up, he came upon one of the engineers—Tim, he thought his name was. They ran for the emergency line at the end of the corridor. He hoped that the lines had not been routed exclusively to the Control Room.

Dylan listened to the panicked security guard explain that the Control Room had been taken over. Since this was a federal reservoir, he needed to call DHS. A series of clicks later, he heard, "Elle Hardwick here; go ahead, Officer Owen."

"Ma'am, Dylan Owen here, Page, Arizona, PD. We have information that the Glen Canyon Dam has been the subject of an attack. Reports are that the Control Room has been taken over with four, maybe five casualties."

"Officer Dylan, stay on the line. We have an asset there, an FBI agent, Greer. I'd like to patch him in." The line clicked.

Dylan found that interesting. Obviously, something had been in the works, and Page had been a target all along. That pissed him off. He should have known about it. Keeping the Page PD in the dark was contrary to post-9/11 protocols.

Dylan had the line on speaker, and the other two duty officers listened in. Dylan volunteered, "I've been in the dam many times. If the Control Room has been seized, dam access is limited. It's huge. We could spend hours trying to locate someone inside."

Elle broke in. "Officer, yesterday, a radiological device was detected in Phoenix. Three to five males, Hispanic or Middle Eastern in appearance, spent the previous night in a home that was contaminated by severe radiological exposure. Either they are transporting material for radiological dispersion, a dirty bomb, or they have a nuke with a breach in its containment. We think it's the latter, as no one would knowingly expose themselves to this extent. They would have to know they would succumb to the radiation before they could carry out an attack."

The officers sat in silence. Dylan managed to ask, "Ma'am, who am I talking with?"

"Elle Hardwick, CIA. We've dispatched a NEST team to your location. There is a chance that the same group is behind the attack on the dam," she said.

A few moments of silence followed before Greer chimed in. "If they have a nuke, why waste it in the middle of a desert?"

Franklin spoke, "Franklin Harbour here, also with the Agency. Zach, the nuke is likely a low-yield portable weapon. In a metropolitan area, it would have a devastating effect on a square mile or two, but it wouldn't level an entire city. But taking out the dam there would bring devastation to millions. The dam is the first in a series of dams on the Colorado River. We've been told that if Glen Canyon were to have a catastrophic failure, a wall of water could sweep downstream, potentially toppling Hoover Dam, Davis Dam, Parker Dam, Palo Verde Dam, Imperial Dam, and on and on. The water supply for Arizona, Nevada, and Southern California would largely be cut off, and millions would be without electricity for months or years. Hoover and Glen Canyon alone generate eight and a half billion kilowatts a year, supplying three million people."

They listened in stunned silence while Elle explained. "A nuke of this size would probably bring the dam down. But due to its mass, it isn't assured unless the bomb is placed in the upper half of the dam, where the concrete structure is narrower. They likely know this. You are to concentrate the search in the upper half of the dam."

Then Elle described the worst-case picture. "If Glen Canyon goes, a wall of water several hundred feet high will rush down the Grand Canyon toward Lake Mead. At capacity, the active, or releasable, volume of the reservoir is just over twenty-four million acre-feet of water, eight hundred billion gallons or so. Our sources tell us no one knows what that volume of water would do when it hits Lake Mead. Mead is apparently very low, not nearly at capacity. It might just fill and spill, or it might overtop the Hoover Dam. The briefing sheet says dams are not made to be overtopped;

their structural integrity fails. If Hoover fails, all succeeding lower dams will fall like dominos. The intricate balance of water, power, agriculture, and municipal supply for the southwest quarter of the nation will cease to exist."

Sarah added, "And that's only half of it. Southern California will be deprived of four and a half million acre-feet of water a year, devastating Southern California. Arizona supplies through the Central Arizona Project might be safe, but no one knows. Worse, Las Vegas would simply cease. The water level in Lake Mead now is so low, the supply of water for Las Vegas is in danger of reaching the level of its intakes. If Mead fails, Las Vegas literally would be left high and very dry."

Everyone knew this result would push the country into decades of depression, triggering a worldwide economic calamity.

Shaw had been on the line listening despite the sounds of lower Wall Street. This was about water, electrical production, maybe both. The plan was to disrupt the economy, not kill all at once. It made sense. The cells in Europe were all trained in engineering.

Sarah phoned Shaw on the other line. Shaw merged the calls as Sarah explained, "The FBI is tracking an informant's cell phone east of Los Angeles. That phone just went active. The informant dialed the number given by the FBI. It is muffled, like it is in the informant's clothing. They were able to make out just a few words: 'former...help me cut the fence.'"

Elle asked, "They are forcing the informant to cut fence? What fence? Sarah, get a map of all installations DHS has a threat matrix on in that location."

Shaw thought, then spoke, "Not informer. The word was 'former.' Jeez, they are after water and electricity. The word has to be 'transformer.' Get a map of all large electric substations in that area."

DHS was on the line and broke in. "Mr. Shaw, this is Bill White at DHS. Three of the major transmission lines in the grid intersect or nearly intersect in that area. The Western Area Power Administration's line comes in from the southeast, Pacific Gas and Electric's DC line comes in from the north, and a third line comes in from the Rockies. They converge near the large wind farms east of Palm Springs. If the substations are disabled, it could cause massive blackouts in a three-state area, with rolling blackouts possible in other states. And these would be long-term events—several weeks or months to repair."

"Agent Davies, are you on the line?" Shaw asked.

Davies replied, "Yes, I'm here with my team and your two additions, Agents Corre and Culbert. We are at the airport outside of Palm Springs. I've just ordered our bomb-disposal people from LA to meet us here at the airport. ETA about twenty minutes."

It would take DHS that long to get the list of potential targeted substations to them. The suspects would be long gone. They were playing catch-up, Shaw thought.

Sarah broke into the conversation. "Everyone, they think they located the FBI mole. A senior technological officer, Allison Matsif, a five-year veteran. Before that, she was with Rytec Technology for two years, based in Silicon Valley. Graduate of Caltech. She was born in the Georgian Republic. She was scheduled for a polygraph. Someone noticed she left her desk and reported it. They chased her on foot, and she was struck by a car three blocks from the FBI building. She died on the way to G. W. Hospital."

Shaw spoke. "OK. That's good and bad. We need one of them alive. Let's focus on the immediate threat. Brian, you work with the FBI field team and bomb disposal team to find the California bombs and get them disarmed. Agent Davies, can you track down the cell phone signal and take down this bunch? Kathy, I want you going along," Shaw ordered.

"My thoughts exactly. The cell phone was stationary for about forty minutes in a residential community east of Palm Springs but is now moving on the interstate east. I'll have the CHP meet us at Blythe Airport. There are nothing but farm exits for a hundred or so miles until there," Davies said.

Shaw added, "We have a drone up that should be able to identify the car from which the cell signal is coming. But it's imperative that we get at least one of them alive. We need answers."

CHAPTER 69

LAS VEGAS, NV

She couldn't sit in the office any longer. Carol strapped on a radio and removed her holster from her belt. She checked her service nine-millimeter and put it in her purse, which she threw over her shoulder. She turned and remarked to Josh and Anna, "I can't sit here. If something happens in this town, it'll happen on the Strip, and then, within a short four to five blocks. If we go out and walk it, we might get lucky, stop something before it happens."

"But we have no reason to believe Las Vegas is even a target. The ones we were following are now in LA or Palm Springs, and the other threats are in Page and New York," Anna said.

"Yeah, I know. There isn't intel on Vegas, but then, why does the Bureau want us to stay here? They must feel as though ancillary or follow-on attacks are a possibility here. Besides, just sitting here is driving me nuts," Carol said in an exasperated tone.

"Well, it beats sitting here. Besides, I've never seen Las Vegas. Come on," Josh said to Anna, walking toward the door.

Anna shrugged, stuffed her Beretta 70 into the tight belt holster in the small of her back, and pulled her blouse over it.

They parked at the Fashion Show Mall. Carol had been to Vegas plenty of times and remarked, "If anything happens, it likely will happen from this point south to City Center and the MGM; that's about a mile and a half. Besides the Wynn, there across the street, and the Venetian and Palazzo Hotels just to the south, nearly all traffic is on the west side of the road. Just a heads up: it will be hard spotting someone suspicious; the sidewalks will be jammed with people who, uh, look 'out of the ordinary.'" She laughed and walked toward the street.

Josh and Anna looked at each other, wondering what she meant by that last comment. After walking several hundred feet, they understood it all too well.

Josh walked the east side of the Strip on the sidewalk outside the Venetian and Palazzo. Anna and Carol walked the west side past the Treasure Island Pirate Ship toward the Mirage. A mass of what was clearly identifiable as "odd" confronted them. Who could possibly "look suspicious" when nearly everyone looked bizarre? Obese men in shorts and wife-beater shirts, overweight, middle-aged women in heels and yoga pants. Drunk barely twentysomethings with two-foot-high cocktails, and roaming packs of college kids. It was a scene. People having fun. Something for everyone and everyone looking for something.

Josh approached two men of Middle Eastern descent who appeared agitated. Josh gripped his nine-millimeter in his waist holster through his shirt and listened in. They were heatedly arguing over how much the Eiffel Tower looked like the real thing.

Anna was trying to grapple with the onslaught. Carol was used to Vegas; she perused the crowd for someone out of place among the misplaced. The crowd waited patiently for the Bellagio fountain to erupt. There, a man, maybe thirty-five years old, sweating profusely, struggling to walk but intent on being someplace. He could just be a crazy person, or he could be something else.

Carol watched him approach and whispered in Anna's ear, "There, eleven o'clock, approaching man in tan shirt, blue jeans."

Anna looked over and saw the man. He was briskly walking, not looking at anyone or anything, focused on getting somewhere, his gait staggered. Was he was drunk, or high? Just another overserved tourist, she thought. The man's eyes met hers, and they both knew otherwise.

Amante didn't know if he could make it back to get the other backpack. He felt horrible, the heat was withering, and he was burning up. He had planted the first backpack and was headed back when the woman caught his attention. She was good looking, vaguely familiar, and looking only at him. She wasn't a tourist. Her shoes told the story—neither walking shoes, sandals, or heels. No, these were crepe soled. Only crazy people and police wore shoes like that. She had her hand on her hip, no purse, an isosceles stance. Amante pulled his weapon before Anna could see his arms through the crowd. Two quick pops, and Anna was down.

Carol drew but didn't have a clean shot in the crowd, which had panicked, running in every direction.

Amante grabbed a young girl, no more than twenty. Her eyes wild with surprise and fear as her head was yanked back, her body thrust between Carol and him. He saw Carol in a firing stance. He pushed the girl forward. The girl had the sense, or fortunate reaction, to twist from his reach, leaving a clump of her blond hair in his hand. As soon as he realized she was out of his reach, he felt the hammer of two nine-millimeter rounds striking his body. His last thoughts were of the heat of the sidewalk and the strange coldness enveloping his body.

"Agent down. Need ambulance at Bellagio Fountain, street side. Suspect down. Josh, hurry," Carol screamed into her mike.

Anna was hit at least twice; she knew it was serious. One chest wound, another a shoulder wound. In less time than she could imagine, she heard Josh next to her. "Stay with me, Anna. The ambulance is coming; stay with me, dammit." There, in his arms, Anna looked up, her eyes became still, her breath stopped.

Carol was going through the pockets of the dead suspect. Some cash, a prepaid cell phone, and a room key. No identification. The room key was at least printed with the Rivers Hotel logo. Las Vegas police were on scene almost immediately, one of the virtues of extensive surveillance cameras. They ran to the site yelling, "Everyone stand back. You, get away from the body, stand, arms above your head."

Carol raised her hands, her credentials high. "FBI, FBI!"

The officers lowered their weapons. Carol continued. "Get away from the body. The perpetrator may be radioactive. Don't touch or move him without radiological hazmat procedures."

That stopped the police in midstride. Carol went on to explain. "This man is a fellow agent, and the deceased woman is a 'friendly.' This entire operation and shooting must be kept quiet, at least for now." Despite objections, she told the officer in charge, "We need to leave immediately. It's a matter of national security. We need transport to the Rivers Resort now."

The senior officer, a man of perhaps thirty-five, wanted nothing more than to get away from the "hazmat victim," remarking, "I'll take you; get in my car. Jimmy, you wait here for backup and the CSU. Don't touch anything, and don't broadcast this over the radio. Everyone has scanners in this town. Use your phone. No one leaks this to the press."

At the Rivers, Josh, Carol, and the officer went past the six or seven people in line waiting to be checked in. Between Carol thrusting her FBI ID in front of the clerk and the officer, the young woman at the front desk went wide-eyed. Without hesitation, she took the key and fed it into the reader. "Room 3213, Mr. Ibrahim Shastani, checked in yesterday for a two-night stay. I can have security open the door for you."

Carol thought for a split second whether a warrant was required for entry into a hotel room and immediately snapped out of it, telling the girl, "We have reason to believe the guest has brought substances into the premises that endanger the building and its guests. Get security up here immediately, give me a key to the room now, and direct me to where the room is, please."

That was all it took. All innkeepers know that if a guest causes a disturbance or potential problem to the hotel or its guests, they have the right to enter and eject the guest. The girl handed over a key and gave directions to the elevator.

A second hazmat team had entered the hotel from the service entrance so as to not cause panic. The design of every hotel in Vegas required a circuitous voyage through a casino to get to the room elevators on the off chance the guest would play another game or two on the way. The Vegas police understood the effect of charging through a casino; every hotel had emergency access corridors that were protected from the public. The officer radioed the hazmat team to meet at the room.

The hazmat team captain, dressed in a breather, accessed the room. The breather was completely ineffectual to radiation, but Josh felt the captain likely knew that and needn't be reminded. "Radiation levels are not that high, but higher than background. Wait at the door until we complete our search."

The team went through the room, paying particular attention to the backpack lying on the closet floor. "Radiation sweep is complete. Levels are elevated but safe. My guess is that someone had a radiological here and left. It's not here now. But that backpack appears to contain bomb materials and military-grade explosives. Looks to me like HMK. That shit's multiple times more powerful than C-4. Better get the bomb squad in," the captain said.

Carol called Shaw in New York, who conferenced in Franklin. This was bad news. Attacks were being coordinated in so many locations—New York, LA, Palm Springs, Arizona, and now Vegas. How many more cities had they missed? Shaw shuddered at the thought. A coordinated attack on half a dozen or more US cities was incomprehensible. This was beyond the home-grown jihadi, or even Al Qaeda's abilities. Who was behind this? What *state* was behind this? Shaw asked himself.

CHAPTER 70

Mike, a young officer only three years on the force, and Dylan met Greer and Sandy at the dam's Visitor Center parking lot. Several tourists were standing and taking pictures, disappointed that the Visitor Center and dam tours were closed. "Hey, what's with the dam being closed? We drove seven hours to see it. There's no one here but some weirdo by the door who threatened us and told us to get lost," said a young a twentysomething with a tank top and tattoo of what could only be described as a bar code on his shoulder.

"There's a security issue with the bridge and dam; best you leave the premises. Sorry. But where did you see the fellow who told you to leave?" asked Dylan.

"The guy's over on the far right side of the Visitor Center, the side away from the parking lot," he replied.

Dylan nodded to Mike, and the two approached the Visitor Center. There, a man was slumped on the step. "You, sir, are you all right? Do you need assistance?" asked Mike.

The man jerked up, surprised out of his stupor, raising a gun. He fired three rounds erratically. Mike pulled his Beretta and fired twice, both shots striking the man, who slumped. Dylan and Mike slowly approached as Dylan radioed the event in. Dylan stopped midsentence. The man was grotesque. Patches of his scalp were bare, bleeding. His tongue was swollen, slightly protruding from his lips. Large, ulcerous, red sores were all over his face, neck, and arms.

"Don't touch him and stand clear. Kick the gun away, but don't pick it up," Dylan told Mike.

Greer ran to Dylan yelling, "Don't get near him. A NEST team will be here in thirty minutes. They'll arrive by chopper. Can you clear an area for them to land? If I'm right, the man is radioactive. Don't get near him."

As if line dancing, Mike and Dylan reacted to this in unison, stepping back two steps. "Jeez, radioactive? What's going on?" Mike asked.

"I know as much as you. Get those tourists out of here. There are only three vehicles in the lot. One of them is probably his and radioactive too. And block the entrance to the parking lot with a patrol car," Dylan ordered.

Greer called Franklin, getting Sara Tashkent. "This is Agent Greer in Page, FBI. Connect me with Franklin or Shaw, please. We've had a shooting at Glen Canyon Dam, and we believe we have a radiological footprint at the dam."

Sara replied, "Wait one for Mr. Harbour, Agent."

The line clicked, and in seconds he had both Franklin and Shaw on a conference line. "Go ahead, Agent," Franklin said.

"Sir, there's been a shooting incident between Page PD and a suspect at the dam. The suspect has radiation sickness symptoms. NEST team is en route. Their ETA is thirty minutes. We'll check the suspect's vehicle, but given the reports that an intruder has taken over the Control Room, I think we have to assume the radiological is already inside the dam," Greer reported.

Shaw broke the silence. "Bob, we need a tactical team to make the assault, not the locals. Page has an airport. I suggest the FBI's LA tac team be brought in."

Zach responded, "I thought of that, Shaw, but it would take two-three hours to get them onsite. This could be over in an hour."

Shaw knew Greer was right, but the dam was huge—many, many corridors, many levels. It would be like finding a bomb in a high-rise. The only hope was to assault when the NEST team came onsite, using their detection equipment to guide the search. The NEST team was composed of six individuals, two scientist-technicians. That meant four combat-trained men plus Greer. The local PD wasn't trained in antiterrorism or urban assaults.

"Agent Greer, Franklin Harbour here. I've listened and unfortunately think you're right. We don't have three hours to sit around waiting for the cavalry. When the NEST team gets there, you are authorized to commence a search to locate the weapon. Use all necessary force. I'll call the Page PD and make sure they understand the gravity of this."

Greer replied, "Yes, sir, I understand. Sir, two of Page PD are here with me. They know what's going on, and we'll have two more officers before making the assault."

In the heat, the body looked as if it was already beginning to bloat. "What's happening? Is everyone all right? I heard there was a shooting."

Greer turned around to see Sandy walking toward them, having parked her pickup in the west parking lot.

"We're fine. But it's probably best if you stay out of this, Sandy," Dylan said.

"Bullshit. In case you haven't noticed, this is federal property and in a federal park. It isn't Page PD turf," she retorted, the last words fading when she caught sight of the grotesque form lying beyond Dylan on the ground.

Greer stepped forward and calmly said, "Listen, we are going to need everyone onboard for this. The NEST team will be here in under thirty minutes, but a tac team won't get here for hours, so we are it. There's a nuke in the dam, and it's obviously leaking radiation. When the NEST team gets here, we need to locate it and get it a safe distance away. Dylan, how many officers can you get here in twenty minutes?"

"Four; two officers are away on training, so four, counting me from PD. But I can get Chip Baye. He's a tribal officer, well trained, former marine," Dylan responded.

"OK, that will have to do. With the NEST team, that makes ten. It should be enough," Greer instructed.

"Eleven. I'm coming. It's a federal facility...it's my job," Sandy said firmly.

Neither Dylan or Zach liked it but knew the outcome would be the same whether they argued or not.

They spent the next minutes inside the Visitor Center studying the drawings and scale model of the dam. An elevator led from the Visitor Center to the floor overlooking the generator floor, but along the dam crest were two more entrances, staircases, and elevators. Those access points allowed unlimited access to all floors. Without knowing where the bomb was, an assault plan was pointless. From the appearance of the dead suspect, the NEST team should be able to locate the bomb.

The vibration of the silver Sikorsky 76 reverberated the windows at the Visitor Center as it came in. Greer walked to the chopper as it was winding down, yelling over the chopper's roar that a briefing would take place as soon as the team unloaded its equipment.

When everyone was present in the Visitor Center, Dylan instructed, "Eddie, you and Chip secure and guard the outside of the dam. Eddie, take up a position at the Visitor Center parking lot and keep onlookers at bay. Chip, take up a position on the dam crest with an AR15 to be in a position to subdue anyone attempting to get in or out of the dam."

Zach then spoke. "Have the Sikorsky pilot rig a cable and container to transport the weapon to a remote location away from the dam if we find it. If it is leaking radiation, as they suspect, there won't be an opportunity or time to disarm it. We will conduct a secure search floor by floor with the NEST team out front with their radiation sensors. Since there are only two vehicles in the lot, I think we can assume that we will be dealing with no more than six suspects. Everyone monitor and report. No attempts at a solo takedown. If a suspect has a detonator, he has to be taken down by a head/neck shot where the shot immobilizes muscle control, preventing a triggered detonation."

Dylan added, "Two of us will have that task—one of the NEST team members who is the designated marksman and Jim Redhouse. He's our sergeant and the best shot in the county."

Zach then said, "Cell coverage inside the dam will be nonexistent. We need to stick together or use radios. There would be no way to effectively communicate inside thousands of tons of concrete except by direct voice or hand signals."

They entered the western crest stairwell and proceeded down. The air was cold, musty. A few feet away, the water backed against the dam had a temperature in the forties, keeping the concrete cool. Almost immediately, the NEST team picked up a radiation signature. The readings were stronger in the staircase than on the floor, so they proceeded down, past three floors without a trace of anyone. They had descended about a third of the way down the stairwell when the detection spiked and then dissipated. "Is the bomb moving?" Dylan asked.

"We have wildly fluctuating readings," the NEST team member said.

They proceeded down several more floors, and the sensors showed the source again getting stronger. Again, the detection seemed to go away and then reappear. "It's the ventilation pumps in here. We're chasing ghosts. Is there any way to shut off the ventilation system?" asked the senior NEST technician.

Greer tried his phone. No signal this deep into the massive dam. "One of your men needs to go back out and contact the BuRec, see if there is a way to remotely shut down the ventilation pumps," Greer said to Dylan.

"No, it'll take too long, and we don't even know if it can be done remotely. I'll take two men and get to the Control Room down at the Generation Level. I've been there before," Dylan responded.

Greer nodded his assent, and Dylan tapped Mike and Terry, both Page PD officers in their twenties, to go with him. Despite his age, Terry was a combat veteran, two tours in Iraq. Dylan wanted him with him if there was going to be an assault on the Control Room. Mike was a nerd. Two years at Brigham Young in software engineering. More than anyone, he likely would know what to look for once in the Control Room. They descended the staircase for the Control Room, several hundred feet below.

The NEST team stopped, with Greer and Sandy conducting a floor-by-floor search. The floors were massive. Long corridors, some with yellow hospital-like tiled corridors, others bare concrete with bare light bulbs inside metal cages providing lighting that cast long, eerie shadows. The bowels of the massive structure.

Dylan and his team neared the Generation Level, where they could hear and feel the whirling of the massive generators. It was deafening. Communication became impossible. Hand signals took the place of words. Terry took the lead, having been trained in house-to-house combat. There, they could see the Control Room shielded in glass across the room and up a half flight of metal steps. If anyone was looking out the windows, they would be easy targets from an elevated advantage point.

They ran twenty feet to a point behind the nearest generator, then another twenty feet to the next generator. They were massive concrete-and-metal elevated round structures, nearly thirty feet high and thirty in diameter. Imposing, red-topped, round, black metal machines. They spun from the force of hundreds of thousands of gallons of water per minute turning turbines deep beneath them.

There was no cover for the last thirty feet and the ten or twelve steps up to the Control Room door. They would be exposed to fire from an elevated position. Terry yelled into Mike and Dylan's ears for Mike to position himself with the assault rifle and cover their advance, to suppress any fire coming from the room.

They watched one figure pacing back and forth in front of the windows, every once in a while peering out. He seemed to have a timing, as if he was walking a repeated distance nervously. Five, maybe six seconds away from the window each time. They could see no one else. Motioning to Dylan, Terry walked his fingers and then counted down three, two, one. At zero they ran for the steps, making it without discovery. They lay low while the shadow above them paced over their heads. They then crept up the stairs. There was no doubt the sound and vibration from the generators masked any sounds they might make, but the vibration of footsteps on the metal staircase might be different.

Terry remembered the simple small mirror he had fixed to a slender metal wand he carried in Iraq, wishing he had it now. Without it, he could not peer into the room undetected. He had no idea if the door was booby-trapped, if there was one or a dozen armed men in the room. Whether there were friendlies in the room. They were about to assault the room blind.

Terry reached for the doorknob above his head, hoping it was unlocked. It was. He turned the knob, as he motioned to Dylan to scan the left side of the room while he took the right. Dylan would be first in, given where he was crouched.

Again—three, two, one. The door swung open, and Dylan leaped into the room and lay prone on the floor, taking aim on the pacing man, who began to swivel, raising a handgun. A split second later, Terry was in, looking for a target to the right. But the split second was all that it took. Two bursts from the Beretta both found their target. Dylan felt two jolts from his right, as if someone had hit his hip and torso with a baseball bat. He fired, hitting the pacing man. Terry saw the muzzle flashes at the same time he pulled the trigger on his Smith and Wesson, taking the shooter to the right down. Terry swept the room. "All clear," he yelled, grabbing the weapons from near the two suspects. Both suspects were down, one clearly dead with a head shot from Dylan's weapon.

He swept over to Dylan, where a pool of blood was forming on the tile floor. "Dylan...Dylan...buddy, stay with me. You're going to be all right; stay with me," Terry yelled.

Mike ran into the room and saw the scene, closing the soundproof door so they could hear once again.

"Dylan's hit. Find a phone and get an ambulance now. Then find the ventilation pump controls," Terry yelled.

Terry went over to the wounded shooter who had shot Dylan. He was conscious but bleeding badly, one to the stomach and another to the shoulder. He'd bleed out in minutes. Terry had seen it all before. He got close to the man and said, "Where is it? It's over. You're gut shot, you're dead. Tell me where it is."

The man smiled through clenched bloody teeth, spraying blood with each breath. "America is over, Allah Akbar."

Terry slapped him across the mouth with his weapon, teeth and blood spraying across the floor.

"Here, here, I think I found the pump controls. They're shut...I think," Mike yelled, staring at the control desk.

Three hundred feet above, the NEST team felt the cold draft subside, and the sensor began a stabilized reading. "We're a go. Dylan's team must have done it. Start the track," Greer yelled.

The NEST team took off to the stairwell, the sensor recoding a stronger signal. That meant the source wasn't on their floor; it was either above or below. They went up two floors, and the readings were noticeably weaker. So they reversed, descending the stairwell, watching the readings steadily climb. As they neared the next floor, the readings spiked. The NEST team leader donned his rebreather and sealed his helmet after first telling Greer and Sandy, "You two, back topside. We'll take it from here. It's too hot."

Sandy needed no second warning. She turned on her heels and grabbed Zach's arm, heading in the other direction before he could protest. What a job, Greer thought. These guys trained years for this, and when all was on the line, when their lives were on the line, they didn't hesitate to head into the unseen danger. There was nothing he could do anyway.

After a climb of four levels, they sat on the stairs. Breaking the silence, Zach said, "Dylan got the job done. He's a good man."

Sandy didn't know how to feel. She was drawn to Zach, yet still felt for Dylan. She feared for both and wanted both. She felt comfortable with Dylan, but that was it—comfortable. His daughters came first, and sometimes there was no room for her. She wanted children, and Dylan had made it clear, he was done. Done with more family and probably done with marriage. The dating pool in Page was slim, so she stayed in an awkward, sometimes comfortable place with it.

The radios were good for a few floors, particularly in the staircase. They could hear the heavy breathing of the NEST team below them. Then, "There—ten meters, the wheeled bag," came the voice over the radio. The distinct Texas accent of the NEST team leader was heard. "Cut it loose, and let's get it topside. Bill, I'll take it from here. You guys get topside and get the others out of the way. Get the chopper keyed up."

Greer and Sandy heard the sound of heavy footsteps scrambling below them on the metal stairwell. "We heard," Greer said into the radio. "Going topside!"

This time it was he who grabbed Sandy's arm and pulled her up the steps. They ran six levels up and burst out of the door and into the blinding sun and heat of the day, arms raised as they both remembered Jim Redhouse was posed with his elk rifle for any target emerging from the dam.

Greer called into the radio for the pilot to get to the stairwell and hover to pick the device up. He could hear the chopper blades beginning the familiar whomp, whomp, whomp and saw it rise from the parking lot, a cable unfurling below it. When it was at a sufficient height for the cable to not catch on anything, the chopper angled over to them and hovered with the cable perhaps twenty feet over their heads. The two advance NEST team members came out of the door sliding their rebreathers and helmets back. They started communicating with the pilot, who inched the cable down. The cable was shielded, as the blades were generating sufficient static electricity to create a current strong enough to kill. Sandy and Greer were ordered back to the edge of the dam near the steps to the Visitor Center. Upwind.

A few long minutes later, the two remaining team members came out with the device. A black, wheeled duffel bag, about four feet by three feet in size. They clipped the carabiners onto the bag and encircled it in a light-gray fabric, which Greer assumed was a lead fabric of sorts.

The chopper pulled away slowly over the main channel of the lake. The decision on where the device would be left had been a political one, made two thousand miles away. The logical location would have been to the east, away from populated areas and water supplies, but that would have placed it in the Navajo or Hopi Nations, and that raised so many jurisdictional and political considerations that it was out of the question. Downriver would have been in the Grand Canyon—again, out of the question. The decision was made to leave it in a narrow canyon in the Carcass Canyon Wilderness Area, immediately to the north. Radiation could drift over Lake Powell with its sun bathing tourists and possibly populated areas such as Moab, Blanding, or Montecito, Utah. There was no correct location. The Agency and DOD experts thought with the containment damaged and leaking, the yield would be sufficiently low that it would be contained in the canyon. In a wilderness area, population impacts would be minimal. The chopper headed over the horizon and out of sight, staying low to minimize the air burst EMP effects should it go off along the way.

The NEST team leader watched it go over the horizon as he attempted decontamination in the portable shower. He knew he had received a size-able dose, but he hoped for the best.

CHAPTER 71

EAST OF PALM SPRINGS, CA

Franklin read the summary page to the others in the room and on the line. "Seven potential targets East of Palm Springs. Targets included four electric grid substations bringing power into Southern California from the Southwest, Rockies, and Pacific Northwest, all converging at or near Cathedral City, and an additional target, the Julian Hinds Pump Station, belonging to the Metropolitan Water District of Southern California. That pump station's combined seventy-five-thousand horsepower pumps lifts a half-million gallons every second up 441 feet to where water flows by gravity to thirsty Southern California. Each of these is a probable and logical target, not well defended. The closest airstrip is actually at the pumping station, which is just north of I-10."

"All right, we'll take them down there on I-10. We'll land at the Hinds Pump station in under ten minutes. CHP has three patrol cars inbound to that location. Have them deploy tack strips to immobilize the vehicle," Davies said. "Just make sure we take at least one or two of them alive. We need to know what they know, who they are, and their plan. And remember, we have an informant in the car. Treat him as a friendly. I'm sending a picture of him now," Franklin said.

The drone had been above the vehicle, monitoring the phone signal. A new-model Audi A-8. The high-resolution images clearly showed four occupants, three males and one female. The open and flat landscape made surprise difficult, but there was one rock outcropping that the highway cut through. No more than ten feet high, it could hide the patrol cars and officers. They would have snipers hit the engine block the instant the car hit the tack strips. A fifty-caliber sniper round would cause the engine to seize and stop almost immediately. By landing at the pumping station airfield, they could also cover that target, just in case.

They overflew two patrol cars that had already converged at the outcropping. The third car raced toward the airstrip, no more than two miles away. When they landed, Davies and Kathy Corre ran low from the chopper to the state patrol car. "We don't have much time. The drone shows the car about eight miles away, just over five minutes out," Kathy explained in their run to the car.

They got to the outcropping with under two minutes to spare. Kathy took up a position on the passenger side with Davies. Two state patrolmen took up positions in the median, while the third, using a Remington 700P, a modified elk rifle with a Leopold scope, lay prone on the top of the rock outcropping. Davies would count down the vehicle to the tack strip for the marksman's benefit.

They could see the Audi approaching. Each lay still in the oppressive heat. "Four, three, two, one—FIRE," Davies counted off as the shot rang out.

The car lurched sideways, smoke billowing from the tires and engine block. The car skidded off the right side of the road just beyond where Kathy Corre was at ready. As the car drifted in a skid, Kathy could see a woman in the front passenger seat, eyes fixed on her. She didn't appear surprised, scared, or angry. It was an unemotional, empty, fixed stare she'd seen only one time before, when she was in an Australian shark cage, and she was the prey.

The car came to a stop not more than thirty feet past their position. The woman jumped out, crouched on one knee, and fired three rounds, two hitting Kathy Corre squarely. Davies fired, striking the woman in the neck and chest. The driver jumped out, firing on automatic. He was less trained or more nervous than the woman had been. Most of his rounds were wild. Both officers opened up on him, and he went down.

A second man rolled out of the rear passenger side door. His fire was accurate, and one of the officers went down, struck in the leg. He could see the other officer had dropped back and was trying to outflank his position while Davies and the officer with the rifle pinned him down. The man then started firing back into the vehicle. It was obvious that he didn't want anyone taken alive who could reveal details. The fourth occupant stayed in the car. That would be the informant, Davies concluded. The man crawled back toward the car just as the Remington 165-grain .308 round struck the shooter's skull, exploding it in a pink mist.

The shooting stopped, the only sound coming from hum of the drone several hundred feet over their heads. "Pedro? Pedro Miraz? This is the FBI. You're safe now; come out with your hands above your head. It's over," Davies yelled.

Pedro raised his hands through the rear window and crawled out, stumbling on a knee before going down on both knees. The officers ran over to him, cuffed him, and pulled him up to his feet.

Davies ran back to Kathy. She was slumped, eyes fixed. A round had caught her in the chest; she had likely died instantly.

CHAPTER 72

NEW YORK CITY

The glass box surrounded by hundreds of men, women, and children exploded. A brilliant yellow flash and exploding glass shattered the lazy, warm afternoon and so many lives. Glass shards impaled pedestrians a block away. Inside, the scene was worse. The staircase and elevator leading down were covered in corpses, blood washing down the stairs. At the store level, body parts and pieces of flesh dripped from the walls. A few survived, protected only by masses of people less lucky.

Shaw was reviewing the information they had on the Yonkers attackers at the NYPD's Counterterrorism Division's team at the LMSCC, the Lower Manhattan Security Coordination Center, when the news came in. "A conventional blast…heavy casualties, an estimate of three hundred dead, twice that injured, many children and teenagers. Jeez, it's the Apple Store. They targeted a damn Apple Store," Division Chief Dipracto, listening to his phone, reported to the others.

Stunned silence. Each person left to his or her own emotions. To some, the thought that children and teenagers had been intentionally targeted brought revulsion. But to Shaw, it made perfect sense: Western trappings, personal communications, and social media all had spawned the Arab Spring and democratic ideals endorsed by the young. All were antithetical to those who wished only to rid the world of choice, to maintain religious dogma over personal choice…to rule, suppress, and control.

Five minutes later, Division Chief Dipracto received a second report, an explosion in a subway station in midtown. The bomb had evidently been shaped, as it did little damage to the station or the scores of people waiting at the station. Instead, it had destroyed the main electrical grid to three subway corridors in midtown. Dozens of subway trains had come to a halt. From Fifty-Seventh Street south to Canal, three of the four north-south lines were shut down. Manhattan's subways were suddenly immobile.

Shaw squinted and said, "A nuclear weapon placed to eliminate water service to Manhattan, now transportation, and an attack on commerce and tourism...they are trying to incapacitate Manhattan, create a rolling sense of fear. What's next? It has to be the financial center; it has to be the banks or stock exchange." Chief Dipracto picked up the phone and ordered additional roving patrols in the Financial District.

A few seconds later, another report came in on the radio. "All units, Times Square. Another bomb detonated in Times Square. Initial estimates are more than two dozen civilian casualties."

Across town, Officers Jim Iannor and Pete Repeni were an hour into their overtime shift when dispatch brought the news. All shifts were extended indefinitely, creating an overlap, strengthening the force. They and seven other cars were redirected below Canal Street for an increased presence in the Financial District. "I can use the overtime this month. Nance wants to redo the area under the staircase as a nursery," Pete remarked.

"Me, too, but just not today. I just wish I hadn't promised Lynn I'd go with her today to her brother's place. He's not doing well again." Jim sighed.

They drove south on First Avenue. The radio was buzzing. First the suicide blast up in Yonkers, then the bombing at the Apple Store on Fifth Avenue. Traffic swelled. Many businesses had let their employees off, closed doors. The city wasn't sure how to react to the uncertainty caused by multiple random dispersed attacks. Reports and rumor swirled across the Internet and social media of attacks all through the city, most false, all terrifying. Then the cell phones started shutting down due to the load level. The word over the radio was that another bomb had been located not far from the site of the earlier suicide blast. The bomb squad wasn't being called in to disarm it, they were being called in to relocate it. That said everything. It was too dangerous to evacuate surrounding areas and disarm it. "A WMD, from the sounds of it," Jim said.

Pete couldn't believe that his New York, again, had become a war zone.

Despite gridlock, they made it to Fulton, where traffic had come to a total stop. After fifteen minutes, Jim radioed dispatch. "Dispatch, this is car 1134. We aren't moving here. Total gridlock. We are proceeding on foot to the Financial District."

People walked with a sense of purpose. It wasn't panic, more a forced march. There were no suspects to watch out for. Pete spoke to Jim, "We are to observe 'anything out of the ordinary'...show the force is out. I tell you, on a day like this, *everything* is out of the ordinary!"

On the way south, they learned of the latest bombing in midtown. The reports were that terrorists were targeting bridges and the subway system, cutting Manhattan off. The city would grind to a halt. With traffic gridlocked and the subways stopped, it wouldn't be long until the city erupted in panic and anger.

They walked around the corner on Nassau just as a flash of light and brown dust with embedded dark objects erupted at the other end of the block, followed a millisecond later by a blast of air and a deafening sound. Jim's experiences from Iraq kicked in. He looked around not at the point of blast, but as he had been taught. People were running in all directions—except one, a woman who calmly put her cell phone back into her pocket and walked away. People didn't put their phones away at such a time. They used them. Used them to record pictures, or to call relatives, loved ones. She was calm, while others ran. *She* had detonated the bomb.

"Pete! The woman, three o'clock—jeans and a white blouse. She's a perp. Watch the crowd while I stop her. If she's not alone, I'll probably need cover." Pete always trusted Jim's instincts. His gun was already out down by his side.

Jim walked briskly across the street, approaching her from the side and a bit behind. "You, woman in the white blouse and jeans. Freeze, hands on your head! Feet apart! NYPD," Jim yelled.

The woman glanced back at him as anyone might to see if he or she was the one being talked to. The woman stopped, wide-eyed, placing her hands on her head. Jim walked up behind her and frisked her for a weapon, not finding any. He began to relax a bit. Perhaps he'd made a mistake.

Pete looked around, watching for anything, anyone suspicious or paying close to attention to the "arrest." People were still running, walking briskly away from the bombing and past Jim and the woman.

It sounded like small pops. Jim was falling, the woman still with her hands on her head, and people running past, men with briefcases, one woman with a small wheeled bag. Then the woman with her hands on her head took off in the crowd. Pete ran the thirty feet or so to Jim and then saw the woman with the wheeled bag turn and fire. He swept his gun up, but there were too many civilians around her. He ran past Jim and after her, yelling into the mike on his shoulder, "Officer down, corner of Nassau and Wall Streets. Two suspects. Both women in their late twenties, early thirties. One in jeans and white blouse, one brown hair, women's business suit, with small wheeled bag—like a legal case."

The woman with the gun and bag was falling behind. She yelled something that sounded Slavic or Russian to the other, who grabbed the bag and ran while the woman in the business suit stopped, swept around, and fired. One round hit Pete in his hip, feeling as though someone had swung a baseball bat. He went down but rolled and took aim at the woman. On his stomach, he tried to control the pain and his breath. He fired two shots, striking the woman twice. People were screaming and in panic. He couldn't move, but yelled into his radio, "Second officer down; I'm hit. One suspect down, other suspect in jeans and white blouse with wheeled bag eastbound on Wall Street."

In the Command Center, listening to the officer's reports in rapid succession, NYPD reacted to the fact that two more officers were down.

They had to get the other woman before she set off whatever was in that wheeled bag.

ETA for the chopper to get to the wheeled bag in Yonkers was five minutes. Assuming it took five to secure a line to it, safe distance was another twenty-five minutes. The decision had been made to cross Long Island with it. They couldn't let it go off in Long Island Sound; it was too populated and the water too shallow. They needed to get it over Long Island to a site south of Freeport, Long Island, just north of the main shipping channel where the water was over four hundred meters deep. The shipping channel was being cleared now by the Coast Guard and Navy. If it went off in under thirty minutes, it would be devastation on a grand scale.

CHAPTER 73

LOS ANGELES, CA

The directed charge worked exactly as designed. The iPad program functioned perfectly. The two charges detonated simultaneously on the support columns, and a millisecond later, the directional charge in the trunk created a vertical blast wave. I-10 collapsed onto I-110, instantly crushing twenty-seven cars, one semi, and all their occupants. Another dozen cars and trucks were unable to stop before piling into the lower I-110. Seconds later, LA traffic began to back up, stretching in four directions for miles.

Nearly 150 miles to the east, Pedro sat on the side of the road sobbing. Despite being given his Miranda warnings, he freely described his past life. He had redeemed himself in Davies's eyes. Without his cooperation, none of the cell would have been caught, free to carry on more attacks.

One of the CHP officers yelled for Davies to come over. He handed the radio to him and heard the familiar sound of Shaw's voice. "Davies, I hear you've been successful. Good work. But it seems two of your group's weapons have hit their mark. We've learned that about fifteen minutes ago, charges were detonated in two electric substations. A rolling blackout is now washing over all of Southern California, from Santa Barbara south to the Mexican border, and as far east as Phoenix. Without power, LA will become a tinderbox. It hasn't been ten minutes, and we already have reports of looting. We just heard a second attack in LA has disrupted traffic, collapsing a portion of the interstate system. Without power and transportation gridlock, this is going to get bad quick. Does your informant know of any more follow-on attacks? We need to know who was involved, who directed this, and what their end game is."

"I understand. And sir, I'm sorry, we lost Agent Corrie. She was killed in the takedown," Davies replied.

Shaw's breath stopped, and he uttered only, "Thank you, Agent." He hung up and sat back, a hand over his eyes.

CHAPTER 74

LAS VEGAS, NV

A white brilliance of heat and concussion erupted in every direction. Shrapnel from the metal trash can was propelled at nearly the speed of sound into the soft flesh of hundreds of tourists. Where a second before the party atmosphere of the Strip had pervaded, now pain, panic, and gore were everywhere. Body parts were scattered for hundreds of feet in every direction. Hundreds lay on the hot pavement. Later, they would find a hand on the top of the Caesars sign.

CHAPTER 75

MIAMI, FL

The detonation threw several cars into the air, glass exploded from windows for several blocks, and a geyser of water erupted fifty feet into the air. Blocks away, another explosion killed a young woman and her two children who were walking on a sidewalk, and water from an open main swept them away. Within minutes, entire blocks were flooded. It would be a matter of minutes, perhaps an hour, until the water storage reserves were depleted and Miami taps stopped flowing.

CHAPTER 76

PAGE, AZ

Sandy and Zach sat on the dam gazing out over the peaceful lake. The news had arrived that Dylan was dead, six hundred feet below. He had died assaulting the Control Room, which had led to the location of the weapon. He had saved thousands of lives, including theirs. Sandy sobbed, her face buried in her hands. "What am I going to tell his girls? I haven't—"

Her words were cut short by a bright flash lighting the bottoms of the clouds on the horizon. A few seconds later, the ground vibrated, and the water in the lake shook, casting ripples across the surface and releasing trapped gas from the sediment below, bubbling to the surface. Then a distant roar and the appearance of a slender, iconic mushroom cloud in the distance. Zach's radio reported that the NEST team had failed to make it to safe distance. More sacrifice.

Staring at the cloud, Greer quietly said to Sandy, "On US soil...this changes everything. We're at war."

Sandy leaned her head onto his chest, feeling numb, whispering, "With who?"

CHAPTER 77

ACROSS THE COUNTRY

The news channels were now 24-7 reporting, "ATTACK ON AMERICA," "AMERICA UNDER FIRE," "A COUNTRY UNDER SIEGE." Anchors were reporting the attacks in Manhattan, Yonkers, Las Vegas, Los Angeles, Palm Springs, and Page, Arizona. Al Jazeera America, fast becoming a major news contender, was broadcasting sources reporting radiological threats in New Jersey and Arizona.

Panic was everywhere. The president had ordered a close of the exchanges and banks. Grocery stores across the nation were scenes of pandemonium. Looting occurred in nearly every major city. The National Guard was mobilized in forty-seven states; only Alaska, Hawaii, and Delaware didn't call the Guard up.

Markets across the globe tumbled. US forces moved to DEFCON 2, prepared to strike any country that felt America's misfortune invited aggression or any country found to be complicit. In turn, the strategic forces of Great Britain, France, Germany, Russia, China, India, Australia, and both Koreas went on high alert. Schools let out, shops closed, the economy ground to a halt. Not since the Kennedy assassination or perhaps the Cuban Missile Crisis had America been so galvanized. The goals of the aggressors had been achieved. And the worst was yet to come.

CHAPTER 78

YONKERS, NY

The NYPD chopper had lifted off from its hover with the bag dangling a hundred feet below. It arced off to the east over Pelham Bay on its way across the Long Island Sound, then abruptly south on a course over Hempstead and Merrick on its way to the drop site. The closet location allowing a minimum depth of three hundred meters was twenty-eight miles offshore. They had tied two hundred pounds of dive weights to a line attached to the bag. It would sink fast once the bag was submerged; zippers were left partially unzipped to allow air to escape. If the weapon detonated on the way, most of Long Island would have a very bad rush hour.

Shaw pulled up a map of the country on the screen with red blinking markers identifying radiological threats and orange circles identifying conventional attacks that had occurred. He said in a low voice, "Too many attacks. What attacks are coming? When they going to end? The woman in the jeans and white blouse is still out there with the roller bag. It's astonishing she hasn't been located, what with all the surveillance cameras in the Financial District after 9/11. She's either gone to ground or planted the bomb and changed clothing." NYPD was swarming over the area. If she was still there, she'd be found.

Shaw couldn't stand staying in the Command Center any longer with the woman so close. He had full communications, so what did it matter if he was on the street? he said to himself. Sitting and watching a few blocks from where everything was coming down was not an option. "Elle, Shaw here. I'm on the street. Use this comm frequency. I'm also sharing the NYPD tactical frequency. Do we have anything on the jeans lady?"

Elle had been running her partial face recognition through all data-bases. They had a partial face shot off a low-resolution ATM camera outside the Bank of America on Wall Street. "We have tentative hit on her ID, unconfirmed. She shows up as Marza Umarov, a Chechnya student at Politecnico di Milano, in Milan. She was reported missing from classes three weeks ago, along with her boyfriend Papilli, a.k.a. Phillipe Kadyrov, also missing. Kadyrov trained in the Pakistan Northeast Territories, 2004–2006. His brother was killed last year in Syria outside Aleppo. In another minute or two, we will send NYPD and you pictures that we have on the two," Elle reported.

Shaw arrived at the corner of Nassau and Wall Streets and scanned east. Where was the next target? It could be anywhere—the subway, the stock exchange, any number of banks and financial houses. Just then, the familiar voice of Assistant Commissioner Weller resounded in his earpiece. "Agent Ellis, we have a positive ID on your woman. She was picked up on a cam walking into Trinity Park next to the church not five minutes ago. We have additional cars moving."

"Tell the officers to not—repeat, do *not*—engage her. We have to assume she has a bomb in the wheeled bag—she'll have a detonator on her. We need snipers close to take her with a head shot. She can't be allowed to detonate the bomb," Shaw replied. He pulled up Google Maps on his smartphone, and it was obvious. Running now, he yelled for the driver to go.

He activated his mike. "NYPD, Langley? Shaw here. She's less than two blocks from the Trade Center. She's going to hit that. Get snipers on surrounding buildings. Everything has been about utilities and infrastructure, I think she's going to hit the new transportation hub. They call it the Oculus; it just opened."

The driver swung around Trinity Place and went north on Church to Fulton, getting Shaw as close as possible to the hub. His earpiece told him that snipers were positioning around Towers Two and Three and across Church Street. Officers were present inside the entrances to all buildings, keeping a security ring but not openly visible to the suspect. Shaw tried to look casual, strolling toward the Oculus, the winged above-ground $3.4

billion architectural jewel designed by Santiago Calatrava to resemble a white dove being released from a child's hand. The irony of attacking a symbol of peace, Shaw thought. He pulled out his smartphone and pretended to take a few pictures of the Oculus and new buildings, and then he saw the man in the picture on his phone.

Walking at an angle that would nearly intersect with the man, Shaw reported in his headset, "Male suspect spotted at WTC, northwest corner of Tower Two security barrier, black slacks, blue shirt. Keep an eye out for the woman and bag. She's here somewhere."

Shaw thought how a decade ago, speaking into a headset would have tipped everyone off to the fact he was either law enforcement or a crazy man, but now, everyone with an iPhone had earbuds on.

The male suspect was walking toward the museum and memorials. With the tree canopy there, the snipers would have a hard time. A dozen undercover cops assigned to the NYPD's antiterrorism branch were walking through the memorials. The female suspect had to surface soon. Shaw looked at the time on his phone: 14:55; he always felt it easier to deal with twenty-four-hour timepieces.

"Female suspect spotted in tree line north of the Museum pavilion," the voice came in on his headset.

He didn't want to take his eyes off the male, but he knew the location of the woman was very, very close to him. "Do you have a shot?" Shaw whispered.

"Not yet, not yet, another few feet," came the reply.

Shaw saw the man look his way, and Shaw raised his phone to take pictures of the Oculus from another angle. Pivoting to do so, he saw the woman. He was in between them, not more than thirty feet from either, too close to even whisper into his mike. He began speaking in an aggravated and louder tone. "Listen, I told you...she means nothing to me. I'm close to her, but she has a boyfriend who lives up north. I can't get between them and what they have going. No, that's OK, I'll take care of him...I said I'll take care of him. Listen, I gotta go. I'm taking a few pictures for my folio, but you do what you have to do, and I'll do the same." He looked down at his phone, touching it as if to hang up a call and then slipping it into his pocket. He looked out of the corner of his eye as he turned, walking away from the woman at a forty-five-degree angle toward the man.

The man glanced and then looked over at the woman, who was beginning to walk out of the trees toward the Oculus when a red cloud enveloped her shoulders. A half second later, the shot rang out. Shaw was already in shooting stance, his Glock drawn, when the man turned. Two shots struck Phillipe. Shaw ran to him, kicked his weapon away, and leaned over him, frisking him. He said, "You'll live; you're shot in your hips. You have a choice. Tell me what other attacks are underway and who's behind this, or you'll be on a plane to a country that won't have our notions of constitutional protections."

The man grimaced in pain and spit out, "Lawyer."

Shaw replied, "No lawyers, no Miranda rights. We can question you for twenty-four hours under the Public Safety Exception. If I have to read you your rights, you'll wish I hadn't." Shaw glared at the man.

The man smiled and hissed, "It's beginning."

With the help of two NYPD officers, Shaw grabbed the man and dragged him to a waiting unmarked white SUV. The man screamed in pain.

"Hey, don't you want to wait for an ambulance or EMT?" one of the officers said as Shaw threw the man into the back of the SUV with the driver's help.

"No ambulance needed. This never happened. The only suspect is the one dead back there. You saw nothing else that would cause you to answer questions for the next year or two," Shaw said.

The two officers looked at each other, one of them saying, "You got that right," as the SUV made its exit.

Fifty miles to the east, the NYPD chopper with the duffel slung under it raced to the coordinates given to it by Langley. It crossed south of New Rochelle, across the upper Long Island Sound and Long Island itself. The worst risk was over, as it was now over the Atlantic with less than eight miles to go. The chopper crew readied the line with dive weights and waited for the signal to cut the line. Minutes seemed like hours. "Ready the line. We'll be over the drop site in one minute," the copilot said.

The crew stood at the door, ready to throw the rest of the line and weights out and cut the line from the chopper. "Five, four, three, two, one, DROP, DROP, DROP," came the order. The crew cut the line on "one" as the chopper arced hard and low, north back toward Long Island.

It was close. Less than four minutes after the bag was dropped, it detonated at a depth between 300 and 350 meters, not as deep as planned but deep enough. The detonation caused a plume of water nearly two hundred feet in the air to erupt over a diameter of three hundred meters, but little radiation escaped to the atmosphere.

CHAPTER 79

WASHINGTON, DC

Franklin and Shaw sat before the president at the Pentagon's operational center. There had been a lull, no new attacks in the last six hours. "Franklin, is this over? Have the attacks run their course?" the president asked.

"It's too early to tell, but I'm optimistic. I think it's safe to say the nuclear attacks are behind us. We have since found out from our counterparts in the FSB that the third suitcase-size nuke was accounted for by Russia three years ago. The other nukes are simply too large, too unwieldy, to smuggle in and easily transport," Franklin responded.

Shaw sat silent, staring down at the conference table in thought.

"You don't look convinced, Mr. Ellis. Do you have anything to add?" the chairman of the Joint Chiefs asked.

Shaw responded, "Ah, no, sir. I mean yes. I agree with Franklin that the risk of unconventional attacks is over, but we know there were at least two individuals involved in the Arizona attack who haven't been rounded up, and we have no idea how many were involved in the attack in LA, where no one was apprehended. The LA bomb was sophisticated. And an attack on so many fronts, conventional and unconventional, this widespread, this sophisticated, this well timed...we have just contained a few of the soldiers. We have no idea who the real planners, orchestrators, or financiers of today are. We are no closer now than when this started to knowing the identity or purpose of the so-called Twelfth Gulf Sheik Service."

The silence was palpable. Franklin broke the silence. "Shaw's assessment is, I believe, shared by everyone. We can't let our guard down, and we have a long, hard task of finding out who was behind today. But the successes of the day were the ones that counted. Both nuclear devices have been detonated without mass destruction. The dams on the Colorado are intact, as is the hydroelectric generating capacity and water supply for the Southwest. I'm more concerned with what we tell the American people. If we are honest and tell them that a number of the perpetrators are not only free but unidentified, that we do not know what group or state is behind this, well...it could result in panic, vigilante actions against the Muslim population. If we keep this under wraps, we lose our best means of vigilance—the eyes and ears of the people."

Without answering, the president rose and spoke. "I need to address the nation tonight. Set it up for eleven eastern. It has been a catastrophic day for the country, the world. People are scared. The people need to catch their collective breath. I think we downplay the potential threat but acknowledge a nonspecific threat and emphasize that we, everyone, must maintain their vigilance. That their eyes are needed, but caution against self-action. And I need to get back to the White House and out of this bunker, where I look like I'm hiding."

The president walked to the door and turned to address everyone at attention. "Gentlemen, ladies, you have done our country proud today. Thank you. Now go out and find these people. I want response options."

The president left, and Shaw looked over at Franklin. He had the same look as Directors Tankerfell and Harrence, each pensive and worried. The president's national security advisor, Kate Helmsworth, walked over to where Shaw and the other three were standing.

Shaw spoke first. "The president is feeling compelled to strike. We all are, but this could get much worse if we strike the wrong target, go down a path without a clear understanding."

"I couldn't agree more. But the president will be expected to act. The elections are just a year away. He already has been labeled weak on defense.

It's your jobs to make sure who—not if and not when—he attacks is the culpable player," Kate Helmsworth said, walking away.

After a silence, Director Tankerfell asked, "Who in the room feels like this is going to get a whole lot worse?"

The men stared at one another, watching the Joint Chiefs and military entourage go into overdrive around them.

CHAPTER 80

THREE DAYS LATER, WASHINGTON

It had been three days since the day of the attacks. The cost to the United States economy before the markets were closed was just beginning to be understood. The treasury secretary estimated that it would be in the trillions. That estimate would not to be made public. The markets lost seventy percent of their value and they had yet to reopen. A second worldwide recession, threatening to dwarf the 2007-2010 recession, was thought to be a certainty.

Shaw and Franklin sat before the President, the Joint Chiefs, the Secretary of Defense, the Secretary of Homeland Security, and Director Tankerfell of the FBI listening to a report. "The grid failure left Southern California, Oregon, Nevada, and most of Arizona without power. We estimate that power will not be fully restored for six to nine weeks. We forecast up to 190,000 fatalities. Those in hospitals or the heat of the Southwest will be at highest risk. Within a week thousands more may began to perish from dehydration and disease. Portions of the grid may sporadically fail even after power is restored. Without power, water can't be treated and delivered; sewage can't be pumped and treated," the undersecretary of DHS told the silent room.

The director of the CDC stood from a seat behind those seated at the large oval table. "If I may, Doctor Zeller from CDC. Without adequate water and sanitation, diseases defeated a century ago will return to America's shores. Dehydration and lack of food will take a toll. The human body can go 21-25 days without food, but only three to five days without water".

Admiral Weams spoke. "The Navy has repositioned its hospital and fleet vessels with desalination capabilities along Southern California. Pardon my choice of words but it is only a drop in the bucket. We need food and water stations in place and an airlift inland. The National Guard has been brought up in California, Oregon, Nevada, Arizona and Utah. Food riots have already erupted in over thirty cities and it's likely only a beginning".

The president then lifted his hand and the room silenced. "This was brought on by the hands of a mere dozen or so well-trained terrorists. I'm suspending restrictions on the military operating in the homeland. My constituents can sue me later. We have to restore order, get food, water, and medical assistance to where it's needed. Whatever needs to be done, we need power restored *now* not in six weeks. I want every utility across the country chipping in on this. And I want to address what is on every American's mind. Who was behind this? Have we located the missing perpetrators? What is the latest intel?"

Franklin nodded to Shaw, who stood. "Mr. President, the Agency has confirmed that two, perhaps as many as six terrorists escaped and are at large. We have the name and identities of two; a team from Phoenix living as husband and wife...Ibrahim and Emilia Shastani. We have little else on them. We have DNA on both, facial ID on the man, but only a partial facial ID on the woman. She wore a full niqab, hiding her face anytime she was in public. They appear to have been in the country under student visas for the past decade or so as sleepers. Each of the deceased terrorists finger-prints and DNA are under review; we should have further identifications by tomorrow. As for the others, we have identified two as Chechnyans, three as Syrians, and one as Egyptian. This telegraphs that it was the work of a terrorist organization, not a single state actor. The Agency and NSA are combing through data, transmissions, and satellite imagery that should shed light on who was behind this. In addition, we have received valuable intel from Israel, who provided us with advance notice of these cells and their entry into the States. We are working closely with our partners around the world but this will take time."

"Time is what we don't have," the president said. "Two nuclear devices on US soil; perhaps hundreds of thousands of our people dead or dying.

This is war. I am tired, the people are tired, of extremism, of religious geno-cide. This has to stop now. I want every imam, every mosque, every islamic scholar speaking out against this behavior, condemning these actions. I want them to clean their own houses of this cultural cancer. I want anyone without US citizenship in this country that isn't 100% behind the effort to eradicate extremism expelled from our borders. I don't care what the pundits say. This isn't a war on any religion; it is a war against hate and intolerance". The president's forehead was glistening. No one had ever seen this president's temper and weren't sure what to make of it having seen it. Those in the room glanced at each other as the meeting adjourned. It was a call to action, but at what cost Shaw wondered.

CHAPTER 81

ONE MONTH LATER, GEORGETOWN

Miami had erupted in riots lasting three weeks. Water had been unavailable for just five days, but it turned the city into a battleground. It had been random when the first pipeline to be repaired turned out feed Coral Gables, South Beach, and downtown. It brought claims of racial bias, which fed anger and frustration.

Zach and Sandy sat on a warm Sunday morning reading the New York Times in a small café in Georgetown. The headlines told a story of continuing misery in the Southwest. And the stories weren't just in the west. The article described the New England fishing industry which already reeled from government regulations and overfishing, being decimated. It was not because of any threat or government regulation; the detonation site was hundreds of miles from the fishing grounds. But perception overtook reason. People were convinced by baseless rumors spread over the Internet that the Atlantic's fisheries were spoiled by radiological contamination.

Zach put the paper down holding Sandy's hand as he spoke. "The news doesn't get any better. The press paints a dreadful picture and even they don't know the half of it. I need a day without news, without the office. I need a day with just you. I leave in two days for Israel. I'm thinking maybe you could come over to Israel for a visit, ...or longer."

Sandy looked in his eyes, seeing again the vulnerable side to Zach that had attracted him to her. "We have this afternoon. Maybe a movie or walk along the canal, that sounds good. But not all the news is that bad. I heard that Glen Canyon Dam is going to be okay. Reclamation performed a near miracle, retrofitting the eastern spillway in just two weeks; not the four months they originally had that scheduled for. Evidently the releases from Lake Powell are resulting in Lake Mead increasing its capacity, which is a blessing for Las Vegas and the lower basin states."

She caught herself again talking about the events. Zach was right, they needed a break. They needed to just be together. It had been hard on Sandy to walk away from Page after Dylan's funeral, but there was nothing holding her after Dylan's daughters moved to their grandparents in Flagstaff. Every walk, every encounter in Page was the same. People avoided eye contact or, worse, offered heart-felt condolences that brought more tears to the surface. There were too many memories. She knew she needed a fresh start.

When Zach had suggested coming east with him when he left the FBI for the Agency, she said yes – on the condition they take it slow, with separate apartments. She didn't know how long she could take the urban bustle of DC. Her roots were elsewhere. The Park Service was proud of her actions. It marketed her as a symbol of protecting the National Park System. They gave her a pick of assignments. She had told them she needed time and the agency had agreed to temporarily transfer her to the DC headquarters after a three-week leave of absence.

She never acted on impulse before. She never failed to map out her goals and life in detail before acting. Part of her struggled with taking off, to a city, with a man she had literally just met. But part of her acknowledged that Zach was different. He was open, caring; the type of man she had always wished would walk into her life. "Let me think about Israel," she finally said.

Zach's move from the Bureau to the Agency was without hesitation. When Franklin and Shaw debriefed him, they implored him to join the Agency. It took him by surprise. He knew nothing of clandestine work; he was an investigator. But the Agency was given the charge of learning who was behind the attacks – anywhere, at any cost. Zach was been offered broader counterintelligence powers and responsibilities than he ever would have been given in the regimented organizational structure of the Bureau. He jumped at the opportunity. His only hesitation was an acknowledgment to himself that he would never lose sight of his relationship with Sandy, if she would have him.

CHAPTER 82

LONDON

Shaw had whisked Philippe offshore to a site where the host country turned a blind eye to enhanced interrogation. Elle and her counterpart in MI5 communicated with that government's intelligence service on a daily basis. The rendition had been done with the tacit approval of the president and the directors of the CIA and FBI, although no record of it would ever be found. After the Snowden debacle, sensitive communication was no longer digitized.

The foreign government's intelligence service liaison was Major Hassan, whose report was cold and short. Everybody has a breaking point and Philippe had his. He revealed a handler located in London. Two days later the handler was taken into custody after MI5 persuaded the imam of a mosque in the Borough of Westminster to lure the man to prayers. He was met by Shaw, Elle and three MI5 British Secret Intelligence Service officers.

Elle stood before Agent Martin of MI5 who spoke in a matter of fact British tone. "It seems as though your man had no reluctance to talk. He identified three contacts, one in Iraq, and two in Qatar. One is linked to a radical Sunni faction which sprung up after ISIL went to ground. As you know, the organization metastized into a myriad of new splinter groups after coalition airstrikes eliminated the group's leadership. This file provides the details of the interrogation. Of interest to me was the connections to the Gulf."

"Thank you Agent Martin, the Agency is eternally grateful to MI5 and the Crown. I look forward to reading the full report. I hope you will excuse me," Elle said. She turned on her high heel and walking briskly away as only she could.

EPILOGUE

After the withdrawal of all United States troops from Iraq and a year or more of measured airstrikes in Iraq and Syria, ISIL had gone underground. ISIL engaged in a covert asymmetrical war against the West and Gulf States. Follow-along groups pledging allegiance to jihad sprang up around the globe. Warfare enveloped all of eastern Syria, western Iraq, parts of Jordan and across Northern Africa. The jihadists' successor groups announced an interim government in the shadows of the Internet which it labeled the Caliphate. It modeled this on the first reign of the Prophet Mohammed in the seventh century. Jihadists controlled or threatened access to the Euphrates River tightening their grip and influence from Turkey to the gulf. The use and denial of water as a weapon was confirmed.

A year of coalition airstrikes led to a call for enlistments and revenge against US, European, and Gulf States and their citizens. It was a war against terrorism waged by jihadist groups founded on religious intolerance. Like all wars of religion, this one was based on readings of text written centuries after the teachings had occurred. The written word was limited at the time of the World's religions' founders; centuries later, teachings were memorialized and recollections fought over. This conflict would be no different. The Prophet Mohammed had died in the year 632 A.D. with his followers divided over whether a successor should be chosen by the community or by relation. The Shi'ites, the literal translation of which means "followers of Ali", sought the son-in-law of Mohammed's rule. The majority selected a successor not by blood, who was assassinated less than thirty years later. And so, after nearly fifteen centuries and the name of religion, blood flowed.

America was finally beginning to piece the puzzle together. Ayatollah Ruhollah Khomeini deposed the shah, releasing a Shia revival. The Soviet invasion of Afghanistan led the West to train jihadists in combat. The

United States' invasion toppled Saddam, creating a power vacuum in Iraq. And the so-called Arab Spring set factions against factions, sponsored by gulf nations trying desperately to stay a step ahead of the tide. The United States' subsequent trail of indecision signaled instability. And the proxy war in Syria engaged in between Shia Iran and Sunni Gulf countries, created a cauldron of conflict nurturing terror on a global scale. Centuries of sectarian violence kept in check first by five hundred years of Ottoman Empire rule, colonial imposition, and ruthless dictators became unleashed. The world was teetering on edge of global religious conflict.

It came as a surprise to everyone but Russia and a few of the Gulf countries that one of the first things the underground Caliphate had done after the elimination of ISIL's leader, Abu Bakr al-Baghdadi, was to attempt an act of statehood by extending an olive branch to the European Union. In return for Assad's followers leaving power, it offered secure natural gas pipeline routes from the Gulf States to Turkey through Ukraine, for a financial royalty to support its activities, pledging that it would not project attacks outside Syria's borders. The Russians had backed Assad, in part to ensure its natural gas monopoly in Europe. Now the Russian economy, already battered by its missteps in Ukraine and Syria, crashed. Absent its natural gas sales to Europe, Russia's economy was that of an unstable developing nation. Its nearly thirty-year experiment with free markets was replaced with rising nationalist sentiment throughout the former Soviet Republic.

Over the past year, the Middle East and North Africa transgressed into a sectarian war. World War I had been the unintended consequence of mistakes and treaties. World War II had been forged by the resurgence of nationalistic identity. This conflict, which had all the potential for World War III, was founded on religious dogma, fed by sponsor countries waging a war for commodities and religious ideology.

All indications were that the attacks on America had been forged by a Shia-led faction funded by Hezbollah and its parent Iran. The principle figures were traced to Lebanon and Syria who solicited the help of a rogue former Soviet-era intelligence officer furnishing nuclear arms on the black market. A man who had since been eliminated by the Russians.

America was growing impatient in its search for retaliation. Shaw was one of the sole voices questioning the conclusions that were being rushed. The reports he was receiving from Mossad were backed up by Zach's weekly reports. He found himself asking whether the trail was too obvious, too orchestrated. The story too complete. Life and investigations seldom played out in linear progression. Franklin, Director Harrence and Director Tankerfell agreed, but their voices were overshadowed by the politics of an election.

Projections were that it would take decades for the United States to recover. The common man had lost half of his accumulated wealth. America's borders were now secure to the point of a fortress at the urging of a bipartisan Congress - the same Congress that in the same term, forged a landmark immigration bill that recognized the dangers of politicizing issues that needed solving. Additional support was given to Mexico to eradicate the cartels for their role in the attacks. Mexico's economy would be strengthened as a buffer and strong partner with America and Canada. America no longer felt protected by oceans. The psychological toll on the common man was immeasurable. America had, as perhaps no time since December 7, 1941, a steely focus.

And in a small café off Al Muntazah Street in Doha, Qatar, nine men met over strong tea and croissants. The eldest of the three at the head of the table sipped tea and said in a low tone, "The Americans are following in the steps foretold. Soon they will respond with a fury".

The youngest, a man to his side with a scar across his forehead, nodded and, added, "The Twelvers will at last be eliminated!"